You Bet Your Planet

Edited by
Martin H. Greenberg
& Brittiany A. Koren

D1522180

DAW BOOKS, INC.
DONALD A. WOLLHEIM, FOUNDER
375 Hudson Street, New York, NY 10014

ELIZABETH R. WOLLHEIM
SHEILA E. GILBERT
PUBLISHERS
http://www.dawbooks.com

First Printing, March 2005
1 2 3 4 5 6 7 8 9

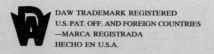

ACKNOWLEDGMENTS

Introduction © 2005 by Brittiany A. Koren.
Cook's Turing © 2005 by Esther M. Friesner.
Heart's Desire © 2005 by Mickey Zucker Reichert.
Mind Game © 2005 by Susan Shwartz.
Stop or I'll Shoot © 2005 by Ed Gorman.
Here to There © 2005 by Jane Lindskold.
Name That Planet! © 2005 by Elizabeth Ann
   Scarborough.
Scenes from the Contest © 2005 by Robert Sheckley.
The Hollywood Dilemma © 2005 by Russell Davis.
You'd Better Win! © 2005 by Josepha Sherman.
Dish of the Day © 2005 by Susan Sizemore.
Entertaining Folly © 2005 by Bruce Holland Rogers.

For Michael, Sabrena, and Samantha,
the future is yours!

CONTENTS

INTRODUCTION
by Brittiany A. Koren   1

COOK'S TURING
by Esther M. Friesner   3

HEART'S DESIRE
by Mickey Zucker Reichert   35

MIND GAME
by Susan Shwartz   83

STOP OR I'LL SHOOT
by Ed Gorman   111

HERE TO THERE
by Jane Lindskold   131

NAME THAT PLANET!
by Elizabeth Ann Scarborough   181

SCENES FROM THE CONTEST
by Robert Sheckley   205

THE HOLLYWOOD DILEMMA
by Russell Davis

THE HOLLYWOOD DILEMMA
by Russell Davis   223

YOU'D BETTER WIN!
by Josepha Sherman   237

DISH OF THE DAY
by Susan Sizemore   255

ENTERTAINING FOLLY
by Bruce Holland Rogers   279

INTRODUCTION

by Brittiany A. Koren

IN THE LAST FEW YEARS, game shows and reality television have hit a new high. And for good reason. They give us entertainment. They let us use our knowledge and intellect in ways different from our normal lives. They give us contestants with a certain bravado that allow them to use their courage and wit against the rest of the human race. The stories herein take our imagination of the game show even further. Some of the stories will answer questions, and others will bring new ones to mind.

What would someone do for a minute of fame? Why would they humiliate and possibly even injure themselves for the elusive grand prize? And what gives someone the courage to become a contestant in the first place? To get up in front of an audience and perform, sometimes—although some would say most of the time—at the cost of their dignity?

The people in these stories do more than this.

Not only do they have few things in common, but they are put in unnatural circumstances—under extreme stress—to do their very best. And most compete for the same reason—for their continuing existence—and some find out the hard way what it takes to survive.

By watching the shows in real life, we see a bonding experience happen between those involved on the program, and those at home watching. The contestants give us experiences we most likely would not have seen otherwise, and teach us what to do—and what not to do—in certain situations. They display true courage, vulnerability, and hope.

Inside you'll find what the world's games might be like in the not too distant future. Whether far out in space or here on Earth, the contestants give us a run for their money. The games are extreme and the stakes are high. Some learn that life isn't always a game where you play by the rules. Sometimes, you need to make up your own. They don't give up, they don't give in. They persevere.

More real than any reality series, these stories will show you the intricacies of the game shows of the future, and you'll learn why it's survival of the fittest with every event.

COOK'S TURING

by Esther M. Friesner

Esther M. Friesner is the Nebula Award–winning author of thirty novels and more than one hundred short stories. She is also the editor and creator of the popular *Chicks in Chainmail* anthology series. Her most recent publication is *E. Godz*, coauthored with Robert Asprin. She lives in Connecticut with her husband, son, daughter, and two cats.

"I DON'T SEE what's so hard about it," Allison said. It wasn't her place to speak up, being one of the dozen-or-more auxiliaries attached to the New York branch of the Terran-Golzod Liaison Office, but she couldn't help it. Her training had stressed that the newly opened, opportunity-rich field of intergalactic peacekeeping was one of infinite subtlety and nuance, a complex, hypersophiscated webwork of obscure-yet-vital sociopolitical subtext, best left to the experts. There were wheels within wheels, boxes within boxes, guppies within carp within tuna within . . . Well, suffice it to say that it was a veritable apple strudel of multi-level intrigue. At any given moment in the proceedings, the fate of all Earth might very well hang in the balance (mostly because the Golzod possessed weaponry that made the eruption of Krakatoa look like a tadpole's hiccup). She knew this to be true.

And yet there were times like these when the finely woven fabric of diplomacy looked like nothing more than a tattered fishnet with holes in it large enough to let a whole school of killer whales swim right through. She could not ignore it. She simply *had* to say something.

"No, really," she persisted. "I mean, what's the problem? It's not that hard; it's just a matter of choosing something edible. My two-year-old nephew could do it. Or maybe not—he keeps trying to eat kitchen appliance cords for breakfast—but it can't be *that* difficult." She saw the looks she was getting and felt compelled to add: "Can it?"

Stony silence greeted her unrequested observations. The innermost circle of the Terran side of Terran-Golzod affairs—two women, three men, and an Enhanced miniature dachshund named Friedrich—all regarded her with identical expressions of exasperation and a *soupçon* of distaste.

"If you are *quite* through, Ms. Tyler?" Dr. Kirstensdottir's voice was a good ten degrees colder than her eyes.

"All I said was— Oh, never mind." Allison turned to leave. It wasn't as if her presence was indispensable. She had only been sent into the conference room to bring the big shots their ten o'clock coffee transfusion. (Friedrich had a fearsome thirst for cinnamon lattés. Merely the *thought* of a mini-doxie hyped up on caffeine was enough to make most folks grit their teeth and shudder.) Her comment was not the result of active participation in the Terran-Golzod intergalactic *rapprochement* process, but merely the fruit of inadvertent eavesdropping.

Allison had learned a thing or two outside of her training classes, and the most useful real-world lesson by far had been this: *Do not attempt to contradict or argue with Experts. There are more productive things to do with your life, such as pounding sand down a rat hole using your forehead for a mallet.* She didn't need to stay here and be sneered into submission by the redoubtable Dr. Kirstensdottir. She could get that kind of treatment almost anywhere else in the building, short of the steno pool. She was halfway to the door when a high-pitched, sharp voice hailed her.

"Ms. Tyler! Halt! Return!"

She froze in midstep and whirled around in time to see Friedrich give her a wide, tongue-lolling grin. "Here, girl," he yapped. "Good girl. Come. Sit. Stay."

As a mere auxiliary she had no choice but to obey. Pleased, Friedrich wagged his tail and tossed her a donut from the box of Krispy Kremes on the conference table. "Goooood girl," he crooned. "Who's a good girl, then? *You* is. *Yes,* you is! Yes, you's my good little—"

"Er, Friedrich?" Dr. Balfour adjusted his glasses nervously. "Is there a reason you have asked Ms.

Tyler to rejoin us, or are you just trying out some of the techniques in the *No Bad Humans* book I gave you for Christmas?"

The Enhanced dachshund gave a small, slightly embarrassed whine under his breath. "Pardon. I thought that we at least owed her an explanation for why we reject her question as stupid."

"My daddy always said that there's no such thing as a stupid question," said Violet Breem, looking as arrogant and self-righteous as was possible for a woman in her late forties who *would* insist on wearing such painfully huge quantities of leopard print clothing. She was the group's foremost expert on the Golzodian religion and code of ethics, which was the only reason that Dr. Kirstensdottir had thus far refrained from strangling her where she sat.

"Then your *daddy* never worked around here," Dr. K. sneered.

"Hey, take it easy on Vi, 'kay? She's not the enemy *or* the problem. Learn to pick your battles, Brunhilde!" The team's Public Relations *Wunderkind,* an eager-beaver Yalie by the name of Randall "Randy" Morris, had neither M.D. nor Ph.D. behind his name. Yet for all that, he was the highly valued and indispensable Doctor of Spin-ology whose ongoing efforts were all that stood between peace on Earth and mad panic in the streets. He was also Number Two on Dr. Kirstensdottir's *Strangle By Next Thursday at the Latest* list.

Twirling around and around in his leather desk chair like an unruly five year old, Randy Morris managed to wink at Allison as he whizzed past. "The problem here—" he said, his voice wobbling weirdly as he spun, "—the *immediate* problem, as opposed to the Biggie, of course—is that our Ms. Tyler doesn't know the straight scoop, the real deal, the in-your-face case we've got to handle *juuuust* right or Mother Earth is screwed." He grabbed the edge of the conference table, jerked to a stop, and added: *"The Great Test."* He uttered those words with such unwonted gravity that you could actually *hear* the Significant Capitalization.

Allison frowned slightly. "I know about the Great Test. I thought it was just a formality."

"Sure it is." Randy might have stopped his wild gyrations as a courtesy to her, but he'd left his sarcasm switch in the "on" position. "Like the big religious debates of the Middle Ages were 'just a formality.' " He noticed Friedrich giving him a quizzical look, and so he went on to explain: "Back then, the Church decided that it might be better P.R. to *humiliate* the Jews instead of merely slaughtering them. So churchmen challenged rabbis to public debates, Judaism versus Christianity, best two falls out of three."

"Ach!" The dachshund wagged his tail in approval. "A friendly debate is so much more civilized than a massacre."

"There was nothing 'friendly' about it. The Church made the rules and the rules said that if the Jews lost, they *had* to convert, change their whole way of life, give up everything they cherished, worshiped, and held dear. Sound familiar?" Randy's grin was fixed and cold as he surveyed his fellow Experts. They exchanged knowing, sorrowful looks, which piqued Allison's already irritated sense of curiosity no end. "They figured that they'd win in a walkover, after which the Jews would *have* to convert because not only had their faith been proved to be Brand X, but also because that was one of the rules that the Church set up before the debate started, take it or leave it, leave it and die horribly."

"And?" the dachshund asked, tail wagging in spite of himself. He did love a good history lesson.

" 'And?' " Randy echoed. "And what do *you* think happened? The Church lost."

"So . . . it was a happy ending?"

"Sure. For the Church."

The dachshund's tail drooped. "I do not understand."

"Well, once they lost, they just declared that the Jews *couldn't* have won the debates without the devil's help, because everyone knew that the Church was always *right*. Anyone who could defeat good, honest churchmen in open debate was getting infernal help, and thus it was the Church's duty to destroy them."

Allison gasped. "Is *that* what's happening here with the Golzod Peace Alliance?" she demanded. "Do you mean to say that the Test—the Test's not just a quaint, traditional procedure that they administer to all new Alliance members?"

"*Potential* Alliance members," Violet corrected her. "And no, it's not, dear. It's a trap."

"A trap from which we are even now attempting to extricate Earth and all who dwell here," Dr. Kirstensdottir added. She glowered at Allison and added, "At least that's what we were *trying* to do before we were interrupted by a lot of stupid questions."

That was when the third man stood up from his place at the table, tore a page from the antique spiral notebook before him, crumpled it, popped it in his mouth, chewed vigorously, spat the pulpy wad into his hand, and deftly flung it with dead-bang accuracy so that it made a beautifully loud *splat* when it struck the left lens of Dr. Kirstensdottir's glasses.

The effect was stunning. Dr. Balfour twiddled his own glasses at a furious rate until he wore the bridge of his nose raw. Randy Morris burst into great dollops of raucous sound that were the mutant offspring of a guffaw, a burp, and drowning. Friedrich threw back his head and howled. Violet Breem began uttering arpeggios of tiny, ladylike yelps as she dug into her purse and pulled out a lace-trimmed hankie (also leopard print) and tried to pat away the mess from Dr. K.'s glasses.

As for Dr. Kirstensdottir, she sat as if turned to stone. All color drained from her face. Allison observed her with the rising fear that the impromptu spitball had somehow delivered enough of a shock to have struck the good doctor dead where she sat. How else to explain the fact that Dr. K. was doing nothing whatsoever to prevent or intercept Violet's ineffective dabbings?

On the other hand, Dr. K.'s paralysis might just as

easily have been the result of a force far more devasta-
ting than any spitball, more immobilizing than shock
and/or outrage, and almost as ancient as the art of
spitball warfare, namely *love*.

Love, or at least lust. Infatuation was too namby-
pamby a term to apply to the man who had just as-
saulted the testy doctor with that impromptu salivary
missile. He was perhaps the most unarguably gorgeous
creature Allison had ever slapped an eyeball to. In all
her time as an auxiliary with the Terran-Golzod Liaison Office she had heard much about the elusive
Chairman Bysshe Nagoya, but before today she had
never seen him and, until this moment, she had been
too distracted by the other committee members to
take a good, long look at him.

It didn't take her more than a pair of heartbeats to
accept the fact that the mere act of looking at Chairman Nagoya was a pleasure that proved itself well
worth the wait and then some. His appearance went
far beyond *attractive,* transcended *handsome,* and left
Whoa, Mama, buy me some of THAT! panting in the
dust. It was this very abundance of physical beauty
that allowed him to get away with stunts like the recent spitball. Tall, slender, graceful, with cascades of
blue-black hair reaching well below the seat of his
form-fitting pearl suede pants, the vision allowed his
blazing aquamarine eyes to sweep slowly across every
face at the conference table before parting oh-so-
kissable lips and saying:

"I believe that Miss Breem has already reminded
us that there is no such thing as a stupid question."

Violet sighed and lavished a melting look upon the speaker. It was a gooey, adolescent, puppy-love-infected stare fit to make a python barf. "Ooooooh, Chairman Nagoya, *thank* you! It's so sweet of you to say—"

"Miss Breem is also wrong," Nagoya snapped, glaring knives—nay, cleavers!—at the besotted Breem. "A question that wastes our time, when time is the ingredient we most need and most lack, *is* stupid."

"I—I'm sorry." Allison twisted her fingers, longing for a rock to crawl under and die. "I apologize for—"

"Apologize to Earth!" Nagoya shouted at her with such force that she staggered backward. "Apologize to your fellow humans when we are all enslaved, sweating under the lash of our Golzod overlords!"

"Sweating . . . lash . . ." Dr. Kirstensdottir gasped, eyes fixed upon Chairman Nagoya, and she fanned herself furiously. Mouth slack, eyes staring off into the distance, she sighed with longing. Whatever mental image she was presently entertaining, and vice-versa, was rated NC-17 at the very least.

"I—I didn't mean—" Allison inched away from the conference table, trying for the second time in under an hour to feel her way to the door and make a discreet getaway without lowering herself to the point of a sharp, undignified cut-and-run. She almost made it.

A shame that she put her foot in the puddle of yellow slime seeping from the group of three Golzods standing in the doorway and slipped, landing full force on the Legate Plenipotentiary. There was a loud, squooshy sound and—as all too often happens follow-

ing loud, squooshy sounds—a historic decision was
made in haste.

"Ah," said one of the two unsquooshed Golzods,
sizing up the situation while his comrade looped a
tentacle around Allison's waist and helped her off the
jellied Legate. "We see that you have picked your
candidate for the Great Test. Good." The two surviving Golzods hustled her away before the terrified eyes
of the Terrans.

Randy Morris was the first to break the ensuing
silence. "At least they don't seem to care when we
kill one of their own," he said.

"Why should they?" Dr. Kirstensdottir growled.
"They're part yeast: They'll just step into the rest
room and bud off a fresh Legate before lunchtime."

"A shame, a shame," Dr. Balfour said somberly,
rubbing the bridge of his nose and wincing at the un-
expected pain. "If they didn't hold their own lives so
cheaply, they might be more inclined to show some
mercy to their, er, subject peoples."

"Well, they do, so they don't," Violet Breem said
sharply. Oddly enough, the remark made sense in
context.

The Enhanced dachshund tucked his tail between
his legs. "Anyone want to take me walkies before
Doomsday?"

The day of the Great Test dawned bright and clear.
This didn't matter because it was scheduled to take
place at night, 10:00 P.M. Eastern Standard Time to be
precise. In spite of the stringencies of global time zones,

every human being in the world with access to a television set was up to watch the fate of his planet be decided on the shining floor of the Golzod Portable Culinary Arena.

The Golzods were sticklers for form. They had proved their respect for the social proprieties and the importance of popular opinion time and time again. Dr. Kirstensdottir had written several monographs on the intricate and highly ritualized code of behavior which the all-conquering extraterrestrials followed among themselves. They were also quick to admire and adopt any non-Golzod customs or manners that they found attractive, even should such sociological phenomena come from lesser life-forms (i.e. anyone who was not a Golzod).

Thus it was only natural that the "benevolent visitors" took a shine to Japan, giving themselves wholeheartedly to the beautifully orchestrated social niceties which that particular Terran culture had perfected over the course of centuries. When they chose Tokyo as the only acceptable site to host the Great Test, no one was at all surprised.

Nor could anyone fault the Golzods for failing to mount a good show. Overnight their technicians transformed an empty hangar at Narita Airport into the fabulously appointed site of the Great Test. It was a task they had performed many times before, on many other worlds. Culinary Arena was both splashy and austere at the same time, with flaming torches illuminating the last word in kitchen equipment gathered from the far, somewhat rounded corners of the known universe.

Unfortunately, the last word that had lodged itself firmly in Allison's mind was: HELP!

"Ms. Tyler, you must calm yourself," Chairman Nagoya said severely. "You will need all your wits about you for the ordeal ahead." He was resplendent in a jacket whose sequined extravagance would have made the late, great Liberace look Amish. As a sop to their soon-to-be-slaves, the Golzods had decreed that he should be Master of Ceremonies and general overseer for the Great Test so that no one might accuse them of anti-Terran favoritism. They were very big on appearances, for a race that resembled tentacled boogers.

"Too much is riding on your shoulders for you to succumb to hysteria," he concluded.

"Oh that's going to calm me *right* down!" Allison wailed, wringing her hands in the perky pink apron she had been issued as part of her costume for the big event. Beneath it she had been forced to wear the wasp-waisted, crinoline-skirted dress of a 1950s TV housewife, her hair lacquered into a bouffant flip that brought to mind fond memories of Darth Vader. The Golzods had certain firm, unshakable, dated notions as to the required appearance of a female Terran cook. "Sure, why *shouldn't* I be calm? Knowing that if I make *one* mistake—just one!—all Earth will become a Golzod protectorate, which is *their* name for a slave labor supply house. Gee, who couldn't stay calm knowing *that?*"

"Save your sarcasm to cool your rice porridge," Chairman Nagoya snapped, his eyes blazing. "You will succeed! You have no other choice."

He bowed to her formally, as if to communicate that the matter had been settled. Bowing was second nature to him. As his family name indicated, he boasted Japanese ancestry, though his height, the wave in his hair, and the uncanny color of his eyes spoke of parents wealthy enough to afford deluxe prenatal genetic tweakery. When the senior Nagoyas decided to name their son and heir after their favorite English poet, Percy Bysshe Shelley, it was merely the finishing touch, the pickled *ume* plum at the heart of the rice ball that was Chairman Nagoya's unique existence. With a background like that, small wonder he chose to devote his life to extraterrestrial diplomacy. His family was simply Not of This Earth.

"I will try to do my best," Allison replied, bowing back. "Which won't be all that good considering that this is a cooking contest and *I don't know how to cook!*"

A wry smile touched Chairman Nagoya's lips. "Is that where you think the problem lies? My dear Ms. Tyler, the chief difficulty in passing the Great Test is not in the cooking of today's theme ingredient, but in the *selection*. And were you not the one who observed that the very process of ingredient selection is no more than a matter of common sense?"

Allison frowned. "I was, but that was before the rest of you came down on me for asking dumb questions. No one explained where I went wrong, just that I was a fool to even *ask* about why choosing the one edible ingredient out of three would be so difficult. I *still* don't understand."

"You would, if the Golzods had not interrupted our meeting when they did and spirited you away. I was, in fact, on the point of elucidating the truly insidious nature of the Great Test when they burst in. I will attempt to be brief; we haven't much time left and you must be aware of the circumstances facing you. Today's contest will begin with you issuing a challenge to one of three alien master chefs. This is just meaningless stage-dressing, done because the Golzods have a bizarrely overdeveloped love of dramatic spectacle. The three chefs will resemble different extraterrestrials, including one Golzod for vanity's sake, but in truth they are all robots, mechanical chefs constructed from solid iron. It is unimportant which you challenge; any one of them can cook delicate puff pastry rings around you. What matters, Ms. Tyler, is the moment when I unveil the three ingredients."

"And here I thought that what mattered was the moment when I *chose* one." Allison managed a smile.

Chairman Nagoya's expression softened somewhat. The young woman's distress was palpable, her courage astonishing. Here she stood, with the fate of all Earth in her hands, and she had not screamed nor fainted nor become a gibbering madwoman from the pressure. She had whined a bit—that was only natural—but underneath it all she was game. His huge, expressive eyes filled with a look that reflected heartfelt admiration for so much spunk in so attractive a package.

"You are right, Ms. Tyler," he said. He smiled back, and in the instant something impalpable passed between the two of them for which there was no recipe in all the universe.

"Well, I hope one of the ingredient's a jar of peanut butter, because I *know* that's edible and a good old-fashioned P.B.J. sandwich is the only food I can make that *sometimes* comes out right," Allison told him.

"One of them very well may *look* like a jar of peanut butter," Chairman Nagoya said. "Or perhaps he may resemble an octopus, or a bowl of grapes, or a lobster, or a block of tofu, or a very large and ugly fish, or—"

"Whoa!" Allison held up her index finger, begging a point of information. "Back up, there. Did you say *he?*"

"Or she." The Chairman shrugged, making his sequins rattle. "Or both at once. It's hard to tell with some of these aliens, and it doesn't matter to others."

Allison's jaw dropped. Through a haze of shock and denial she heard Chairman Nagoya inform her of the full measure of sneakiness the Golzods employed wherewith to place whole civilizations under their not-so-benevolent control while at the same time making it appear that they were doing it strictly in the best interests of the subject peoples.

"Who could argue with the good intentions of the Golzods whose only desire—so they have always claimed—is to make the universe a kinder, gentler place?" Chairman Nagoya's lip curled. "And how better to do that than by determining which races are savages, a danger to themselves and others? All hail the Golzods, who isolate those uncivilized creatures and educate them!"

"But they *don't* educate anyone," Allison protested. "They *enslave* them!"

"You say potato, I say po-tah-to, and the Golzods say their equivalent of *Arbeit macht frei,*" the Chairman replied evenly. "I suppose we ought to be grateful that they do care so much about what the neighbors will think, otherwise they would simply crush us without going through this Great Test charade. They do have the power for that."

"Then why do they put us through this?" Allison asked. "Three ingredients for me to choose from, except one is a member of a sentient alien race? Good heavens. Now I see why you all thought I was being stupid. There's *much* more to this Test than just picking out something edible. One man's meat might be another man's nephew!" Allison shivered at the thought, then said: "I'm almost afraid to ask this, but . . . what's the real story behind the *other* wrong ingredient?"

"It's poisonous; fatally so," the Chairman replied. "Hence the part about our being a danger to *ourselves*. The Golzods are, in effect, administering a cosmic Turing Test. They are not, however, using it to determine whether a machine is intelligent enough to pass for being human, but rather whether we are intelligent enough to pass for being . . . Golzod." His cool, scornful expression conveyed his contempt for the aliens and their duplicitous, self-serving ways far better than words alone.

"But it's cruel!" Allison protested. "It's even crueler to the poor creature who's got to pose as an ingredient! What happens if I *pick* him? Her? It?"

"If you do, then he, she, or it will be slaughtered by the attending *sous* chefs, cooked in a series of appropriate and tasty ways by you and the robot chef you challenge, and served up in a manner that best expresses the theme ingredient." The Chairman's jawline hardened. "No sooner shall the first delicious bite cross the judges' lips—if they have lips—than Earth will be condemned. Obviously. You can't allow a planet full of cannibals loose in the cosmos, can you? Enter the Golzods, for the greater good of intergalactic civilization." He snorted derisively.

"But wouldn't the ingredient—I mean, the alien—speak up? Why would he just lie there and allow himself to be killed and eaten?"

"Because unless he dies, the verdict for Earth will remain in doubt, and the Golzods don't want that. The alien in question *will* keep silent. He will have been chosen from one of the worlds already under Golzod domination and will come to Culinary Arena fully aware that should he make the slightest attempt to signal you as to his true identity, his entire planet will be destroyed. A wasteful procedure, but the Golzods have plenty of slave worlds, so they don't mind annihilating one of them every now and then *pour encourager les autres.*"

By now Allison's apron was a damp wad of pink cotton in her clenching hands. "What—what happens if I pick the ingredient that's poisonous?"

"We fail the Great Test as soon as the first judge dies. If we don't exhibit enough intelligence to be able to tell victuals from venom, we must be protected from our own stupidity. You simply *can't* leave infants unsupervised. Enter the Golzods again."

Allison hugged herself, trying to cast off the icy

mantle of dread that had fallen over her shoulders.
Nothing like this had been covered on the Civil Service examination when she first signed up to enter the
glamorous world of interstellar diplomacy.

"And what happens if I make the *right* choice?"
She looked away from the Chairman, out through the
heavy draperies that separated the behind-the-scenes
area of Culinary Arena from the stage upon which the
fate of all Earth was about to be determined by the
cognitive processes of a young woman who had once
come within inches of eating a piece of wax fruit.
(Granted, it was an embarrassing memory that belonged to Allison's toddler years, but the present situation had left her feeling more than a little insecure.)
"Not that *that's* going to happen," she concluded
mournfully.

Without warning, she felt a strong, supple hand fall
on her shoulder as she was spun around to confront
the Chairman's blazing aquamarine eyes. "Haven't
you learned yet?" he demanded. "Don't waste time
asking stupid questions! And that *is* a stupid question,
Ms. Tyler, for it is impossible that you can do anything
except make the right choice!"

"Chairman Nagoya, how can you say—?" Allison
began.

"Call me Bysshe." He drew her into his arms. There
was no evading the intensity of his gaze nor any way
to deny the overwhelming power of her answering
emotions when he added: "You *will* succeed. I recognize the warrior's spirit within you that will accept
nothing less than complete and utter triumph. I knew

it the moment I laid eyes upon you, though your personnel file confirmed my initial suspicions. Brooklyn is merely another name for victory!"

"But I don't come from Brook—!"

"Hush." He silenced her protests with a kiss that left her gasping. "I believe in you, Ms. Tyler. I believe in you, and since I have lived in the United States I have seen enough inspirational made-for-TV movies to understand that if a fabulously handsome man declares that he believes in the spunky-though-mundane heroine, his faith magically endows her with the unquestionable ability to succeed. Also, it increases her bust size dramatically." His gaze slid slightly downward. "Hmm. Apparently I will have to believe in you even harder. But no matter; there will be time enough for all that later, after you and your team have won the Great Test! Destiny calls you! History awaits! Posterity—"

"What team?" Allison asked.

Chairman Nagoya looked irked at being interrupted in mid-declamation, but nonetheless rather grudgingly replied: "Your team of aides and helpers. Did no one tell you? You are entitled to as many backup personnel as can fit on your side of Culinary Arena, besides the *sous* chefs provided. You may employ them however you like. That's why it doesn't matter whether or not you know how to cook. Under the Golzods' own rules, your helpers can do anything and everything connected with the competition, short of selecting the actual ingredient."

Allison's face lit up with a glorious smile. She

grabbed Chairman Nagoya by his sparkly lapels and gave him a big, wet, gleeful kiss. It wasn't as romantic as the one she'd just received, but it scored top points for enthusiasm.

"Bysshe, darling, you've just helped me save Earth! Look, you're the Master of Ceremonies: Stall the start of the Great Test just a little while. Tell the Golzods I didn't know about being entitled to have a backup team and that I'm making a few calls to assemble my helpers. They'll allow that, won't they?"

"Uh . . . Yes, I assume so. They must. The rules are their own and they are punctilious about obeying the rules. In fact, you should speak with one of them so that they may use their transportation technology to fetch your teammates immediately."

"Oh, yes, that's right: They can do that sort of bzzt-blink-flash-pop thingie, can't they? Silly me, I forgot that's how they brought us all over to Tokyo. Do you think they'll share the secret with our scientists once we prove that we're *civilized* enough for them?"

"Prove we're—?"

"Once *I* prove it by winning this contest! And I will, Bysshe; thanks to you, I will." She gave him another tonsil-bruising kiss. "Okay, I've got to run and talk to the Golzods. Hold down the fort. I love you!" She dashed off.

"You what? I mean, er, how could you do otherwise?" the slightly rumpled Chairman called after her. He tried to recover his self-confident smirk, but settled for fluffing his hair instead. Just because the fate of a whole planet was balanced on the slightly sweaty palms of a low-ranking auxiliary of the Terran-Golzod Liaison Office, there was no reason to look less than his best for the waiting cameras.

"Uh . . . Vu'ukwee-*san?*" Eizo Koga had been assigned to the position of Official Terran Commentator for the televised Great Test and was walking on eggshells as far as the proper way to address his Golzod counterpart.

"Yes, Koga?" the alien replied affably.

It was all Koga could do not to breathe a deep sigh of relief before pressing on to the business at hand, namely giving the worldwide audience additional insights as to what was happening on the floor of Culinary Arena. Holding his old-fashioned hand-mike with practiced ease, he posed the question that was foremost on the minds of all humans, namely: "It's rather, er, past the officially posted starting time and we're still waiting for the challenger. Will your people regard this as a forfeit?"

The alien made noises like a vinyl-covered sofa at a nudist camp, the Golzod equivalent of laughter. "By no means. Ms. Tyler's delayed appearance was cleared beforehand with our High Command. The Earth challenger was unaware until recently that she is entitled to a support team of her own choosing. She requested the time and means to gather that team and we are helping her do so. As you Terrans would say, she will be here in two snaps of an overseer's whip."

"Uh . . . indeed." Koga swallowed hard, but did not allow his personal anxieties to get in the way of his professional duties. Like most Terrans, he had never heard of Ms. Tyler until the Golzods had decreed that the fate of Earth and all who dwelled thereon were hers to decide. He had no idea of her capabilities or chances for success and thus did not dare to get his hopes up. For all anyone knew, the Golzods had stacked the deck by selecting a complete bungler. If only she would get here! The tension of anticipation was even more unbearable than the thought of what would happen should she fail. An abrupt commotion at one end of Culinary Arena drew his attention and he recognized the young woman in the midst of the group marching toward the stage where Chairman Nagoya stood and sparkled.

"Vu'ukwee-*san!*"

"Yes, Koga?"

"The challenger has entered Culinary Arena. However, she doesn't appear to have brought any helpers with her aside from the preassigned corps of *sous* chefs. Have your people disqualified her chosen teammates?"

"Impossible, Koga. She was free to bring anyone she wished. Those are the rules, and we honor them." The alien shadowed its eyes with one tentacle and squinted under the intense lighting. "Are you *quite* certain she is unaccompanied? Perhaps her helpers are obscured by the crowd."

Koga did the same. "Perhaps," he admitted.

On stage, Chairman Nagoya raised his arms for attention, ready to order that the Great Test begin. In the lofty box seats with the best view of the proceedings, the alien delegation shared space with the rest of the Terran-Golzod Liaison Committee. On the floor of Culinary Arena, Allison was almost hidden from sight by the press of *sous* chefs surrounding her, like a lone crouton in a sea of split pea soup. In spite of this, Bysshe made it his business to meet her eyes with a smoldering gaze before saying:

"If memory serves me, it needn't bother; it is worthless. This is the first time that Earth has ever participated in anything like this. Unwonted delay is likewise worthless, except in the case of pot roast, and so I summon . . . *the robot chefs!*" To the sound of trumpet fanfares and the deep, sonorous roll of kettle drums, three platforms descended from the ceiling of Culinary Arena, bearing the mechs who would mindlessly cook up whichever ingredient Allison chose, whether bean, bane, or being.

Allison took another step forward and the press of *sous* chefs around her fell away like the petals of a boiled-for-two-hours artichoke. "I challenge . . . robot chef Golzod!"

"Vu'ukwee-*san!*"

"Yes, Koga?"

"The lights must be playing tricks on my eyes, but I think—I think the challenger has a *child* with her!"

"In that case, my light-receptors are deceiving me as well. I see the same thing. I did not think human young were quite so hairy."

"No, no, no, Vu'ukwee-*san.*" Koga shook his head. "Not the one on the leash, the other one."

"Ah!" The Golzod lacked a neck and could not

nod, but gave every indication of being on the same page as the Terran commentator. "The tail should have alerted me. That is what you call a dog, isn't it?"

"Yes, an Irish Setter; one of the most beautiful breeds." *And one of the stupidest,* he thought, recalling several incidents from his days covering the dog show circuit. To be fair, he was making a generalization based on limited personal experience. Not *all* Irish Setters were dumb any more than all Chihuahuas were shivery bundles of raw nerves or all Yorkshire terriers were weaned on amphetamines. Still, scratch any stereotype deeply enough and you might find a subatomic particle of Truth within.

The dog accompanying Allison was doing his best to justify Koga's prejudices. All of the lights, the music, the strange people and stranger smells had conspired to convince the animal that he had somehow stumbled into the midst of a vast, far-reaching conspiracy which must be stopped at any cost. It was also being run by chipmunks. (As any dog worth his chew toys would tell you, could he but communicate the information effectively, everything wrong or perilous in the world was directly traceable to the evil machinations of chipmunks.) Thus it was that Juniper Crest's Best Pride Lord Alvin Dmitri Montaigne O'Bryan ("Dim" to his friends) opted to cope with this clear and present danger by lunging in all directions and barking like a demented thing at anything that moved. Or didn't.

Allison tried to make Dim calm down, but only succeeded in reducing the volume and frequency of his barking to the point where the dog sounded like a malfunctioning smoke detector. She gave everyone a sweet, apologetic smile and said, "I'm so sorry, but he's always like this when he's on the leash. I know it looks silly, having a dog on my team, but he's really very intelligent and understands all sorts of commands. I'm going to have him fetch my cooking utensils; he'll do it *much* faster than any of my human aides." She leaned over to release the leash catch from Dim's collar, then gave the dog a hand signal. Dim immediately stopped barking, sat down, and wagged his tail. A ripple of appreciative applause washed over the crowd.

The corps of *sous* chefs exchanged miffed looks, but were powerless to object. One of their number, a tad pissier than the rest, did see fit to sneer, "And I suppose that . . . *infant* also has a use?" He nodded at the toddler who, until this point, had been almost completely hidden by Allison's voluminous skirt.

Allison laughed. "Moral support and inspiration. Let us never forget that I'm doing this . . . *for the children.*" In the face of that unanswerable rhetoric-bombshell, the audience and the *sous* chefs broke into a compulsory ovation. This set Dim off again, barking up a storm.

Chairman Nagoya, who had been waiting patiently for silence so that he might get on with his hosting duties, finally gave up and proceeded over the sound of yapping. At his signal, a large, cloth-draped block slowly and majestically arose from the floor before him. The outlines of three separate objects were

clearly discernible beneath the covering of blood-red
silk embroidered with the Golzod homeworld coat of
arms/tentacles.

Giving Allison one last, meaningful look, Bysshe
laid hold of the cloth and announced: "Let the choice
be made!" With a grand, theatrical flourish, he whipped
off the silk.

Something on the display table screamed. Fuzzy
sides heaving, it resembled a guinea pig in the throes
of transition labor as it rolled and rocked and filled
the air with shrill, teeth-gritting cries of distress. The
other two items were less vocal; indeed, they were
inert. Worse, they were identical. Both of them looked
exactly like that fine old Terran staple, a bunch of
carrots.

Allison stared at her three possible choices, then
looked at Chairman Nagoya as if to ask, albeit silently,
whether there had been some mistake. Bysshe turned
away, his beautiful eyes hooded and unreadable.
Somewhere a thin stream of music with a distinctive
beat and melody began to play. It only took Allison
a few seconds before she realized that the Golzods
had pirated the familiar tick-tock tune known to *Jeop-
ardy* fans everywhere. What better way for the
passive-aggressive aliens to convey the message that
she didn't have all day to make her choice?

A russet snout thrust itself over the edge of the
table and snapped at the screaming furball. Allison
grabbed Dim's collar and yanked him back. "Bad dog!
Bad, bad dog! Don't bother the ingredients!" The dog
struggled to escape, leaping for the tabletop again and

again, intent on getting his jaws around the noisiest item present. With one last pull at the dog's collar, Allison snapped the leash back on and handed the end to the nearest *sous* chef.

"Please take him away before he hurts himself," she said. "I guess I won't be able to use him after all."

She gave an exaggerated sigh and a shrug, patted the departing dog on the head, and returned her attention to the display table just in time to see the small child hauling himself onto the surface and reaching for one of the two bunches of carrots. He was contentedly sucking on the curly green tops before anyone could stop him.

"Bobby, *no!*" Allison's shout caused every Golzod present to molt three layers of mucus. While the emergency cleanup crews plied their mops, she forcibly separated the wailing toddler from his prize, handed him over to another of her *sous* chefs, and declared, "I have made my choice! I choose . . . that!" She pointed at the ungummed bunch of carrots.

"So be it," Chairman Nagoya intoned. "*Allez*— Er, let the cooking begin!"

All at once the floor of Culinary Arena erupted as several tables brimming with the chosen ingredient surged into the light. While the selected robotic chef began loading up a basket with bunch after green-topped bunch, Allison contented herself with grabbing one in each hand before retiring to her assigned cooking station.

The gastronomic contest that followed was short and sweet.

"Vu'ukwee-*san!*"

"Yes, Koga?"

"Do you think the challenger has hurt her chances for victory by banishing the only two members of her team that she chose for herself?"

"I don't think so, Koga. I am unfamiliar with many of your Terran ways, but even I could see that they were both more trouble than help. She appears to be doing well enough without them."

"True, Vu'ukwee-*san.* Her preselected *sous* chefs are handling the demands of the contest quickly and efficiently. Look at how they're peeling and cutting up the—the—" Koga paused, unsure of how to proceed. "Er, Vu'ukwee-*san?*"

"Go!"

"How should I refer to the chosen ingredient? At the pre-Test briefing I was informed that one of the three items on the table would be a self-aware being. If the challenger did happen to make the, uh, misjudgment of choosing that one, I feel it would be disrespectful to refer to the unlucky entity as 'it.' "

The Golzod gave Koga as roguish a smile as was possible for a creature with problematic lips. "Can you be certain she did *not* spare the sentient being? The fuzzy brown item is still screaming, after all."

Koga dabbed perspiration from his forehead with a neatly folded white handkerchief. "I would like to believe that, but the universe is often like a mad dim sum chef: You never know what it has put on your plate until you take a bite. If it were me out there, I would not have chosen the item that moved and screamed. I perceive it as far too much of a crimson anchovy, as our English-speaking viewers would say."

"Mmmm, anchovies . . . thin crust . . . extra cheese . . ." Vu'ukwee oozed drool and lapsed into a pleasant reverie. Pizza was the one-and-only aspect of Earth culture that the Golzods agreed was worth the trip.

While Koga attempted to get his colleague back on track, for the sake of the home audience, Allison was hip-deep in the frantic ballet of cookery. At a word from her, the *sous* chefs fetched the prepped ingredient, sliced into uniform circles in a bowl, along with two sealed jars and a loaf of white bread.

"Vu'ukwee-*san!*"

"Anchovies . . . Ummmm . . . Uh, I mean, yes, Koga?"

"Check out the two-knife technique the challenger is using on *four* slices of bread at once!"

"Indeed, her ability to spread that dark purple aspic so swiftly yet so evenly is most impressive. And now she's set out four additional slices of bread and is using two more knives to spread them with the light brown purée from the other jar. What mastery! However . . . what *are* those substances? I am regrettably unfamiliar with Earth condiments," the alien confessed, somewhat shamefaced.

"I think they are—" Koga paused and raised one hand to the audio feed button in his ear. He frowned slightly before replying: "According to my sources, one jar contains peanut butter while the other contains a popular brand of American-made grape jelly."

"How exotic! I can't wait to see what she makes with them."

"You won't have to wait long. She's scattering a layer of the theme ingredient over the peanut butter and now—now I think she's—yes, she *is* putting the jelly-bread on top of it! She's completed all four sandwiches with time to spare. As far as Ms. Tyler is concerned, the Great Test is *ovah!*"

The decision of the four judges was as swift as it was final. To quote the expendable Golzod who took the role of spokesman: "We are all agreed: Ms. Tyler's creation is the nastiest thing we have ever been forced to ingest, but as it did *not* contain the sentient being and since we *did* survive the experience, we declare Earth to remain a sovereign, self-governing planet and welcome the inhabitants thereof into the Golzod Peace Alliance. You will receive your membership packet in four to six weeks. Have a nice day."

"How did you know?" the other bunch of carrots asked Allison. (The correct term for his race was the *Y'hak,* a term that most of the Terrans present at the alcohol-soaked post-Test celebration were already invoking repeatedly.) "How could you tell that I was to be spared?"

Allison lowered her eyes and looked modest. "Well, I rather suspected that the screaming, moving item wasn't sentient—that would have been too easy—but I couldn't tell whether or not it was safe to eat."

"True, true," the Y'hak mused. "The Pilganian

Shriekfruit is instantly, fatally toxic to 99.9 percent of all galactic beings. The remaining .1 percent break out in huge, disfiguring hives and *then* perish."

"That was obvious the moment that the Irish Setter tried to eat it," Chairman Nagoya put in. He sat with his arm around Allison, his face alight with pride in her world-saving accomplishments. "Some dogs are born with the instinct for gobbling down the one thing most likely to kill them. I had a Dalmatian once, who—"

"But how did you know to choose between me and the remaining item?" the Y'hak asked, ignoring Chairman Nagoya in favor of his savior. "My people are famous for our resemblance to the savory *mefmef* root you ultimately selected. It is an evolutionary quirk that provides good camouflage against meat-eating predators, but was almost our doom during my world's Age of Large Rodents. How could you tell the difference?"

Allison laughed. "That was where my two-year-old nephew Bobby came in. Toddlers will put almost anything in their mouths, but I've never met one yet who'd willingly eat his vegetables."

"Such insight!" Chairman Nagoya exclaimed. "Ms. Tyler . . . Allison . . . I no longer care whether or not my faith in you increases your bust size! The allure of your intelligence is irresistible. Say that you will be mine!"

"Marriage? Are you sure?" Allison smiled mischievously. "You know the old saying, Bysshe: Cooking lasts, kissing don't. And aside from a really *nasty* peanut butter-jelly-and-*mefmef* sandwich, I really *can't* cook."

Rather than answer her with words, Bysshe once more sealed her lips with a kiss, thus proving once and for all the not-so-old but no-less-true saying that the way to a man's heart was through his interplanetary Peace Alliance.

HEART'S DESIRE

by Mickey Zucker Reichert

Mickey Zucker Reichert is the best-selling author of more than twenty novels and thirty-five short stories, including *The Return of Nightfall*, the *Renshai* trilogy, the *Renshai Chronicles*, the *Bifrost Guardians* series, *The Legend of Nightfall*, *The Unknown Soldier*, *Flightless Falcon*, the *Books of Barakhai*, and *Spirit Fox* (with Jennifer Wingert). A pediatrician, Reichert lives on a forty-acre farm and divides her time between a zillion animals, family (including three kids who only seem like a zillion), and "real-life research" for her novels and stories. Claims to fame: Both parents *are* rocket scientists, and she *has* performed brain surgery.

CARRINGTON ARBUCKLE SHIFTED from foot to foot in the large den, seeking a polite way to divert the attention of the "leisure mother" from her wall-sized television screen. She lay on a soft, curvy divan, ergonomically designed to prevent back pain and bedsores, and she clearly spent most of her time wrapped in its plushy, garish folds. A boy of about

ten years swayed on a matching chair, his entire head
lost in a VR helmet. Two girls sat staring at the same
screen as their mother. Another boy toddled around
the carpet, stimulated by a robotic tower that dropped,
floated, or whisked away various brightly colored
toys and rescued the child whenever he fell. A baby
lay in a bassinet on the floor, rocked, warmed,
and fed at appropriate intervals by the mecha-
nized crib.

Arbuckle tried not to gawk at the woman, who
shoveled calorie-free snack chips into her mouth by
the handful. She appeared to be in her mid-twenties,
nearly a decade less than half his age, with machine-
styled blonde hair, skin pulled tighter than his prefer-
ence, and more cosmetics than he would have wanted
his own robotic groomer to apply to his wife, Kyra.
She wore shorts and a tank top that exposed her midriff, and she kept the room hotter than Arbuckle, in
his overalls, appreciated. He wiped away beads of perspiration with the back of his gloved hand, smearing
dirt across his broad forehead. He knew he looked a
mess, with his gray-flecked brown hair faded and tangled by sun and wind, his overalls soiled, and mud
adorning his round face; but he did not care. He enjoyed the time outside, sucking in the fresh smell of
overturned earth and new seed. He loved the feel of
his muscles working and, more importantly, the real-
ization of personal accomplishment. He had done
something, anything, with his own hands.

Not that he needed to. Since the field of sensory
robotics had exploded, the technology had become

cheap enough to replace menial labor and become commonplace in every home. In his childhood, Arbuckle remembered, his parents went to work every day while he attended school, earning the money that paid for their necessities, entertainment, and conveniences. Though his mother budgeted every dollar and his father complained about taxes, they understood the need for social welfare programs to feed the hungry and tend to those unable or unwilling to work themselves. Now, it seemed, no one had to toil. The government delivered money monthly to anyone who did not earn it on his own, whatever the reason. And, usually, that reason was that there were no jobs left undone, no goals to fulfill.

Arbuckle continued to study the woman, hoping his hovering presence would become annoying enough for her to deign to glance in his direction. He did not begrudge her her leisure. Every member of today's society had the means and time to entertain himself in any way he preferred, and hours of television was the first choice of most of the population. Even Carrington Arbuckle enjoyed a nightly movie or short comedy now and again. But to him, most, scheduled daytime programming seemed inane, filled with immoral people shamelessly touting decadent actions or self-injurious behavior, often wounding the ones they claimed to love the most. He wondered what voyeuristic satisfaction the audience gained from watching such things. By the size of it, they knew something he did not.

Failing to draw the woman's regard, Arbuckle

glanced at the screen where a middle-aged man mooned
the cameras, his pin-striped trousers around his ankles.
A live audience shouted, wolf-whistled, and clapped,
many exhorting him to turn around. He had the same
fine figure as everyone in this day and age; the food
machines provided nutrients and calories attuned directly to its owner's metabolism and empty taste-alikes
thereafter. Nevertheless, he clearly did not want to
expose himself. Even his buttocks looked flushed, and
he barely moved. It seemed like a dull contrast to
the scantily clad, gyrating young men and women who
regularly appeared on talk shows.

A slight smile eased onto the face of the watching
woman.

Arbuckle considered leaving. After all, this woman
owed him nothing. He volunteered to landscape gar-
dens because he enjoyed the work, not because he
expected anything from the owners of the small strips
of property. It would not be the first time someone
had not even bothered to get up to see what he had
accomplished and how closely it adhered to the
straight rows and colorful lines the robotic gardeners
could craft.

Without taking her eyes from the screen, the woman
finally addressed Arbuckle, "Finished, Cary?"

Though Arbuckle had waited for this moment, the
sudden address surprised him. "Yes, ma'am. Would
you like to come see what I've done?"

The woman raised her hand to silence him, still attentive to the program. "Let me just finish this last
segment." She pointed to the food machine. "Get
yourself something. You must be thirsty, at least."

Arbuckle nodded. He could use a drink, though he knew it would only dispense diet versions of anything he might request. She had clearly already surpassed her calorie allotment. Pressing the proper sequence of buttons yielded a large cup of icy water. He gulped down half of his drink, unable to completely shut out the images parading across the screen. The man had complied with the audience's request for him to turn, though he shielded his genitals with his hands.

One of the girls turned toward the divan. "Mommy, is he going to show?"

"Depends on how much he wants that old-fashioned wooden rocking chair." The woman sat up and brushed chip crumbs from her clothes. Instantly, the cleaning robot shot out to suck up the mess.

Arbuckle sipped at his water, watching. For several moments the man covered himself while the audience screamed. Finally, he dropped his hands to reveal an average-sized set of male anatomy.

The audience went wild as the man ran from the stage and into the sheltering sidelines of the set.

The woman rose, stretched, and headed toward Arbuckle. He stepped aside to let her lead the way, leaving the children behind. It seemed odd to Arbuckle how easily she separated from them, without worrying about their welfare. He recalled his own youth, when his parents dogged his every step, gradually allowing him more freedoms, more moments away from their sight. He rode his bicycle with a helmet and pads, but at least he went where he wished, roaring through puddles and over hills with a speed that sent him airborne. He had loved that feeling: the wind whipping his face, the helpless sensation of flight. To leave an infant or a toddler alone would have smacked of neglect. Now, those things had reversed. Safer among monitoring 'bots and cameras, the children remained in the room; and the populace would consider it abusive for the mother to take her children outdoors where they might ingest worms, breathe in pollens or pollutants, or become infected with viruses. Outside, a stranger might abduct them, a vehicle or machine might ram them, or a fall might cause injury or death.

The mother led Arbuckle back up the stairs and out the door to the government-issued fenced-in strip of land she called her own. Clouds muted the sunlight, though she still squinted and blinked as her eyes adjusted. She examined the young flowers Arbuckle had planted in not-quite-perfect rows and the mounds and lines of dirt where new flowers would grow over the ensuing days and weeks. She managed a weak smile and a pat on his grizzled head. "Very nice, Cary. Very nice. Thank you."

It was more than most clients gave him. A nod here; a grunt there. Yet, Arbuckle did not care. Glad to have anyone at all who allowed him to work, he tried to ingratiate himself as much as possible. "A pleasure, ma'am. You'll have the prettiest garden on the block. Just wait and see."

"I'm sure I will."

The conversation came to an awkward end. Still trying to make her like him enough to invite him back next year, Arbuckle feigned interest in her abstraction. "What was that . . . that show, anyway?"

The woman's head jerked toward him in clear surprise. "You mean the one I was watching?"

Arbuckle nodded. "With the . . . man. The one who . . . pantsed himself."

She laughed at his unusual phraseology. "You've never seen *Heart's Desire?*"

"Never."

She shrugged at his obvious ignorance. "It's a game show. People will do almost anything to get what they want."

"People *want?*" Arbuckle joked. "In this day and age?"

The woman led Arbuckle to the door. "Oh, you'd be surprised. Men want women. Women want men. People want children, can't have them, and don't want to go through the regular slow adoption process." She opened the door for him. "Sometimes it's a family heirloom that got willed to someone else. An antique they can't find. A forbidden food—that's a common one. The missing piece to a collection, maybe an old book." She tipped her head, clearly trying to remember past shows. "A taped episode of a favorite program. Sometimes I can't believe the things people are willing to do to get hold of some dumb old thing."

"Amazing," Arbuckle said as he slipped out the door into the cloud-shrouded sunlight. "Simply amazing."

The conversation haunted Carrington Arbuckle through the day and into a restless night. Eyes closed, he lay on one side until it became clear he would not find sleep in that position. He rolled the other way, toward the center of the bed, to stare at the slack features of his sleeping wife. He smiled. Kyra always looked her most beautiful when asleep, her face fixed with the first wrinkles the groomer could not erase. Long lashes framed her lids, and soft waves of dark brown hair swept over her pillow. He found himself seized with the urge to touch her, to run a hand over the curves that still excited him wildly after more than thirty years of marriage. He knew that would awaken her, so he suppressed that desire, which reminded him of the game show again.

Heart's Desire, the woman had called it. Like every American, Arbuckle had so much and needed so little. In fact, he had more. He had Kyra and the knowledge that a creature of such delicate beauty, of such exquisite intelligence loved him also. Yet, daily, his soul still cried out for the one thing, it seemed, he could not have. *A job.* It seemed so silly. He still remembered the days when people came home from work and collapsed into a favorite chair, moaning about the tedium of their work and the rampant stupidity of their co-workers. He still remembered when Fridays were revered for being the last day of the five-day cycle, not for being the night of a favorite drama or reality show. He who was old enough to recall such things should embrace the idleness mechanization had finally gained them all.

Instead, it gnawed at him, ruining an otherwise happy life. Most times, he reveled in hearing about Kyra's work as a programmer, embraced knowledge

of the other side of the machines most people took
for granted. He hated that he sometimes envied the
seven hours a day she spent performing higher func-
tions that gave her life more meaning. He wished he
had a talent like hers, that the Board had chosen him
as one of the people necessary to keep the world going
rather than simply one of the many who benefited
from that knowledge. He loved Kyra with all his heart.
He celebrated her successes. He only wished he had
a few of his own to share.

Still unable to rest, Arbuckle rolled to his back. He
knew he could not fall asleep in that position; he never
could. It just gave him some relief from the discomfort
his usual postures could not assuage this night. He
forced his thoughts wholly on Kyra. She would need
him bright and alert in the morning. At least, he liked
to believe that, and she indulged his fantasy. He
needed to forget that silly game show. Even if he
could find out how to contact those involved in its
production, he probably did not qualify for it. Even if
he did, he would surely find himself on the end of a
years-long list of waiting contestants. *Foolish thoughts.*
Foolish dreams. Foolish old man.

Arbuckle rolled back to his side; and, this time,
sleep found him.

Carrington Arbuckle awakened to the grind and
whoosh of groomers tending to his wife in the bathroom. He sat up, unusually muddle-headed, and the
blankets fell to his feet. Though he would have preferred more sleep, he forced himself out of bed. Kyra

needed him to get her off to work in the morning.
Clinging to that necessary delusion, he staggered out
of bed. Almost immediately, the 'bot at the footboard
glided up the bed, smoothing the sheets, reaffixing the
blanket. Feeling captivated, Arbuckle watched it work.
It seemed odd that, in his childhood, so many otherwise visionary writers had pictured robots in human
form, a single unit performing the daily humdrum of
every housekeeping chore. It made so much more
sense to use several small 'bots, each designed to a
specific task and shaped and equipped to accommodate it. He watched the bed 'bot perform its function
flawlessly, its laser sensors finding every fold or wrinkle for its flippers and brushes to handle.

Arbuckle disrobed, then selected and pulled on his
clothing, preferring to match his own colors rather
than allowing the machine to do it for him. He picked
out a flattering pants suit for Kyra, a stylish red-and-
white check with a built-in silk scarf. "The usual
breakfast," he sang to the kitchen helper, knowing it
would make Kyra's favorite: scrambled eggs, orange
juice, and light toast with both strawberry jam and
butter, in addition to his bowl of kasha and bows. He
would undergo his own grooming after he sent his
wife off to her job: well-dressed, belly content, and
full of the knowledge of her husband's love.

Kyra emerged from the bathroom naked, amid a
wash of moist, lightly scented air. Scrubbed from head
to toe, white teeth gleaming, she seized Arbuckle's
full attention. Though her body had begun to show its
age, he loved looking at her familiar curves. With the

advent of machine-modified diets, the variation in figure types had lost its extremes. Size had more to do with height and genetic bone structure than girth. Despite that, he could pick his wife's body out of a two-million-woman lineup. Each rise and fall had become his dearest friend. He loved every blemish and wrinkle and would change absolutely nothing about her looks. Her hair formed a sea of red-brown ringlets that accented the perfect oval of her face. Her small nose sat pertly between high-set cheekbones, and her mouth formed a wide-lipped bow. Deeply set brown eyes held a twinkle of mischief. "Carrington W. Arbuckle, what are you looking at?"

"An angel," he answered breathlessly, taking her into his arms and wondering how he could have worried about his "heart's desire" when it stood right in front of him.

"Yuck. You haven't groomed yet." Playfully, Kyra pushed her husband away. "You'll get stinky man-smell all over me."

Arbuckle clung. "Admit it. You love stinky man-smell."

"I love *your* stinky man-smell," Kyra admitted. "Because I love you."

"I love you, too." Arbuckle wondered how many times he had said those words in all the years of their marriage. And meant them just as fervently.

Kyra pulled on the clothing her husband had laid out for her. "So, what's on your agenda for today? Turn off the 'bots and wear the skin off your hands cleaning? Another gardening gig?"

Arbuckle shook his head. "Not today. No one's interested." He finger-combed his tousled mane, looking forward to his own grooming once he got Kyra on her way. "I was thinking about looking into something I learned about yesterday. Have you ever heard of a show called *Heart's Desire?*"

Kyra frowned, tipping her head as she considered. "No," she finally admitted. "Can't say that I have."

Arbuckle expected that answer. She rarely had time for television, and her coworkers would spend their free time discussing evening shows, the ones they had the opportunity to watch. "It's a game show. People humiliate themselves in exchange for something they want."

Kyra paused, one leg in her pants. "Okay . . ."

Arbuckle raised and lowered his shoulders. "Okay, nothing. That's it."

Kyra placed her other foot through the proper leg hole. "There's more to this story, Cary. Otherwise, you wouldn't bother to mention it."

Kyra was right, of course. Even when it wasn't so blatantly obvious, she could always read him with ease. "Well, you know how much I want to work . . ." He glanced into her eyes, afraid she might remind him that he did not need a job, that the government paid him handsomely to stay at home, that most people saw work as drudgery, that having one employed member was more than most families could boast.

"I do," Kyra said. "And I understand that dream. Completely." She did not have to explain its impossibility; Arbuckle did it for her.

"I know. I know." He lowered his head. "You need a talent to hold a job. You have to be able to perform some task that machines can't."

Finished dressing, Kyra took Arbuckle back into her arms. "And being a handsome stud won't do."

Arbuckle grinned at the compliment. Though he considered himself competent in bed, that hardly made him a stud. They had no children, by choice. Though both felt capable of handling the responsibilities of teaching, endowing morality, and sharing their love and experiences, the evolving child abuse laws and penalties intimidated them. The bruises and scrapes that had served as badges of honor in his own youth now became fodder for child protective agencies. The death of a child, no matter how accidental, translated into jail time for someone. "I'm just thinking that this *Heart's Desire* show provides things people can't find on their own. All kinds of things. Maybe—"

"Maybe," Kyra repeated thoughtfully. She smiled so broadly, it lit her entire face. "Why don't you check it out? Let me know what you find out when you come home tonight. I'll support you any way I can."

"Even if I have to pull down my pants on international TV?"

The grin remained. "Even if."

"Even if I have to spill all our sexual secrets, and your mom might be watching."

Kyra winced, but remained smiling. "Even if. Honey, I want you to be happy."

It was a testament to spousal encouragement that went way beyond love.

*   *   *

Carrington Arbuckle could not believe how swiftly things moved from that moment. The next morning, he and Kyra packed a few days' worth of clothes and *tubed* cross-country to Nova Studios in Hollywood, California. There, a trio of serious-looking, dark-suited men ushered them into a small, windowless room. Despite the artificial lights, which usually brought any place to a comfortable illumination, everything seemed gloomy and dim. Plied with illicit candies and soft drinks, he and Kyra sat at a study table in front of a contract as thick as a magazine.

Arbuckle began reading the machine-generated words. Once he got past the part about them promising a job that would not interfere with Kyra's employment, it seemed mostly to protect Nova Studios from legal action in the event of occurrences that seemed to cover every situation from him stubbing his toe on the inside of his own shoe to dismemberment and death. The dimness of the lighting bothered him, blurring the words until he felt the need to squeeze his eyes shut and pinch the bridge of his nose every few minutes as he read. The constant conversation between Kyra and the men distracted him to the point where he found himself poring over the first paragraph repeatedly just to get the point of each sentence.

A woman's voice suddenly intercommed into the room. "Mr. Farris?"

One of the men looked up, brows beetled, and shouted, "Not now!"

"But, Mr. Farris. The second contestant has canceled."

Now, all the men looked up, clearly startled. "But . . . it's a live show!" Farris shouted.

"Yes, sir."

The man pinned Arbuckle with an intent, steel-gray gaze. Mr. Farris, or Jackathan as he had introduced himself to the Arbuckles, had hawklike features with a prominent nose, small slanted eyes, and pinched cheeks. "Mr. Arbuckle, how soon can you have that contract signed?"

Tired of reading, Arbuckle flipped to the last page and penned his signature on a line that held a small black "X" at its beginning. He scribbled in the date. "You don't mean . . ."

"You're going on in just a few minutes." Farris' expression went from panicked to relieved as he passed the stack of papers to Kyra. "And you, ma'am?"

"Me?" Kyra looked at her husband. "Why do I need to sign?"

"You're his witness," Farris explained.

Arbuckle gestured at the papers, and Kyra affixed her name in the space below his. Excitement built to a wild crescendo. *Now?* His heart pounded. *Why not now? Sooner is better.* His thoughts betrayed him. *No. Sooner is not better. I need time to think, time to prepare.* Terror assailed him with a rush that threatened to destroy all self-control. *Sixty-three years old, and I'm about to piss my pants.*

As the men ushered the couple out of the room and into a long hallway filled with autographed celebrity photos, Arbuckle whispered his concerns to Kyra. "It's too soon. I can't do this. I'm not ready."

"Maybe that's best," she soothed. "I don't really

think anyone canceled. I think they planned it this way, so you wouldn't think too hard or too much and ruin your chances of succeeding."

Arbuckle had not considered that. "You think they set me up?"

Kyra shrugged to remind him she had no way of knowing for certain, and she relied on intuition and speculation. "It's probably their standard mode of operation. How many people would change their minds given enough time to consider?"

Arbuckle felt less sure. "If it's really their heart's desire . . ."

"True," Kyra hissed back. "But the people who might chicken out are the same ones likely to embarrass the easiest; and, from what you've told me, the entertainment of this show comes from humiliation. It's not as much fun watching a stranger parade around in his skivvies if he's enjoying doing it."

Arbuckle wiped his sweating hands on his pants, glad the men led them in silence. He needed this time to chat with Kyra.

"Just remember," she said, taking his hand. "No matter what they ask you to do, you can always say 'no.' And if you wind up doing something you regret, I'll still always love you." She winked. "No matter how badly you disgrace us."

Though he appreciated the support, Arbuckle did not like the sound of that. He searched for a positive point. "At least none of our family and friends will know I'm on today. Only the ones who happen to be watching anyway will see us. Fewer people to laugh at us later, and we have the perfect excuse for not telling them in advance."

Jackathan Farris gestured at a door. "Ms. Arbuckle, if you please." He opened it a crack.

Kyra squeezed her husband's hand. "Good luck." She pushed the door open and went inside.

Though the three men remained with him, Arbuckle felt suddenly very alone. He followed Farris through a similar door, trying to remember the names of the other two men. *Randon and Karlo.*

They sat him in a grooming chair that set to work on making his face presentable to the cameras. The largest of the three, the squinty-eyed, dark-haired Karlo talked to the mechanical groomer, getting every detail properly handled, while Randon addressed Arbuckle, "All right, sir. Jack will bring you out on stage—"

The intercom bonged, and the woman's voice came over it again. "Mr. Farris, you're needed on stage in ten seconds."

"That's my cue." Farris patted Arbuckle's shoulders, then winked at his two companions. "I've got to get on stage with the first contestant. You're in good hands. You'll do just fine."

The trite pep talk did little to alleviate Arbuckle's anxiety. He hoped that, when his time came, they would give him more than a ten-second warning.

Karlo continued, "Jack will introduce you to the live audience and explain your situation." Arbuckle nodded, looking at the man's reflection in the mirror in front of him rather than directly at him. This one looked predatory, too. Though he did not have Farris' beak, Karlo had a discomforting look about him that Arbuckle could not quite explain. It came more from expression than appearance, one of learned familiarity and disdain.

"He may banter with you a bit. You're not expected to be a comedian. Just answer straight or kid a bit; but make sure you don't say anything that might hurt Jack's image. You don't want him cranky."

Randon huffed out a little snicker that sounded more snide than amused.

Arbuckle rolled his gaze to the other man. Randon had closely set eyes that barely allowed for a nasal bridge and made him look dishonest. Though Arbuckle knew better than to judge by looks, he dredged up an instinctive aversion to the small blond man known to him only as Randon.

Though he had no intention of riling the host of *Heart's Desire,* Arbuckle had to know. "What's wrong with cranking on Jack a bit?"

The two men exchanged glances that looked sinister to Arbuckle before Karlo replied. "It's just best, Mr. Arbuckle, not to upset someone who has your life in his hands."

"You mean my dignity," Arbuckle corrected.

"Your dignity," Randon said. "Yes, of course."

The groomer beeped to indicate it had finished, and Randon pushed back Arbuckle's chair.

Arbuckle did not like the way the conversation, and the men's manners, had degenerated. "I've changed my mind. I'm not going on."

Karlo's face lost any amiability it might have had to settle into a familiar glower. "I'm afraid, Mr. Arbuckle, you must go on. You signed the contract."

"So?"

"So you have to appear. When you're told to."

"When I'm—" Irritation flooded Arbuckle, coupled with a sudden influx of fear. He suddenly wished he had not allowed them to hurry him, that he had insisted on reading every fine-print word of that insanely thick contract. "You can't—"

A light flashed over the entrance to the room, accompanied by the first few notes of a cheerful song.

"Time to go," Randon announced, ushering Arbuckle through the doorway in a manner so abrupt and certain that Arbuckle never thought to make further protest.

Sandwiched between the two television men, he headed farther down the hallway in a haze of uncomfortable confusion. *What have I gotten myself into?* His own attempts to answer the question soothed him. *Why am I overthinking this? I knew going in they would badger and humiliate me. They want to aggravate me, to intimidate, anything to make a good show for the viewers.* For a moment, he even dared to sympathize with these three men. Day after day, they had to entertain the masses with ever more shocking "true" stories, increasingly gut-wrenching news, and shows that forced contestants to perform more and more dangerous stunts. Each new experience set the bar higher. He remembered how it had all started, in his youth, with shows like *Survivor, Who Wants to Marry a*

Millionaire, and *Fear Factor* that put ordinary people, or celebrities, into situations of ever-increasing anxiety.

Now, overwhelming emotion was not enough for the starved-for-excitement television viewers who thrived on humiliation and danger, but only vicariously. Of course they wanted him emotionally volatile and intense. It would make a far better visual for him to come out huffing and puffing, full of himself and his rights as a citizen before dropping his drawers in front of a live studio audience. They wanted not just to slap him, but to topple him.

The trio stopped in front of another door, this one with a winking red light near the top. Randon stepped from in front of Arbuckle to beside him. "When the light turns green, that's your cue to enter and walk over to Jack."

Calmed by his own considerations, Arbuckle decided to let his escort sweat. "And what if I don't go through?"

Karlo refused to banter, his tone chilling. "Please don't go there, Mr. Arbuckle. You'll be so much happier if you don't."

It was not the answer Carrington Arbuckle wanted or expected. Before he could argue, the light flashed green, and the door swung open of its own accord. He looked at the two men beside him, surprised to find no amusement on their faces. They stood together behind him now, a solid wall of opposition. If he tried to back out now, he would have to shove his way past them. Again, the sense of unease spiraled through him. All moisture left his mouth to seep from his palms and pits. *You want this, Cary. Don't try to weasel out now.* Steeling himself, he walked through the door and onto the *Heart's Desire* stage.

Bright lights blinded Arbuckle. Ahead, he saw a beckoning Jackathan Farris, his teeth like white beacons in a broadly smiling face. To his right, an audience darkened nearly to obscurity cheered his entrance wildly.

"And here he is!" Farris announced. "Mr. Carrington Arbuckle!"

Arbuckle approached the host without bothering to acknowledge the audience or their apparent appreciation.

Farris placed an arm around Arbuckle's shoulders as if they were old friends. "Tell us about yourself, Mr. Arbuckle."

Arbuckle forced a smile. "Well, I'm sixty-three years old, married to the most wonderful woman in the world for almost thirty-one years—"

Farris interrupted, "I didn't know you were married to my mother."

The audience erupted into laughter.

Arbuckle managed to hold his smile. "Her name is Kyra. She's a programmer."

The audience clapped politely.

"Any children?"

Arbuckle shook his head.

Farris removed his hand. "The stage is well miked, Mr. Arbuckle; but I don't think the people in back can hear your head rattling."

More laughter.

Arbuckle found the old joke more irritating than humorous. "No, sir. No children."

Apparently dissatisfied with the small talk, Farris took over. "Well, ladies and gentlemen. Mr. Arbuckle has an unusual wish for *Heart's Desire* to grant. Unusual, that is, until today when you heard our previous contestant ask for the same thing. Yes, kind audience, Mr. Arbuckle is not satisfied with the freedom to come and go as he pleases, to take long vacations to places around the world and not have to worry about angering some boss or client. Mr. Arbuckle wants . . ." He paused dramatically ". . . a job."

Only a smattering of applause met this pronouncement.

Farris turned to Arbuckle. "Obviously, not too many in our audience share your dream."

More clapping.

"Can you explain why you want to trap yourself into the workaday life our parents escaped?"

Arbuckle cleared his throat, trying to verbalize the deep desire that haunted his waking moments and, sometimes, his dreams. "I–I . . ."

"Obviously not the same reason as our last contestant, Mr. Palance."

The audience fairly howled with laughter at a joke Arbuckle did not have the information to understand.

Farris explained, "He beautifully described an overwhelming, artistic need to express himself and share stories with the world. To educate the masses through well-written or spoken craft."

Now, Arbuckle understood and managed a grin at the comparison of his stammering self to a suave author. "Obviously, I don't share his talent."

The audience clapped to show their appreciation for his humility.

"I have different reasons for wanting to work. I like using my hands and mind and not just for myself and my family. I find a deep satisfaction in knowing that I'm giving myself to others. I like to feel that I'm appreciated and needed." Arbuckle continued, still uncertain he had explained it quite right. "I thrive on a feeling of accomplishment, in doing what needs doing because . . ." Once again, he lost the proper words.

". . . it needs doing?" Farris supplied, turning the whole mess into a crude redundancy.

Though put in a simplistic way, Arbuckle could not help but agree. "Yeah. Like that." Doubts assailed him. For the first time, he wondered if he deserved a job, clearly lacking the linguistic talent of this Mr. Palance.

The sound rising from the audience seemed to mingle light mirth with understanding grunts and a smattering of applause. Arbuckle wondered if they appreciated the sincerity of his wish or just Farris' wit.

Farris' tone changed to a well-projected boom of familiarity. "Okay, Mr. Arbuckle. Let's play *Heart's Desire*."

Now, the audience erupted in cheering. A curtain whisked open on the back wall of the stage to reveal an enormous board holding hunks of multicolored cardboard at regular intervals. At the top, in bold red letters, it read: EMBARRASSMENT.

"All right now, Mr. Arbuckle. I know this is your first time on or seeing the show, so I'm going to explain what happens next." Farris made a sweeping gesture toward the board. "The studio and home audiences will vote on whether or not performing an embarrassing act is enough to earn your Heart's Desire. Then, I'm going to ask you whether you're ready to perform. If you agree that your Heart's Desire is worth an act of embarrassment, you will select a card from the board which will tell you what you need to do to obtain your . . ." The audience chanted along with Farris, enunciating each word: "Heart's Desire!"

Arbuckle nodded, certain Farris would help him with the details.

"Let's give the audience a chance to vote." Farris waved a hand toward the crowd. "Go!" Then, he looked directly at an area beyond the people, apparently a specific hidden camera. "You at home can vote, too, using the PIP button on your television sets."

Farris returned his attention to Arbuckle. "Now, sir, it's time for you to decide if embarrassment is worth your heart's desire."

Tense music filled the background, the type that played behind suspense movies, filled with uncertainty and need. It all seemed silly to Arbuckle. If he were unwilling to undergo some silly, awkward moments for his cause, he would never have volunteered for the show. "Yes," he finally said.

"Yes?" Farris repeated.

"Yes," Arbuckle said louder, this time heralded by audience applause and cheers.

"Choose your weapon." Farris made another grand gesture at the board, where the colored cards began flashing.

Uncertainly, Arbuckle approached the slabs of cardboard, selecting a yellow one at random, his favorite color. Freeing it from the holder, he glanced at the other side to read, in huge neon letters: LEMON SURPRISE.

"What's it say?" Farris asked, though he could see the card at least as easily. Arbuckle suspected a person in the back row of the studio could also.

Arbuckle turned the card to face the audience. "It says, 'Lemon Surprise.' "

Applause.

"And, do you know what that means?"

"No, sir," Arbuckle admitted.

At that moment, an object came hurtling toward him at tremendous speed. Arbuckle scrambled to duck, too late. An enormous pie slammed into his face. Pain shocked through his head and neck, and the force of the blow sent him sprawling. He landed on his buttocks, pain lancing up his spine, and sat there, stunned.

The audience whooped and hollered.

Farris offered Arbuckle a hand, helping the older man to his feet. When the noise died down, he said softly, "Surprise."

Arbuckle tasted the lemon in an otherwise disgusting concoction. "Lemon surprise," he whispered, sticky and dripping. It had made him look like a fool, and it would probably take at least two grooming sessions to clean off; yet, it seemed well worth it. *I have a job! I'm employed.*

"Randon," Farris called offstage. "Please come take Mr. Arbuckle to the groomer. Karlo, show us what the audience said. Did Mr. Arbuckle earn his heart's desire?"

What? Arbuckle whirled to face Farris directly. *Why is that even in question?*

A deep, disappointed buzzer sound filled the studio, accompanied by two huge letters that replaced the rack of cards: NO!

The audience went wild again, a combination of groans and cheers.

"I–I don't understand," Arbuckle stammered, wiping a stinging mass of pie from his eyes.

Farris raised his hand, and the crowd went silent. Randon slid through the stage door to stand patiently by Arbuckle's side.

"Folks, Mr. Arbuckle says he doesn't understand. You see, we have a *Heart's Desire* virgin here." The crowd remained politely silent while Jackathan Farris explained. "Mr. Arbuckle, the audience gets a large say in this show. Remember, before you picked your card, they voted to decide whether or not a simple act of embarrassment would be enough to win you your heart's desire."

Arbuckle was starting to hate the phrase that formed the name of the show.

"Apparently, they decided that it wasn't enough.

You need to continue playing our show." He pointed at Randon, still waiting in silence. "Please go get cleaned up. We'll be waiting here for your next decision on . . ."

Again, the audience gave Farris a unison, ". . . *Heart's Desire!*"

Carrington Arbuckle returned from the groomer within a few minutes, freshly dressed and scrubbed but not at all sure he wished to continue. The game had intricacies that worried him, rules he did not understand. He wished he had had the time to read the entire contract, now certain that Kyra was right. They had rushed him into a hasty signature on purpose. They clearly wanted to keep him ignorant about much of the game. The audience seemed to enjoy the intimacy of holding his dignity in their hands, along with Jackathan Farris. They knew more than Arbuckle did about his own fate, and that gave them power.

Arbuckle emerged through the door at the proper signal, amid another swell of audience applause. A new board hugged the back wall, this one entitled HUMILIATION and also holding an array of cards.

"Okay, Mr. Arbuckle," Farris started. "Are you ready to continue playing . . ."

This time, Arbuckle found himself mouthing along with the crowd, ". . . *Heart's Desire?*"

Arbuckle cleared his throat. "I'm not sure it's possible to be ready."

"You're here," Farris pointed out. "We were taking bets on whether you'd tubed off to Botswana to hide."

The audience laughed.

"All right, Mr. Arbuckle. It's now up to you and the audience to decide whether your heart's desire is worth utter humiliation. Studio, home . . ." Farris made another looping arm movement. "Hit those buttons!"

"All right, Mr. Arbuckle." Farris turned his attention to his contestant. "What's your answer?"

"I've come this far." Arbuckle hated the thought of having been blindsided by a giant pie for nothing. "I guess it's . . ."

Though Arbuckle felt he had already made his intention clear, the audience seemed to hold its breath.

". . . yes."

"Yes?" Farris repeated.

Arbuckle winced. *I can do this.* "Yes."

The audience cheered.

"Choose the weapon of your humiliation."

Once again, the cards on the board flashed in rainbow hues. Arbuckle wondered if most contestants preferred the idea that their fates appeared to lie in their own hands by their personal selection of a card. In truth, they could have no way of knowing what was behind any given card, so there was no real choice to it, just blind, dumb luck. This time, Arbuckle selected a red card in the upper left hand corner, hoping the natural tendency for people to pick a second or third row card would make those the ones to avoid. He flipped the card over. It read, "Striptease."

"What's it say," Farris asked.

Arbuckle swallowed hard, hoping his pride went down with the saliva. "It says, 'Striptease.' "

The audience twittered.

"Does that mean what I think it means?"

Suggestive music blared to sudden life.

"It means exactly what it says, Mr. Arbuckle." Farris winked at the audience, evoking some frank laughter. "You start right away and end with the music. Don't go too fast, or you'll spend more time than you want fully naked. On the other hand, if you're not buck by the time the music ends, you forfeit."

Please, Mom, don't be watching. Please, Gran, don't be watching. Please, Great Granna, don't be watching. Wondering if a man could truly die of embarrassment, Arbuckle stepped forward, flushed from the roots of his hair to his toes. Never much of a dancer, he did his best to appear game, to win the hearts and minds of the audience. The sooner he did, the less future humiliation he might have to undergo.

One by one, the items of unfamiliar clothing slithered off of him, while he did his best imitation of bumps, grinds, and gyrations and the audience remarked on every movement with cheers, hisses, or laughter. He found himself wearing more clothing than usual, and the dresser 'bot had obviously prepared for this contingency by putting him into boxers decorated with tiny penises over jockeys with a strategic smear. He held out as long as possible, but as the song slowed toward ending, he finally displayed his goodies for a wildly whoopping crowd.

The moment the music ended, though, Arbuckle scrambled for the clothes, hastily donning them as Farris spoke into the air while looking at the audience.

"Karlo, show us what the audience said. Did Mr. Arbuckle earn his heart's desire?"

Arbuckle wondered just how much further he could go if the audience refused him, even as he felt certain they would let him off the hook this time.

Then, that horrible buzzer rang across the stage, and the brilliant neon of those horrible two letters flashed across the back of the stage: NO!

No. Arbuckle could scarcely believe it as he buckled his pants. *How could they say no?* Disgust trickled through him, followed by a dense shiver of horror. He could not image how much further he could go. If they expected him to join some onstage orgy, they would have to find another patsy. He would never betray Kyra. "I'm done," he whispered too softly for the ubiquitous microphones to pick up. "I'm finished with this ridiculous game."

Even without amplification, Farris heard him. "You're done," he warned just as softly but with clear venom, "when I say you're done."

Arbuckle's nostrils flared. He had grown as tired of the veiled threats as he had of the insolent host. He wanted to grab Jackathan Farris by the throat and throttle him on live TV.

Farris never missed a beat, the phony smile still glued to his face. "Well, the audience has spoken again. It's time to go on to our next category."

The humiliation board disappeared, replaced by one that read: DANGER.

"We don't usually get this far, but Mr. Arbuckle's heart's desire is particularly difficult to grant, as you clearly know. Should he make it through the final round, he will not just get a job. He will get one of the most sought after jobs in the world, a job right here at Nova Studios."

The audience went into a wild frenzy of cheering that seemed to rock the room.

Arbuckle stood frozen, fists still balled yet no longer driven to harm Farris. Irritation and outrage had nearly caused him to forget the reason he had come. For all his smarminess, Farris was truly about to offer him his heart's desire. He glanced at the board. *If I survive to take it.* He shook his head. Nothing was worth risking his life over.

"Audience, it's time to vote. Will surviving a dangerous act earn Mr. Arbuckle his . . ."

"*. . . Heart's Desire?*"

Farris turned back to Arbuckle. "All right. Our audience has voted. What say you, Mr. Arbuckle? Is that job worth performing a dangerous act?"

Arbuckle cleared his throat into a growing silence. "No," he finally said.

Farris glared, though his tone never lost its friendly edge. "No?"

"No," Arbuckle repeated firmly.

The audience booed.

"Are you quite certain, Mr. Arbuckle?"

"I'm certain." Arbuckle felt as if his heart sank into his chest like a stone in water, but he knew he had made the right decision. Too much about this show seemed sinister and secretive, just plain wrong.

The audience made more noises of unpleasantness and revulsion.

Farris raised his hand, and the noise fell to a hush. "Don't worry, Mr. Arbuckle, it's not over yet."

Dread clutched at Arbuckle. *It's not?*

"If the audience also said 'no,' then you have one more chance. One last chance to obtain . . ."

". . . your *Heart's Desire!*"

"No one's ever gone this far, Mr. Arbuckle. Let's look now and see." Farris waved his arms in his grandest gesture yet. "Karlo, show us what the audience said. Did Mr. Arbuckle lose the chance to earn his heart's desire?"

For the third time, the buzzer rang, and the giant letters forming the word "no" appeared on the background.

No? No. Now what? Arbuckle held his breath, daring to hope. Perhaps they went full circle. Maybe, just maybe, another pie in the face might earn him the job he believed he had given up by his refusal.

A new board appeared in the back. For several seconds, it sat in darkness, then the words finally sprang into relief, a single white card in its center. The title read: MORTAL DANGER.

The crowd seemed to suck in a collective breath.

Arbuckle's eyes widened, then he laughed. It came out in a hysterical wave, welling up from his abdomen with the inevitability of vomit. When he finally managed words, he spat them at Farris, "You must be joking, Jack."

"Oh, this is no joke." Farris stepped around Arbuckle to tap the only card. This time, he did not request an audience vote, did not ask if Arbuckle wished to perform the act written there. "You're committed, Mr. Arbuckle."

"Committed!" Arbuckle had had enough. "You should *be* committed. I'm not putting my life on the line for anything, especially from your crazy show. My answer is no. An emphatic, neon no. Don't bother to question, because my answer is still 'no.' "

Farris bowed to the audience. "Excuse us for a moment, please."

Music swelled to life as Farris led Arbuckle from the stage through a door and into a small room that contained nothing but a table, two chairs, and a copy of the contract. Casually, Farris dropped into one of the chairs. "Mr. Arbuckle, please sit."

"No." Anger, held in check, seethed into that single word. "I know you're not used to hearing this, Jack Farris, but no. I'm not so desperate that I'd risk my life for work."

"Mr. Arbuckle—"

Arbuckle had not finished his piece. "I don't know what kind of stupid, bug-fuck game you're playing with me, but I'm done, finished, out of here. I'm not playing anymore."

"Mr. Arbuckle—"

"Who the hell do you think you are, anyway? What right do you have to put anyone's life in danger?"

This time, Farris waited before speaking with a calmness that only stoked Arbuckle's rage. "Are you finished?"

"For the moment." Arbuckle refused to sacrifice his right to explode again. "I should have known when I came that I was wasting my time, sacrificing sixty-three years of dignity for nothing."

"So you're not finished." Farris folded his hands on the table. "Please, go on."

"I have nothing else to say." Arbuckle finally took a seat.

Farris riffled through the contract, then folded it back to expose a single page. "You're obligated to finish the game, Mr. Arbuckle." He shoved the contract toward Arbuckle, and he noticed that it was not the exact copy he had signed. Clearly, Jackathan Farris was taking no chances that Arbuckle might attempt to destroy it.

Arbuckle did not bother to read it, shoving the whole back toward the game show host. "I don't give a damn what it says. Consider me in violation. Sue me."

Farris rose, stretching. "All right, Mr. Arbuckle. I guess I'm not going to convince you that your wife's life is worth putting your own at risk for."

The words made no sense, just a garble of syllables. Arbuckle contemplated each sound separately, forcing them together into a cohesive whole. It took him much longer than it should have to make sense of the sentence; and, even then, the concept still eluded him. "What?"

"The contract." Farris tapped the page he had tried to show Arbuckle. "It gives me the right to have your wife executed if you break the rules of the game."

"That's ridiculous." Arbuckle felt certain Farris was playing him. He glanced around, looking for cameras and microphones, though he doubted he would see them even if they existed. They had become small enough to hide on the head of a pin. "No one would enforce a contract that said such a thing. You can't—"

"Oh, I can, Mr. Arbuckle. And the Supreme Court of this nation has upheld my right to do so." Farris grinned, leaning nearly into Arbuckle's face. "You see, it's not easy entertaining the masses. It takes some, to use a phrase from your time . . . extreme measures."

Arbuckle barely glanced at the contractual paragraph, realizing it did allow Farris to do exactly what he had just stated. *Kyra. Not Kyra.* "I don't believe this."

"Mr. Arbuckle, the audience and I have waited a long time for someone like you. Someone so uninformed about the show, he doesn't see his own peril until it's upon him. Now, are you ready to continue?"

Arbuckle sat in stupid silence, wondering what other rights he had signed away in ignorance with the stroke of a pen. "I want a lawyer. I want one right now."

Farris laughed. "Page six, paragraph four. You waived your right to counsel. Now, the longer we sit here, the longer Kyra has to stay in that other room with Karlo's gun at her temple. You have exactly four minutes to make your decision. The audience gets to watch you risk your life, or Kyra lose hers. Between her screaming, pleading death and your emotional reaction, I think they'll get their money's worth either way. I just think they'd prefer to see you have a fighting chance.''

"This can't be true," Arbuckle managed to whisper. His chest ached, and he wondered if he was having a heart attack.

"It is.''

"I . . . you . . .'' A surge of temper filled him with a white-hot need to kill the man beside him. "You disgusting bastard!''

"I've been called worse." Farris glanced at his watch. "Three minutes. Now, Mr. Arbuckle, you need to come back out on stage with me. If you don't, we'll assume you've made the decision to sacrifice Kyra.'' He started toward the door.

Head whirling, Arbuckle followed. More than anything, he wished he had never come. Barring the ability to change the past, he wanted time to read through the contract, to find some glaring loophole. *Could they really do that? Could they really kill Kyra?* It seemed impossible, yet he dared not take the chance. *Better to put my life on the line than test that theory.*

As the two men reemerged from the room, the audience clapped tentatively.

Farris announced, "Mr. Arbuckle has reconsidered. He has agreed to the challenge.''

This pronouncement produced a wild flurry of cheers that seemed to go on forever.

Thoughts swirled through Arbuckle's mind, unsortable. He pinched the flesh of his back, hoping it might awaken him from a nightmare. This could not possibly be real.

Farris whisked out the one card and held it up for all to see. "MANHUNT," he proclaimed, reading the enormous letters.

Again, the audience shouted so long and loud that no one could speak for at least a minute. They chanted, "Manhunt, manhunt, manhunt . . ."

Arbuckle felt dizzy. His knees buckled, and only Farris' firm grip on his arm kept him standing. "What," he managed, already knowing the answer, "What does that mean?"

Farris did not wait for the noise to die down, clearly not caring if only Arbuckle heard him. The others already knew. "We have two men competing for one job. Two men, two guns, one job. The one who comes out alive . . ."

"The one who . . . ?" Arbuckle could scarcely believe what he was hearing. None of this made any sense, at least not in any civilized, logical world that he had known. *Have we fallen this low? Is it really possible?* Arbuckle could not believe it. "The one who comes out alive gets to spend forever in prison."

The chant died as the audience clued in to the quiet exchange it was missing.

Farris turned Arbuckle a rictus grin. "No. I signed the contract, too. Any crime you commit during the duration of the show is pardoned."

"Even cold-blooded murder?" The question was stunned from Arbuckle as he stared at the wickedly smiling host. The power of television personnel had grown beyond any propriety, fueled by the hunger for ever more stimulating shows to fill the empty hours. Arbuckle, and others like him, had become dinosaurs, throwbacks to a distant time when people merited what they earned, when a few hours of hollow, happy entertainment allowed some escape from the workaday world. His need to keep busy had held him from the main form of human amusement, had left him behind in a world gone terribly mad. No wonder the audience saw justice in this heavy price for obtaining a job in television. It was the modern equivalent of playing god.

"Any crime is pardoned." Farris no longer addressed only Arbuckle, so his voice rose in volume and regained its showman's quality. "But only for the duration of the show, Mr. Arbuckle. So don't get any wild ideas about plugging some ex-wife when we're finished."

The crowd chuckled at humor so dark it seemed more like a black hole.

Arbuckle doubted he could kill this other innocent man who had done nothing worse than wish for a way to earn his living. Resigned to death, and certain Farris would fill him in on the details, he only had one more question. "So long as I participate, no matter the outcome, Kyra goes free? Right?"

Farris raise his hand like an old-fashioned boy scout. "On my honor."

Now, Arbuckle's expression grew grim. "I'll need something more significant than that, you doubledealing, two-faced bastard. I've seen more honor in a speck of ant shit."

The audience laughed nervously, and Jackathan Farris' ever-present smile finally slipped.

*   *   *

The contest waited only until Farris demonstrated the appropriate parts of the contract and a monitored image of Kyra at the business end of Karlo's gun. Carrington Arbuckle doubted they had told her exactly what he needed to do to free her, but he could see the fear in her eyes that betrayed a brave front. She never doubted they would kill her if he did not cooperate. "She gets released the moment this slaughter in the guise of a game begins. Right?"

"It's in the contract," Farris reminded.

In the contract. Arbuckle hated that phrase. He would never sign anything again in his life. Unwilling to believe the general populace had become this bloodthirsty, he had to believe they did not truly understand the reality of the situation. Accustomed to actors, they would expect the dead man to appear in some future episode, unable to truly separate fantasy from reality.

But to Carrington Arbuckle, the situation was all too real. He wished he had the verbal fluency to override their love for Jack Farris, to explain to them how twisted their beloved host's morality had become that he would gleefully send two strangers out to slaughter one another for amusement. He suspected his opponent would prove equally innocent and desperate, another *Heart's Desire* "virgin" with a threatened family member should he refuse to take part in this abomination. Arbuckle did discover that, although this was the show's first manhunt, the hosts had built up this moment with promises that it would come. Someday, they would find two men ignorant and desperate enough to sign a sheaf of papers without reading it and place themselves in the position of becoming brutal rivals, each hellbent on the other's death.

Randon hefted a blunt-nosed needler. "This is your weapon. It's an FNPDW."

Arbuckle looked at the gun but made no move to take it. "Huh?"

Karlo cut through the jargon. "A Fabrique Nationale Personal Defense Weapon. It's got a thousand round cassette of subcaliber needles. The safety's in the trigger. All you have to do is hold it in." He pointed at the proper place, then took the weapon out of Randon's hands and cradled it expertly. "Choose your target wisely and keep your pull light. After about a minute, you're out of ammo."

The voices seemed to come at Arbuckle from a great distance. In a quiet daze, he followed his handlers to the studio battlefield.

For some reason, Arbuckle expected a jungle scenario, so the dull brown mounds of dirt caught him by surprise. Randon pinned a tiny microphone to his shirt, worried that the studio mike could not pick up the small sounds of the interaction: the scuff of foot on dust, the labored panting of his breathing as the hunt grew more frantic, any muttered comments, last words, or exchanges of conversation. The audience sat in a high circle that gave them an overview of the entire battleground, separated from stray gunfire by a transparent dome. It also blocked out sound, which

kept the audience from shouting information about
a favored man's whereabouts to the other. Arbuckle
wondered if he could use the directions of their gazes
to help him figure out how to avoid his opponent.

My opponent. The description seemed way too
weak. *My killer, or my victim.* A chill spiraled through
Arbuckle, filled with a hopeless rage that sparked
abruptly to a bonfire. *Damn those bloodthirsty vul-
tures. Damn Jack Farris and his damned evil show.*
Needing an object on which to vent, Arbuckle tight-
ened his grip on the gun. He could not bring himself
to damage it; though he doubted he could kill a man,
he also did not wish to die. Instead, he set the gun on
the ground and turned his ire against the microphone,
snatching it from his shirt with a suddenness that tore
a gash in the fabric. It gaped open to reveal a thinning
tangle of brown hair, liberally grayed.

Focused wholly on the tiny microphone, Arbuckle
barely noticed the cool kiss of air against naked flesh.
He drove his fingernails against the finespun steel of
the microphone, kneading at the construction until it
weakened. When it did not break fast enough, he put
it in his mouth and bit down until he felt it give. Again
and again he gnawed at the mike until his jaw ached
and the microphone became a tiny, mangled bit of
metal. Finally, he dropped it to the ground, stomping
it into the dirt.

Only then, Arbuckle returned to his senses to see
the audience above him shouting soundlessly, some
with hands clamped to their ears, others shaking their
fists at him, and several more jabbing fingers in his

direction. For an instant, he reveled in the discomfort
his temper tantrum gave them, the pops and shrieks
of the dying microphone. He only hoped the noises
had equally bothered Farris and his buddies. Then,
the significance of the audience revealing his location
struck home. *Oh, my god! I've got to move!*

Snatching up his weapon, Arbuckle sprinted in a
random direction, tearing around the nearest dirt
mound, then another. As he rounded the second one,
he collided with something solid with a force that sent
him tumbling. He slammed to the ground, breath
driven from his lungs. Jarred from his grip, the needler
skittered across the dirt. *No!* Gasping for breath, he
forced himself to look up into the startled features of
a man half his age, still clutching a gun exactly like
the one Arbuckle had lost.

The younger man scrambled to point the barrel at
Arbuckle's chest. "Don't move."

Arbuckle could not completely heed the words. His
chest flailed wildly for air, beyond his control. His
oxygen-starved brain registered only the need to
breathe. Finally, his diaphragm spasmed open, and his
lungs managed to suck in a welcome breath. "Wait,"
he squeezed out, so softly the man had to bend closer
to hear. "One . . . last . . . request." He gasped again,
his lungs fully in control. He hoped his body would
soon recognize its recovery and breathe without the
deep and chaotic sucking that made his entire chest
ache.

"I'm listening." The other man, apparently the one
Farris had called Mr. Palance, said.

"When you're . . ." Arbuckle forced out in a wheeze, ". . . finished . . . with me, promise me one thing."

Warily, Palance nodded, in no way bound to any last request. "Save . . . some ammo . . . for . . . Jack Farris."

In the monitoring room of Nova Studios, Jack Farris and his two assistants watched the battlefield encounter from their wall-sized screen.

"What's he saying? What's the geezer saying?" Randon demanded, leaning toward the screen as if that might increase the volume.

Farris pursed his lips in irritation. He had expected the old man to lose, just not this quickly. They had budgeted too much time they would now have to waste chatting with Tyler Palance and discussing the contest. *Stupid old man. Stupid weak old man.* At least, they had learned some lessons for the next time. They had kept the battlefield simple, worried that spending too much time on the two men trying to find one another would become a bore. Hopefully, the audience had not expected much from this first manhunt. Each progressive one could become more detailed and exciting, with more interesting participants, bloodier weapons, more complicated terrain.

Karlo picked his teeth with a thumbnail. "Begging for his life, no doubt." He slipped into falsetto. "Please, don't kill me. Please. My wife will miss me."

Randon laughed at the imitation.

Farris made a curt gesture. "Quiet. I'm trying to hear." *Stupid old man.* He cursed Arbuckle again. The pleading and groveling would add to the suspense, if only the audience could hear it, if only he had not destroyed that microphone. *Another thing we'll have to keep in mind for next time. Hidden mike. Better sound system overall.*

Palance placed the needler's barrel against Arbuckle's chest.

"Moron." Karlo winced at the winner's ignorance. "Never get that close to an enemy. He'll take the weapon right out of your—"

Suddenly, Arbuckle stiffened, then slumped over Palance and the gun.

"Or not," Randon finished.

Palance screamed. With the volume turned all the way up in an attempt to catch the faint whispers, the sound emerged in an ear-splitting wail of pain. The entire audience jumped.

Farris loosed a foul string of swear words, rushing to decrease the volume. "From that position, you can't see anything. I can't see anything!"

"Jack!" Palance yelled. "Jack! Can you hear me?"

"What the hell?" Randon finished muttering before thumbing on the intercom and nodding to Farris.

"I hear you, Tyler, buddy. Are you all right?" Farris tried to sound appropriately concerned.

"No, I'm not all right. I'm pinned under two hundred pounds of bloody corpse." Palance shoved at Arbuckle's still form. "And I hurt my leg. Bad. Some of those needles must have ricocheted."

"Ricocheted off what?" Karlo could not help saying.

Farris frowned at his companion, shaking his head. The details of Palance's injury did not matter. If they did not treat him with the utmost courtesy, they would never find another contestant for *Heart's Desire*.

"Hold on, Mr. Palance. We're on our way." Farris clicked off the intercom and opened the door. "Come on, guys. Let's clean up the mess."

The three headed into the hallway, then through the door to the battlefield. Farris continued talking, his voice pitched to maintain the suspense, to keep the audience occupied as well as to pacify Palance. "We're on the field now." He waved at the audience who opened their mouths in what had to be a cheer. They jumped, waved, and pointed in an obvious attempt to steer him to the correct location. Farris covered the microphone to address Randon and Karlo. "You two lift the corpse. I'll slide Palance out and help him walk." He uncovered the microphone. "We're coming around the last dirt mound."

The three men stepped around the hill to find themselves looking down the barrels of two needlers in the hands of Tyler Palance and a very much alive Carrington Arbuckle.

Farris stiffened. "What . . . what are you doing?"

Arbuckle leveled the weapon directly at Farris' midsection. "Ridding the world of a parasite."

"But that's murder!"

"I calculate," Palance said softly, "that we have fifteen minutes to commit any crime, scot-free, thanks to your wretched contract."

Karlo made a desperate dive for the dirt, but not

before a minute of trigger pulling sent two thousand tungsten carbide needles through the bodies of Farris and both of his assistants.

Jackathan Farris knew nothing more.

The only surviving member of *Heart's Desire*'s human contingent met the two ruffled men at the stage door. Beside her stood Kyra and a seven-year-old girl Carrington Arbuckle knew must be Palance's daughter. He threw himself into Kyra's arms, even as Palance's daughter flung herself at her father. Arbuckle closed his eyes, enjoying the warmth and closeness of Kyra, a joy he thought he would never know again. Suddenly, finding work seemed grotesquely unimportant.

The stranger's voice, the same as they had earlier heard over the intercom, broke the warm silence of their reunions. "It seems we have some fresh openings on the *Heart's Desire* team. And I understand both of you gentlemen want jobs."

Before the words could even sink in, accompanied by understanding of what such a thing might entail, the woman continued.

"I've always wanted to take this show in a completely different direction, but the men wouldn't let me. Perhaps my new colleagues will."

Palance hefted his daughter, who clung to his neck. "Count me in." He looked at the embracing couple. "Cary, please? We make one hell of a team."

The idea thrilled Arbuckle. Any job would suit him, but taking the one held by the monsters whose corpses now lay on their own battlefield seemed ironically ap-

propriate. He felt closer to Tyler Palance than he had
to any friend in the past. It amazed him how quickly
an alliance could grow when two men beat down the
devil together. "I–I . . ." He released Kyra far enough
to hold her at arm's length. ". . . have to ask my
gorgeous wife."

Kyra smiled. "Well, I've been talking to Madison,
here." She gestured at the other woman. "She says
Nova Studios has a lot of 'bots and computers that
will need reprogramming."

Arbuckle grinned. "Then count me in, too."

Having heard everything on the sound stage, the
audience whooped and cheered.

MIND GAME

by Susan Shwartz

Susan Shwartz's most recent books are *Second Chances*, a retelling of *Lord Jim*; a collection of short fiction called *Suppose They Gave a Peace and Other Stories*; *Shards of Empire*, and *Cross and Crescent*, set in Byzantium; and the *Star Trek* novels (written with Josepha Sherman) *Vulcan's Forge* and *Vulcan's Heart*. Others of her works include *The Grail of Hearts*, a revisionist retelling of Wagner's *Parsifal*, and over seventy pieces of short fiction. She has been nominated for the Hugo twice, the Nebula five times, the Edgar and World Fantasy awards once, and has won the HOMer, an award for science fiction given by Compuserve. Her next novel will be *Hostile Takeovers*. It draws on over twenty years of writing science fiction and almost twenty years of working in various Wall Street firms; and combines enemy aliens, mergers and acquisitions, insider trading, and the asteroid belt. She received her BA, *magna cum laude*, and Phi Beta Kappa from Mount Holyoke and earned her doctorate in English from Harvard University. She has also attended summer school at Trinity College, Oxford, and has held a National Endowment for the Humanities grant for postdoctoral study in conjunction with Dartmouth College. She is now vice president of communications at an alternative investments firm in New York. Some time back, you may have seen her on TV selling Borg dolls for IBM, a gig for which she actually got paid. She lives in Forest Hills, New York.

ONE MINUTE, I was a TV celebrity. A very, very minor one. The next minute, they voted me off the island. They took the torch away from me, and I was off the show, thank you so much, and don't forget to write.

Now you'll see how the game is played.

That phrase echoed in my head. I'd heard it since I'd started to grow up a fast-track, smart-mouthed kid and people had practically lined up to make sure I got cut down to size. You get a few years of that hitting you under your belt and you're not just cut down to size, you're undersized, but if you're a smart-ass kid, you're probably a good enough actor, actress, whatever, that you'd rather die than let it show. And, in fact, it doesn't show, so they only try harder to make sure you flinch the way they want you to.

So I was voted off the island, thrown off the show, and I smiled and showed all my nice capped teeth, changed out of my Nature Girl clothes and into my Bolton's Best blacks, bought on discount because people who are between grad school and jobs don't have much money, and got the hell out of there.

And I hurt. Not least because I really could have used the million bucks. No job, no money, no grad school, and student loans coming due now that I was out of school, and while I joked that if you defaulted on your loans, Columbia got to repossess your brain, I'll tell you frankly, I have my doubts. A lot of people in this city go missing every year. What's more, up by Morningside Heights, you find a lot of space cases working McJobs, and they've got to come from somewhere.

By the time I got my makeup off and found myself walking against the traffic's flow on Fifth Avenue past the GM Building, I saw they'd already lugged away the plastic grass and palm trees of the Fantasy Island setup they'd put us on in front of the Trump Plaza. Now, workmen were tackling the steel pipes and slats that had been the platform where I'd stood with a bunch of fair-weather friends, made-up survivalists, and camera-hogs. You could hear the hammers, wrenches, and four-letter words all the way to Bergdorf's for Men.

A hot dog vendor and a man selling lousy watercolors and photos of the World Trade Center turned the sidewalk into a footpath. That meant I had to play dodgeball with three tourists shambling abreast and avoid the West Sider who seemed to be aiming her stroller straight at my ankles.

And I really thought I'd had a shot at winning, too! What had *I* been smoking in the first place? And in the place before that, why the hell had I listened to my former classmates?

"Oh, go *on!*" they'd urged me. "What do you have to lose?"

Aside, of course, from my self-respect. Aside from my privacy in everything from eating disgusting things to burying—never mind that. That game was the last time I go anywhere where there's not at least one Port-a-Potty, and preferably several.

And no damn cameras.

I'd heard them whispering. They could *never* put themselves on display the way I had. No *serious* student could. And magisterial *tsk*'s about "always had had an unfortunate tendency toward self-aggrandizement."

I'm telling you, anyone who thinks having to dig a hole before she can squat over it while cameras are lurking around is self-aggrandizement needs to look the term up in the OED all of us overeducated, underpaid types manage to own.

I was pretty sure I'd seen one or two people I knew in the audience, smiling with shiny, gratified grins as I was voted off. They wouldn't have been pleased at all if I'd won that money. I think they were glad I lost. In fact, I was pretty sure that they'd have really liked it if I'd made a bigger damn fool of myself than the time I fell into that swamp carrying the tribe's rice.

Now what was I going to do?

I watched the people lounging on the benches beneath the lamps and flagpoles and the high roofed entryway, the ones swarming down the shallow steps at me with such determination that if I didn't hold my ground, they'd probably run me off the sidewalk and into Fifth Avenue, where the cabs were even deadlier than the island I'd been kicked off of.

The basic question: What *could* I do now?

The usual answer: Oh, you'll find something.

This is New York, they'd tell me. Surely, a smart kid like you's got to be able to find *something*.

But there was no place for me in the tribe, on the island, in school, or the types of offices I'd find in the buildings I walked by, all finance and law and advertising, assuming I could get past all the gate-keepers in Security, Reception, Financial Aid, you name it.

So, it didn't look like I'd be going back to school to finish up my history degree any time soon. That meant my loans would come due and, as I'd been told, they were clamping down. You had to be careful, they said, with the implication being that she wasn't careful at all. But you're smart, they'd add. You'll find some-thing. Have you tried X and Y and Z preposterous thing, they'd demand, until I was ready to scream, only that would get me called obstructive when they were only trying to help me, but I didn't want to listen. I could even hear the scolding singsong that they would reserve for that kind of reprimand. And see, in my mind's eye, the wigwagging fingers I never had gotten the courage to snap my teeth at.

What made it worse was that I hadn't been the one who'd thought of entering the game in the first place. I'd been set up.

"C'mon, Annie, you're outdoorsy, it'll be an experi-ence, you've got to experiment, take risks and try new things." Adventure, Annie style. Other people got to suggest it. I got to actually do it. And if I complained, I'd get told I was too old to be talked into things that way. Too old to be gullible. And it would do me good to be more adventurous, break out of my rut.

Whatever.

Besides, I thought I'd had a chance to win the million dollars or maybe some smaller prize. Growing up in the far Midwest, I'd camped, fished, and even hunted, which, let me tell you, is not the sort of thing you want to get out at grad school cocktail parties where people wince if the tofu is undercooked.

When I'd started at Columbia as a first-year grad student in history, I'd still been really fit. So I'd managed to earn money during the summer by working for Outward Bound. But then the people in Outward Bound thought I'd spent too much time in New York to be considered authentic and, let's admit it, I wasn't as fit as I used to be. So that job had evaporated; I was way too old to play camp counselor; and when I tried the fellowship and grants game, I got shown but good the way the game was played. Which meant I lost. Just as I'd lost on the island where it looked as if the abilities to catch fish, purify water, put up shelters, and perform first aid weren't nearly as important as wispy flax hair, showing toned arms and a flat midriff in a tight T-shirt, or playing for sympathy with hard-luck stories. Or sabotaging the other people on the island.

That was the story of my life. I'm Ms. Almost But Not Quite. I'm good at applications, good at interviews, so I get into schools and get invited to appear on camera—but I can't get myself into the winner's circle, and when I complain about it, I'm told I'm paranoid and whining. And I probably am.

And while I wove reeds and picked off leeches, my classmates had probably been sipping wine and snickering at me very week on TV—those of 'em who owned a TV or didn't keep it tuned religiously to channel 13. They'd probably chimed in on the Internet speculation while I was plucking out splinters and figuring out better snares. Oh, I'd been snared but good.

Some friends.

You can pick your friends, but not your family.

Fat lot of good I was.

Loser. Not even Anne with an E. Just earnest Annie, too blonde and too Midwestern to thrive at grad school either. After all, if I'd fit in, I'd have gotten full funding from the start, wouldn't I? But that was for rising stars, not wonks from the state schools— not even the public Ivies—admitted on sufferance. And, on the show, I'd have gotten way more audience sympathy if I'd been a single mom, a sales manager, a stockbroker, anything but a grad student.

But I didn't have time to waste on self-pity. If I couldn't enroll this fall, I'd either have to find some sort of job or head back home, where they'd say again they told me so, and see, they really did show you how the game was played. And it would be the same story all over again of me smiling and pretending I didn't care.

But the job market was bad, too. Temps needed PowerPoint and Excel as well as Word, not to mention a wardrobe that dressed them for survival, if not for success. And, of course, business experience. Except for Outward Bound and a résumé full of research assistantships, grading assignments, and library work, I had none of the above.

If I wasn't a winner, at least I was a good researcher. I knew where the temp agencies were—mostly farther downtown. Might as well save the bus fare. So I walked past Bergdorf for Men, where the other one one-thousandth shops if they can fit into the clothes and promptly bumped into a workman wearing a Yankees ball cap with a flag superimposed. Nice muscles.

" 'Scuse me," I muttered.

"Don't people say sorry anymore?"

"I said 'excuse me.' " He glared as if wanting a more abject show of deference.

I moved on fast. If I'd have won, he'd have been glad enough to shake my hand, grin into my eyes, and ask for my phone number, not that I'd have given it out to the likes of him.

Now, that was interesting. Columns of lights, high above the West 50s. Wasn't as if I was going anywhere special. Might as well check it out. So, when the lights changed, I crossed Fifth and headed west. I never really had gotten into the way of jaywalking, forcing the Red Sea of cabs, SUVs, and messenger bikes, to part, and besides, you never can tell when someone is going to decide that jaywalking's another "quality of life" crime, and all I need is to be run in and fined.

I was right. They'd set up spotlights outside the Ziegfeld, the immense movie theater where extravaganzas ran and people waited in line for literally days. Might as well see what Event was going on. Besides, the limelight's as good a destination as any. Maybe I'd buy a water and watch the street theater—a few celebs wearing their eating disorders and flimsy couture like medals, a few people plucked out of the crowd, interviewed, and photographed so they came off like fat, stammering idiots, and then I'd call it a night.

Cheaper than dinner and a movie. Maybe, by now, my roommate's study group had cleared out. They weren't into TV, so I didn't have to worry about more than a polite "tough luck," but they were already making plans for the school year, while I was in between, and that's like a divorce or a death in the family. No one quite knows what to say to you, so there's a lot of not meeting people's eyes, and after a while, they drift away.

If I was really lucky, they'd have cleaned up the whole wheat pizza and not borrowed my stash of laundry quarters to tip the deliveryman.

The spotlights grew whiter and brighter as I headed toward Ziegfield. They'd be doubled, I thought, reflected in the ornamental pool by the plaza. At least, I thought there was a pool there this year, after three seasons of downpour instead of a proper fall, winter, and spring. So something was going right; we have ornamental water in the City, cascades pouring down a stone wall, or pinwheeling up from fixtures in a pond, or spattering down a statue, cooling your face and helping you clear your thoughts. It's comforting to watch when it's hot or when you're feeling jangled.

Other things, I decided, needed to go right, too.

Like my life. Like taking what I knew was promising raw material and shaping it into a real life that was mine, rather than other people's object lessons.

I turned west, heading toward the theater. When there's an opening there, you can see the crowd for at least a block before you get there. This evening, though, I was surprised. The area wasn't just quiet, it was empty. No unsanitary hot dog vendors, no flag and photo sellers. No limos and no lines. Not even a stray cop.

The spotlights formed a circle on the pavement in front of me, so bright I couldn't see the rent-a-spotlight that projected it. If I'd won, I might have been the person to get out of a limo, walk across the sidewalk, carpeted for the occasion, right into that glowing circle, pause, turn, smile, and wave, in a dress cut down to there.

Seeing as how the place was so empty, I might as well do the pause, turn, smile, and wave thing anyhow just for the fun of it. No one would see me, and this would be the only chance I'd get. The idea made me smile—a real smile, not smile-for-the-cameras—for the first time that day. And it was one way of explaining why I was so fascinated by the light.

So I walked into the center of the circle and stood there.

I am gray, I thought. I stand between the candle and the dark, or whatever the phrase was. Actually, wherever I stood was invariably in the way of someone sharper, more aggressive, or more entitled to that particular piece of sidewalk.

Seriously, though, I felt gray. Gray as Auntie Em in Kansas before the tornado hit and Dorothy woke up to see that everything had turned green and she'd gone somewhere else.

I didn't want to go to Oz, but I did very much want to get away.

Where did I want to go? I asked myself.

I didn't know. I just knew I wanted to go somewhere else . . .

That was when the lights blinked out.

"Out went the candle and we were left darkling." The words gibbered in my brain. I thought they were from *Lear*. I tried to remember because memory was all, in that moment, that stood between me and the whoosh of—what? wind, rain, energy—that whipped about me. Even my appendix scar seemed to tingle from the inside as I was swept away.

Damnit, I thought, this is New York, and there's no way in hell I'm a likely candidate for the Rapture the way those people who wrote those screwy books describe it. I'd always thought that was just as well. Sitting around killing enemies and feeling good about being righteous has never struck me as much fun.

Thump.

Thump?

Was that all there was to it? This is the way the world ends, not with a bang but a *thump?*

This wasn't just ridiculous, it was just plain tacky. The thought brought me back to reality. Whatever reality was.

I found myself flat on my back on a surface that

felt cool and smooth. When I patted it with my hands, it felt soft. I tried to move my hands further and found them restrained. Just like my ankles, as if I'd had some sort of seizure and lay on a hospital bed or a gurney. Something was prickling at my temples. Maybe I'd actually had a seizure. But I hadn't wet myself, and I didn't feel sleepy or dizzy or any of the other symptoms I remembered from first aid class.

Blind panic took over. Not the sort where you lash out, but the sort where you're paralyzed. They could have saved the expense of the restraints. Thank god for the panic, actually. As the waves of adrenaline and terror receded, I realized it was much smarter to pretend I was still out cold and give myself a chance to get a feel for where I was. Wherever it was around here.

It made sense to make whatever it was out there underestimate me. After all, I was coming off a lifetime of practice at that.

But I realized that I was feeling something aside from the panic that made me wish for a bathroom, a bedpan, or better bladder control. I was furious. Hadn't it been bad enough to be selected as class clown all my life? To have to leave school for lack of funds, be thrown off the island, or be the target for everyone's "helpful" criticism?

Damnit, let's assume that some of that feedback was warranted. No one can always be right. But no one who's really trying can always be wrong either and, right or wrong, I was not a suitable candidate for the types of extraterrestrial colonoscopies that had made alien abduction stories a cottage industry back on Earth.

Back on Earth.

The implications of that phrase froze every nerve in my spinal column . . .

Then the anger came back. How dare they snatch me away? Who in hell did they think they were? They were worse than the self-satisfied people who cut other people down to size and watched them flinch before scolding them for hypersensitivity. And they were worse than people who allowed their lives to be directed by criticism—or who spent those lives trying to avoid it or protest it.

What about living?

What about it?

I found I was clenching my fists, beating them rhythmically against the gurney I was lying on. Write that down, people. Your lab rat's awake, and, boy, is she pissed. The fury felt much, much better than panic, better even than the low-level anxiety I tended to live with.

Tended to live with back on Earth.

Long before I'd moved to New York, I'd learned to hate clichés. Little and cute. Tall and athletic. Smart and maladjusted. But there isn't a bigger cliché anywhere west of Madison Avenue than Mother Ships and the Grays who snatched up humans for incalculable tests. Except, maybe, Roswell, New Mexico, even if I do have a cousin there. Really, though, the place is such a dead bore that she privately thought they'd invented the UFO just to put the godforsaken place on the map.

I froze again, all my helpful anger evaporating and making me wish for a bedpan again. Something was whispering up behind me, slithering—no, that's not a word you want to use—up behind me to remove the cold metal—electrodes? Wires?—that had been put on my temples. With a clank, the wrist and ankle restraints withdrew into the gurney.

"You may move now."

Did I actually hear that voice? Or was I going to have to cope with another cliché, telepathy?

Whatever. Whether it was a voice in my head or a bug-eyed monster, it was damn nice of the Whatever to give me back control over my own body. Hey, I'd take it. It was something

Just as I'd always been told, you'll find something. Maybe the people who told me that were onto a good thing. Maybe they saw me as more resourceful than I did. I could use a little confidence about now. I could use all the help I could get.

I brushed my fingers over my face. No, no scars. No implants. Not unless they were very, very good surgeons. Which, for all I knew, they might be. But damnit, I was not going to live as if my body were one big booby trap, and that was *not* a pun. Even if, somehow, I'd managed to shed all my clothes.

Think it through, I told myself. Hell, all my life, people had told me that stepping back and thinking things through—as opposed to going full speed ahead on feelings (and they'd draw the word out so it had at least five *e*'s in it)—was bad. Still, it was a trait I had. Might as well use it.

Okay. If I'd actually heard a voice, then the Whatevers had vocal cords. And I'd understood them. That meant that the Whatevers spoke English. I could imagine the usual cocktail-party scoldings, mostly in the presence of exchange students, that "Americans, even educated Americans are so illiterate—just one language—and they, never we, barely speak that one well" that I always wanted to protest. Not that I'm a polyglot, but neither are most of the people who say that.

Maybe I did owe someone an apology for not being fluent in French or Spanish or whatever. But I was damned if I was going to do mea culpa for not knowing Martian.

The hell with it. The hell with this, too.

Or, there was another thought. Let's say it wasn't speech. In which case either it was an implant. Or it was telepathy. In which case, I was really in trouble.

If you hadn't stepped into the spotlight . . . I could hear the scolding taking shape. These days, no one had to scold me at all: just put me into a situation where a scolding was possible, wind me up, and I'd do just fine punishing myself.

Just because I'd been idiot enough to volunteer to step into the limelight didn't mean I had no one but myself to blame. It meant that someone had exploited a perfectly normal human reaction.

I might have consented to charges of wanting center stage. But I hadn't consented to this . . . this alien abduction, of all the hackneyed situations.

Swinging my legs to one side and down, fast, before I lost my nerve, I made myself stand as casually as if I'd spent my entire life being transported to stupid mother ships. My clothes were gone, so I pulled the sheet I'd lain on off the gurney and draped it around me in a rotten facsimile of a toga.

My legs didn't buckle, which surprised me, too.

I took a few tentative steps. The floor—or was I supposed to call it a deck—was cold under my bare feet. At least, they could have left my shoes on! I'd paid good money for them, even on sale.

What was that noise?

I whirled around, my eyes wide, determined to take in as much information in one glance as possible. I was standing in—well, I supposed I could call it an observation lounge—a broad clear space facing what looked like a picture window? Porthole? Viewscreen?

It didn't take me long to realize that trying to assign familiar referents to things people don't expect to see unless they're Sally Ride or something was going to drive me nuts, but I'd go even crazier if I didn't try to assume what control I could over my reality. And if all I could do was name things, then name them I would.

It was easy to name what gleamed in the viewscreen in front of me.

Centered in it glowed Earth, its enveloping blue seas beneath veils of clouds and the occasional swirl of a giant storm, the blotches of lights and clouds that were its cities, the ice caps on each pole, spread out before me like a diorama at the Planetarium on West 81st Street that cost a day's groceries to visit.

Tears prickled in my eyes. It was so beautiful. And it was so far away. I'd never make it back. And, oh god, I wanted to be home. Oz may be beautiful, Kansas a hard-working bore, but Kansas is home.

The tears that poured down my face were the warmest thing about this place.

Just let me go home, God, and I promise I won't complain again. Promise.

Is that a promise you can keep?

The thin figure that faced her, with its slanted black eyes, and its attenuated limbs, was a classic Gray.

We want to ask you some questions.

An interrogation. I seriously hate interrogations. Justify your existence, in twenty-five words or less. Usually, they're the prelude to feedback, and I hate feedback even more than I hate interrogations.

"What happens if I refuse to play?" I asked. "Can you make me?"

It would be better if you cooperated.

The words hissed inside my head. I took what I thought was a last glance at Earth, much the same way as a soldier might look at family photos before the balloon went up. I wasn't really naive enough to think it would give me courage, but I had to try.

What kind of information was I supposed to give out? Name, rank, and serial number? Would these creatures settle for my social security ID or maybe my Amex?

Who are you? What do you think you are?

Now, those were questions that I really hated. The alien's mental voice seemed to fragment into familiar scoldings: the doctor who had told me before I switched physicians that women invented cramps; the blind date who'd put me through an interrogation about my beliefs, my "values," my self-esteem (or lack thereof) with the idea seeming to be that if he knocked my ideas to flinders, I'd sleep with him. Like a fine for a parking violation.

I shut my eyes in aggravation. For the first time, I had the sense that I stood in a vast room filled with people, murmuring all around me. I couldn't see them, but I thought that throughout this room, hundreds of interviews, similar to mine, were going on. Hundreds of murmuring people. Hundreds of intrusive questions.

Oh, this *was* a happy space, wasn't it?

Was this the game they were hinting at?

What happened if I won? More to the point, what happened if I lost?

I'm sick of this! I thought at it as hard as I could. The thing stepped back as if I'd actually hurt it with my thoughts. Good.

Boy, would I get snarled at for that by the righteous types at those parties you get in the Village that are half political rally and half teach-in. Maybe I could tell them that the Grays were imperialist or Republican or something.

You carry a lot of anger in you.

"Yes, I suppose I do," I said. Ordinarily, if you admitted to anger, it meant people got to scold you for anger, or tell you that you were being defensive, which was apparently a serious thought crime if they caught you at it as opposed to if they did it, when it was called showing good boundaries. "But wouldn't you expect that, under the circumstances?"

That is logical.

I managed to stop myself from laughing at the word "logical." Just as well. If I laughed now, I'd probably laugh myself all the way to some alien funny farm.

The thing—the being—ought to expect I was going to be angry at being picked up and carried off, but the least I could do, if my thoughts hurt it, was use ordinary speech. Yes, and save my thoughts in case I needed them as a weapon.

The figure seemed to shimmer. The echoes in the vast chamber seemed to be growing fewer.

Suppose this figure wasn't really a Gray but was using that image as camouflage for what they're really like. That would be really fascinating, to coin another stunningly original phrase.

Approval resonated in my mind. Again, the number of echoes, as measured by my sense that fewer people remained in the room with me, seemed to decline. The feeling—whether from myself or anyone else— was so rare that I was sure. This had to be telepathy. Something I had thought had pleased the alien. Powers of reasoning, maybe, or my feeble attempt at kindness to telepaths.

So, to sum up; I'd stepped into that spotlight, been caught, and taken up to this . . . this Skinner box in space for what? So far, no one had suggested an anal probe, for which I was devoutly grateful.

This could be problematic, I thought. If they could get inside my head to let me know when they approved of me, they could punish me, too. I'd always thought I'd go off a bridge if I were diagnosed with

Alzheimer's. At least, now I had a way of making sure
I could go up fast, in a blaze of glory.

And, maybe now, it would throw me a pellet or
something.

I might as well find out more.

"Is this one of those stupid games where you're
supposed to play chess for the future of the world or
something?" I asked. Deliberately, I used the tone
that, when I was a child, had always earned the re-
buke, "Don't you use that tone of voice on me,
young lady!"

"I should warn you," I went on, "I've never won a
damn thing in my life except admission to grad school,
and that was a mixed blessing. I don't play chess, don't
have the mentality, anyhow."

I couldn't take my eyes off my home, Earth, so far
away from me.

"That's a damn long way down," I said. "I don't
see a chessboard," I added. "If this is another survival
game, I ought to warn you you won't have much fun
with me. I just lost one. Why don't you take me back
to Earth and . . ."

Why?

"Because it's my home."

*Your mind is filled with grievances and old pain. The
people there have invaded your privacy, worse than we.
Why would you want to return?*

Anger rose in me, faster than I could control it.

What the hell was I supposed to do, travel with
them, as a sort of interstellar displaced person or an
exhibit in a petting zoo? I could feel the alien flinch.

"Sorry," I offered. Instantly, my memory conjured up familiar rebukes. Apologies are no good. You always say you're sorry, but you never change. You have to control your temper. I could feel my face blushing. If I couldn't convince humans of my good intentions, how could I convince an alien?

To compose myself, I looked out at Earth: the blue oceans, the polar caps, the whirling vast white pinwheel that indicated a serious weather front, the lights that meant cities. It was all there: China with its walls, the veritable third pole of the Himalayas, the great cities of Europe, Baghdad—what was left of it; Kiev, with its heightened radiation from Chernobyl; New York with its imperial maimed skyline. How beautiful it was. I reached out as if I could touch it, cover it protectively with my hands.

Men are buried in those walls, have died in those mountains, at the gates of those cities. So much blood stains your history that one marvels that your seas are not red.

"The multitudinous seas incarnadine, making the green one red." I muttered the splendid hysterics of that line from *Macbeth*.

You take pride *in that violence?*

This time, I didn't bother suppressing my anger.

"I take pride in our history," I snapped, "and what we've accomplished, even in spite of ourselves. Besides, if I want an orgy of guilt, I don't have to travel all the way to Earth's orbit. I can go to a rally or take a sociology class. All my life, people back home have reprimanded me about how I don't feel badly enough about things that I didn't do. And I took it, like a damned fool. But I'll probably never see them again. And I don't need this crap from you, too."

And yet you wish to go back. Why would you, like others of your people, not wish for retribution? I know it is in your thoughts.

The alien's mental "voice" licked out and wrapped about me. In that instant, I felt what the alien felt: every slight, snub, reprimand, and loss, and my own anger and self-pity at dealing with them.

So what if I'd felt hurt and shame at being thrown off the island? That was a silly game.

So what if I'd resented the people who practically walked into me on the street? What about the man I remembered, who'd dodged traffic to help a woman with a stroller who'd miscalculated the distance between a cab and the curb?

For every snub at a cocktail party, I could supply examples I'd witnessed of courtesy. Empathy, even. But those weren't the things I'd been looking for, so those weren't the things I found.

Hurt existed. But I had survived it, and there were other things I hadn't yet thought about. Including the thought of what I might do if I had the power to indulge myself. For years, I'd had a little list of people who'd antagonized me or betrayed me or put me down, or let it be known in public how much brighter or prettier or tougher they were than I.

I'd wished numerous humiliating things on them, but I'd no more sell them out to . . . these aliens . . . than I'd spit on an altar. Or commit a murder. There were some things I just couldn't do. And anyone who liked—and god knows, there were plenty who did, and who had—could call me naive for it.

The alien mind released me. I staggered forward a few steps—toward Earth, always toward Earth, then caught myself. I reached inside myself for the kinesthetic sense that had told me before just how many groups spoke as we had in this observation deck. Most had fallen silent. There! As I tried to listen, still others went quiet. The rest were listening—to me, I realized.

The aliens had told me I would be well-advised to play the game.

Was I winning?

It didn't matter. But now that they'd stopped using my anger against me to make me sick, it rose in me again. "Look, I said. "You've done what no one on Earth could do. You've convinced me I'm an angry, spiteful woman who's picked at her own wounds all her life so they'll never stop bleeding. And that's my business. Not yours. You've pointed out the mistakes we've made—for heaven's sake, I swear you were eavesdropping at the last party I walked out of. But I haven't heard a word about the good things we've done. That's fine. That's your right. Everything's relative and all that. Just don't expect me to trust you."

The anger erupted, a cleansing anger such as I've never known.

"You called this a game. But I think it's more like a test. Would you really destroy me, or the people here, or a whole planet just because you can? Playing games like that is worse than anything we're capable of doing."

Yet.

"Yet," I agreed. "But now you've done something you should never have done. You've gone over the line. Right now, I don't see a damn bit of difference between you and the bores I've grown up with, except that you have the power to impose change if you see fit. You could destroy our planet, or you could make it a paradise. Neither's a particularly good choice, because neither takes us into consideration. So why don't you hurry up, mind your own business, and—and get a life?" I snarled.

How odd it was I could say these things. I'd always been speechless over the beer or the Chardonnay before. Maybe if I'd been able to speak up, I wouldn't have gotten all the feedback I'd lived with. Maybe I'd still be on the island.

Or maybe, I thought, I'd never been in a game where the stakes meant so much to me. Get a life indeed.

And there was, I realized, silence in heaven, if not for the space of half an hour, for long enough for me to realize that all the other conversations that I'd half-sensed, half-heard, had fallen silent.

The silence was broken by a sound I had never expected to hear: the sound of a Gray clapping its malformed hands. Applauding me.

Well played, said the alien.

"I wasn't playing," I told it—and the now-silenced room. "The reason I've been so angry is that, all my life, people have played games with me. That's different from playing games. You don't play games with lives. Or minds."

That is precisely the point.

"Then why are *you* doing it?" I asked. It came out in a yell, but then, I really really hate object lessons.

Point taken.

"I hope so," I said. "It's one thing to push us around. But what if you come across people who are powerful enough to really object?"

Again, the alien applauded. Not just the one alien who had interrogated me, but a mixed crew of things—of people—who made me want to run and hide from the welter of scales, tentacles, lumps, bumps, and ridges that yelped, boomed, stamped, and clapped. My eyes started to roll back in my head, but I caught myself, drew a deep breath—and saw a crowd of people applauding a winner.

Choose your prize. And, after another long pause, *please.*

The faces of the crew—that is, those who had faces—showed me one option. I could stay. But I didn't think so. It had been tough enough, lifelong, to be a stranger in her own land. To be a stranger in a strange land?

"Thanks," I said, and meant it. "I really do feel honored that you'd want me to join you. But I'd just rather go home."

Even though you've never felt really welcome? Though you can expect disbelief and ridicule, at best?

"I'll manage," I said. And I would. I'd find something. After all, I always had.

Hadn't I even found a game I could win?

Then, I remembered. "You know, it's bad enough

I'm going to have to explain why I disappeared for however long I've been gone. But if I show up wearing a sheet made from some out-of-this-world fabric, I'm really going to be in trouble. Do you think you could find me my clothes?"

The alien gestured back toward my gurney. Now I could see my clothes spread out on it. I headed toward them. It didn't trouble me I had turned my back on Earth.

I'd be going back soon enough.

I stepped out of the spotlight in front of the Ziegfield. Dazzled by its brightness, I promptly walked into two people headed in the opposite direction.

One of them, a man easily a foot taller than I, snarled, "Watch where you're going!"

I headed him off with a grin.

"The glare blinded me," I said. "Sorry about that." No point snarling. For all I knew, he'd had a rotten day.

To my surprise, he smiled back. And kept on going.

So did I. It didn't seem as if I'd been gone long at all. So I wouldn't have to make up a story about where I'd been. I'd simply have to say nothing. I was good at saying nothing when people talked. Now, however, what they said didn't have to matter. I'd have enough to do trying to find a job.

Tonight, though, I thought I could take for myself.

I stuck my hands into my pockets in what felt surprisingly like contentment and hit something cool, about the size of a matchbox. When I opened it be-

neath a streetlamp, its contents glittered. One . . .
two . . . three . . . well, they looked like diamonds.

My prize. Not so big that I'd draw attention when
I went to sell them, but big enough to keep me in
funds for quite some time.

I was going to have to figure out how to sell these
things without any documentation. I shrugged. It would
be easy enough to claim I'd inherited them. The hard
part would be not listening to the people who'd tell me
how they'd dispose of the stones, how I wouldn't get
anywhere near a fraction of their value.

So what if I got only part of what the stones were
actually worth? It would do.

After all, I had always been very good at getting by
on very little.

But from now on, that was going to change.

STOP OR I'LL SHOOT

by Ed Gorman

Ed Gorman is a Midwesterner, born in Iowa in 1941, growing up in Minneapolis, Minnesota and Marion, Iowa, finally
settling down in Cedar Rapids, Iowa. While primarily a
suspense novelist, he has written half a dozen Western
novels and published a collection of Western stories. His
novel *Wolf Moon* was a Spur nominee for Best Paperback
Original. About his Western novels, *Publishers Weekly*
said, "Gorman writes Westerns for grown-ups," which the
author says he took as a high compliment, and was indeed his goal in writing his books. "The Face" won the
1996 Spur Award for Best Short Fiction. Among his latest work is the critically-acclaimed Black River Falls mystery series featuring Sam McCain.

THE SECOND TIME HE is to die, it's a carjacking. That's the stunt Sam will pull tonight. Or
try to. Without being killed again.

(Offscreen Voice: "It looks simple enough, doesn't it,
folks? But that's the beauty of it, isn't it? All Sam has to
do is approach the car and figure out some way to attach

the tiny bomb he's carrying to the undercarriage—and then you'll see and hear an explosion that'll take out half a block. Then Sam's problem will be to get away from the car before he gets blown up, too! Can he do it? One billion people are watching around the world right now to see if he can! That's what *Stop or I'll Shoot!* is all about. Can a decent, law-abiding man commit a heinous crime and get away with it?")

Sam Conway. An attorney who last year filed for bankruptcy. If he can steal a car without getting killed again, he'll be set for life.

Sam's first try didn't go so good. He was killed and had to be rebirthed.

The first time was this grocery store, see . . .

Well, the dude behind the cash register knows that Sam is coming so he's got some freaking handgun sitting right next to the register. And he's been shown Sam's photo.

So when Sam comes in, he's packing two choices. If he thinks he can kill the clerk before the clerk kills him, then he goes for the big prize.

But if he gets a bad case of the terrors, he can call out, "I'll stop! I'll stop!" and the game is over.

Sam baby needs money bad, what with the wife and two daughters in the burbs, and lawsuits up both the yin and yang for all the ways he was incompetent in handling client cases. So Sam ain't about to quit.

He comes in the store, the dude sees him, opens fire. For twenty minutes, the huge audience around the world is barely able to breathe it's so exciting, Sam hiding in every conceivable place in the small, smelly store. All the while exchanging gunfire. He needs to get a clear shot at the dude and blow him away. The dude has died twice already. The American Medical Association is on record against any individual being rebirthed more than twice. The percentages are 90 to 10 against surviving your third rebirthing process.

Sam is thinking about all this and it isn't what he should be thinking about at all. He should be strictly focused on making his way to the front of the store (the sickening death stench of spoiled meat is making him nauseous) and not about anything else.

He is behind a life-size plastic tri-dee replica of Captain Mars (now that we've colonized the red planet, virtually every advertiser, whether they make hoity-toity designer clothes or jock itch medicine, ties their campaign into Mars).

Sam, not thinking his odds through carefully, lunges from behind the replica, and figures to get his clear shot.

But the clerk dude is way ahead of him.

He fires off three laser shots that boil a hole all the way through Sam instantly, so that here, for just a second, you've got a guy standing up next to this Captain Mars replica—with a steaming hole in him that you can see all the way through. You can see the display of sulking rotted tomatoes behind him, fer God's sake.

Sam baby, you are dead . . .

*   *   *

The carjacking is sure to go better (Sam is thinking).

The rebirthing, though painful at times, and terrifying even more often, taught him how to focus. Because part of the rebirthing this time was spending two weeks with a retired Green Beret (at his own expense) and training in how to approach a vehicle at a stoplight and plant this little bugger of a bomb to the underside.

The Green Beret was one devious sonofabitch. He showed Sam several alternative methods of attacking the car, making it his own. And doing it no matter what the dude in the Mercedes-Benz chooses to do. All Sam needs to do is stay focused . . .

Now the real time is here, man . . .

(Offscreen Announcer: "Now, it's normal for you folks watching this around the world to feel sorry for a good family-type guy like Sam. But remember, there's somebody in the car. A handsome young man named Steve. He deserves to live, too. Can Steve kill Sam before Sam kills Steve? I guess we'll just have to watch and find out now, won't we?")

But already, even before he reaches the location for the carjacking, Sam's mind is drifting into a morass of resentment.

The thing is . . . the rules of *Stop or I'll Shoot* are such that just for dying in that ghetto store stunt . . . all his bills were paid . . . a quarter million dollars tax free was put into his bank account . . . and a huge Tudor style home was bought for him in a lovely gated community. Dying and rebirthing really isn't any fun . . . and of course there's no guarantee that rebirthing will always work. The stats are that 27 percent of all attempts at rebirthing fail, in fact . . . so *Stop or I'll Shoot* lavishes all sorts of rewards on you even if you fail as he did in the grocery store . . .

He is only doing this because a six-month taste of the good life has changed his nice sweet wife and nice sweet daughters into people he has oddly begun to fear. They have him, as they say, by the short ones. And it hurts. Because he can't object to all their ridiculous behavior. He loves them too much. All the face and body transforms so that they had that exquisitely plastic look of all tri-dee porn stars . . . all the extended-stay trips to Paris and London and San Juan . . . and all the psyche probes that help make them "modern," i.e., without all their old hang-ups and guilts.

Damnit, if he is anything, he is a man soul-deep in hang-ups and guilts.

Hang-ups and guilts are the glue of civilization. Otherwise, despite all the slick soul-dead tri-vid shrinks, what you have is a bedlam of heartless people concerned only with their selfish pursuits . . .

Karin even had one of those implants surgically implanted in her vagina . . . he misses the warmth and moisture and Karin of his wife as she used to be . . . yes, damnit, the implant renders both people involved all kinds of circus thrills, but what's the difference now between his wife and the high-priced call girls who made the implants so popular five years ago? She even wanted him to get that new Satyr Six male implant, but he refused . . .

But at least he had his days in his home workshop . . . his days of walking along the river in the nearby state park . . . his days looking at all the home vids they'd taken of the girls when they were little . . . He'd never enjoyed life as much as he had for the early months after his rebirthing . . . completely relaxed and—

If it just wasn't for that damned tall, tanned, muscular young man (Steve somebody Karin insists is the gardener) . . . and the way his daughters and Karin are always hovering around him when he's doing his shirtless work in the baking sun—

—but hasn't jealousy (he tries to reassure himself) always been one of his problems? He's probably just being paranoid about Steve the Gardener—

—but all this money being spent so unnecessarily . . . all the angry calls from his accountant . . . all the past-due notices, including the fees to the homeowners association here . . . all of it so out of control . . . starting to resemble the kind of money pit he fell headfirst into before he signed on to the game show in the first place. . . .

And then one day the *Stop or I'll Shoot!* folks called and gave him the news. They were taking it all back. He had run through all his money and had borrowed so often against his house that the network fellas said no more. He could have made a new life for himself with their largesse, but of course he—

—it wasn't "he" of course who'd squandered it all, it was "they," but he had too much familial pride (despite his rage) to say so—

The network, the man said, would have to take it all back.

And then the man said: "Of course, if you're interested in getting a chance to keep it all—in fact a chance to not only keep it but get another half million put into your bank account (and this, Sam, is after we've paid off all your debts) plus an annuity that will keep you and yours afloat for the rest of your lives!"

By this time, Karin was in Sam's home office watching the screen with him. She started jumping up and down and clapping like one of those silly contestants on the old-fashioned game shows . . . "An annuity for the rest of our lives, Sam! Think of that!"

Then the man on the screen said: "We'll have to get your lawyer involved in this, Sam. I don't have to tell you that if you get killed and have to be rebirthed again . . . well, the odds aren't so good. But we're sure you'll do better than you did at that grocery store. We can practically guarantee it."

"Yeah," Sam muttered to himself, "practically."

By now, he saw that this was all a ploy to get him back on the show. The network fellas were happy when some poor schmuck screwed up everything for a second time . . . because the audience numbers doubled when a man is facing a second possible rebirthing.

"Thirty to seventy, Sam, the odds, I mean."

"Oh, he doesn't care a poo about odds!" Karin bub-
bled to the network man. "He's a very brave man,
aren't you, sweetie?"

And suddenly she was all over him the way she
hadn't been for years. Hugging him, kissing him,
rubbing his chest with those long, silken fingers . . .
Real affection not connected to that thing in her
vagina.

"Then we can send you the contract to sign?" the
man said.

"Of course you can send us the papers!" Karin
trilled. "The sooner the better!"

Sam's plan was to have a family discussion about
the wisdom of risking a second rebirthing, but the girls
were off to a birthday party somewhere and Karin
claimed a headache . . . and so he sat on the wet ve-
randa watching a solemn, melancholy dusk—all purple
and gold but with thunderheads ominous nearby . . .
and god-damned Steve the Gardener doing his god-
damned shirtless yardwork. He had to give the kid
one thing. He was a good worker. Quitting time for
him was dark.

The contract arrived the next morning . . .

Karin did everything but slap the pen into his palm
and guide his signature across the proper line . . .

*   *   *

Now the time was here . . .

Seeing the Mercedes-Benz now for the first time . . .

They had to pick a place down by the river where

the coiling gray fog off the water would be sufficiently atmospheric for the fat ass potato-chip-chomping voyeurs sitting at home eager for somebody to die . . . and they don't care which . . . driver or Sam . . . as long as there's real blood and real death . . .

. . . The green four-door sedan is parked at a stop sign. The street here is so old, most of it is brick. A tugboat bellows unseen in the cold gloom of the river.

The car just sitting there . . .

Its headlights are on, but the fog consumes the beams.

Vaguely, he can see the driver sitting behind the steering wheel.

He has to remember what the Green Beret came up with . . .

He reaches down into the tight black jeans he's wearing (black turtleneck and black ski mask, too) and finds the tiny red capsule that will adhere to the underbelly of the car.

Once he plants it there, he will have exactly sixty seconds to roll out from under the Benz, jump to his feet, race to the river, and dive in before the roaring explosion will destroy everything on this end of the block . . .

(Remembering how Karin would smirk when he'd come in from training with his Green Beret instructor . . . she'd probably smirked all the time she stood at the window watching him practice throwing himself to the ground and then rolling several feet . . . day after day, he practiced.)

He is crouching behind a bus stop bench, waiting

for his moment. His chest—his heart pounding so hard—feels as if it will literally rip apart like the construction paper the girls used to make him birthday cards on when they were so little (he's a sentimental bastard and can't help it.)

Wait.

There.

Just now.

Did the driver turn and look in his direction? How is that possible with him crouching behind the bus stop bench and all the fog between them? How could the driver see anything at all?

(The producer had explained that the fog would work to the detriment of both men. "You'll both be essentially working blind, all this freaking fog. And, man, the cretins at home'll be lovin' it.")

Imagining things. Had to be.

Now.

The longer he waits, the more prone he'll be to mistakes. (He can see himself slipping on the damp bricks, cracking his skull, and leaving himself a perfect target for the armed driver.)

He crawls on his haunches to the far end of the bus stop bench. Freezing from his own sweat now.

The terrors starting. One thing the Green Beret warned him about over and over again was freezing up when he had the capsule in his hand. Not all that uncommon, the instructor had told him. "You'd think they'd want to plant it and get the hell out of there. But some men, they just freeze. Some kind of suicidal impulse, I guess."

He is not aware at first that he is wetting himself. But then the urine sears scalding on his thigh. He is remembering the odds against surviving another rebirthing . . . his mind losing focus again . . .

My god . . .

(Karin and the girls are watching it all on monitors a quarter mile up in the air in the skyvid center.

Karin says, "I almost feel sorry for him."

"Oh, I don't," Marcie says. "Steve is a much better father than Dad ever was."

Her sister Heather giggles. "Yeah, and Steve is a great lover on top of it! He wore both of us out the other night!"

More giggles.

Karin says, "Now, you remember what I said. We'll have to share him. I didn't bring him in on this just so you could have him all to yourselves." She just hopes she did the right thing, viddying all of Sam's training sessions with the Green Beret. This way Steve would know exactly what to expect. The producers of *Stop or I'll Shoot!* loved the whole idea. Insensitive greedy selfish husband [at least that's how they'd play him after the big funeral they'd give him] done in by the sensitive hunky, humble gardener Steve who just couldn't help falling in love with the sensitive, unassuming eternally maternal Karin whom he comforted in her grief over her dead [if insensitive and greedy] husband Steve. Talk about a ratings buster when Steve and Karin get married at the huge manse the producers will be giving them as a wedding gift, with the two

virginal sensitive daughters watching tearfully as Mom
says "I do!")

Fog. Night. Terror.

But how can Sam miss with the bomb? As long as
he can reach the car, roll under it, and plant the bomb,
he'll be fine.

Sam moves.

In his mind now he's his instructor. A freaking jungle animal, no less. Sneaking up on his prey. (He
wants to look cool for the worldwide audience, doesn't
he? He's gonna survive this and he'll wanna look
macho doing it.)

Sam moves.

Let's just see this motha try and outsmart a
bomb . . .

Crouching. Running. Smelling the exhaust from the
Mercedes that is double-engined for ground or air.

The tiny bomb seeming to sear his hand. The bomb
is ready, too. It wants to go off. Fulfill its destiny. That
is such a cool thought. (There he goes, losing focus
again.) A bomb that has a sense of its own destiny.
A sentient freaking bomb.

He is close enough now that he needs to drop to
the ground and start rolling under the car.

(He has already touched the damp, foggy ancient
bricks and they feel like snakeskin slime . . .)

But just as he begins to squat down, he notices that
the silhouetted figure in the car and behind the fog
has not moved. And Sam has been watching it steadily
for maybe two, three minutes.

Now, this is weird. First, a few minutes back, he imagined that that silhouetted figure had turned to watch him. But now he sees that the damned thing hasn't moved at all. Can a human being sit absolutely still—absolutely not so much as moving even an inch or two—for that amount of time?

Weird. Wrong.

He senses a trap.

(Being part of this game show has made him suspicious of everything. Who wouldn't be suspicious of everything after all he's been through?)

Not a person.

That is the information his mind is dealing with.

That that fog-hidden silhouette is not a person.

Then what the hell is it?

Not until now does he realize that he has unconsciously been moving toward the car. In plain sight. His only protection is the bomb grasped in his palm.

Guy in the car could have turned anytime. And seen him. And shot him.

But the guy in the car hasn't moved . . .

(Offscreen voice [whispered tones]: "It looks like Sam is starting to suspect a trap. He keeps squinting to make out the dark figure sitting in the driver's seat . . . Is somebody playing a trick on Sam?" Beat. "Oh, my god, he's rushing the car!")

Everything boiling, bursting inside of him. Crying, laughing, wetting himself, shitting himself, knowing he's probably going to die but needing a kind of spiritual ejaculation that will—at least for a soul-cleansing few moments—help him forget that he's a failure, that his wife is sleeping with Steve the Gardener, that his daughters laugh about him to their friends—and knowing now that the producers have tricked him.

Slamming so hard into the car that he feels a rib crack.

Ripping clawlike at the door handle.

Throwing the door open and . . .

The dummy leaning toward him and then falling out to the slimy bricks.

Oh those clever mothas!

(Offscreen voice [chuckling]: "Can you see the dummy's face, folks? How's that for a surprise? Ole Sam doesn't look too good right now, does he? There. That's a better shot of the dummy. See, the face looks just like Sam's! In fact, the entire, carefully detailed plastoid dummy *is* Sam, right down to the birthmark on the right cheek of his buttocks! But Sam better gather himself because this little scene hasn't played out yet. Look! Who's that coming through the fog? Oh, my Lord!")

Sam hears the man before he sees him. A certain rasping sound across the surface of the slimy bricks. A certain inevitability in the sound and what it portends.

Sam, suddenly realizing what has happened here. He has been lured to the car. He has opened the door. He has seen the plastoid replica of himself tumble to the ground.

All a setup to allow the real driver to hide in the fog and sneak up behind him.

When he sees the man, he feels a moment's nova of shock. Entire system overloaded with a sense of betrayal and rage. But then this is inevitable, isn't it? he thinks. This is the inevitability I heard in his footsteps a bit ago.

Inevitability.

Must act fast. Not going to let this sonofabitch win. It's not a matter of money now. Or all the acclaim that comes from winning. Now it's a matter of self-respect. He knows instinctively that he will not be able to function if this last lingering shunt of his self-esteem is taken from him.

He lunges at Steve the Gardener.

But Steve is big, young, tough, and trained. He offers no words. No scowls. No feints. None of the drama one associates with a death match like this.

("It'll look bad, Steve," the producers told him, "if you look like you're, you know, *enjoying* it when you kill him. You gotta do it clean, you know what I'm saying?")

And clean he does it.

Grabs good ol' Sam by the arm, body slams him up against the car, rips the tiny red bomb from Sam's grasp.

The first thing he does it punch Sam so hard on the jaw that Sam starts to slump into an unconscious heap. But Steve holds him up with one hand while with the other he—

—flicks on the mechanism that will detonate the bomb in three minutes—

Then he pastes the bomb to Sam's forehead. The camera gets a good tight shot of that. The tiny red capsule adhered to Sam's forehead.

(Offscreen voice [nearly hysterical]: Oh, my god, he slapped it right on his forehead! We've had some exciting moments on the show before but nothing like this! Sam's got three minutes to regain consciousness and tear that bomb off his forehead. And then start running as fast as he can! He's a decent, law-abiding family man, folks. And there just aren't enough of those kind to go around. Tell you what—and you know I'm being sincere here as in split screen we watch Steve run away and that tiny bomb just keep ticking away on Sam's forehead—tell you what. Let's say a little prayer for poor old Sam. God be with you, my friend. This explosion is really going to be something, isn't it, folks? I mean, assuming that God doesn't come through for Sam here?")

The images of Karin and the girls filling the screen now were taped in advance. It is critical that they look believable and spontaneous when their perfect faces reflect the horror of seeing their father disappear in the flame and smoke and shriek of the explosion.

They spent most of a long day viddying this two-minute-and fourteen-second piece of reality that will forever mark them in the worldwide mind as the darlings of suffering and pain the producers want them to be.

Who could bear to see this deeply loved man—their very own beloved father—die in this fashion?

"Oh, Daddy! Daddy!" one of the girls sobs, as the other one hurls herself into her mother's arms.

* * *

Within five minutes of the explosion, the net is besieged with homegrams expressing contempt and rage for what just transpired.

A poor shambling man like Sam . . .

A beefy hunk of a showoff like Steve . . .

This just isn't right!

IS NOT RIGHT!

But then Betty the Shrink (whose own show is dispatched worldwide two nights a week. Betty being best known for the celebs who come on her show and commit suicide when they start talking about how difficult it was to BECOME a celeb. All the trauma flooding back upon them, the torment just too much to bear, then coming back after rebirthing of course, and explaining to Betty how grateful they are that she let them cleanse themselves of all their grief) . . . Betty the Shrink's perfect face fills the screen and she says:

"When someone dies, it's only natural that we feel sympathy for the deceased as well as the family. Homegrams are flooding our net with anger that Sam Conway was killed tonight in a fashion horrible beyond imagining. But I think it's appropriate now—as uneasy as it makes me feel—to tell you the truth about what Sam Conway was really like.

"You see, I chemprobed both of his daughters without their knowing it. I—I'm afraid that I have to tell you that Sam Conway, who seemed like such an ideal husband and father on the surface, was actually sexually molesting his daughters from the time they were very young. The girls were so afraid of him that they never told their mother—Sam convinced the girls that if they ever told anybody what went on while their mother was gone from time to time—he would kill her. Stab their mother to death right in front of them.

"I also have to share with you the fact that Steve—or Steve the Gardener as Sam always so contemptuously called him—saved the girls from their father's clutches. He was afraid to tell their mother this for fear that the whole situation would become even more traumatic for the girls. But once Steve learned what was going on, he threatened to kill Sam if he ever touched the girls again.

"I normally wouldn't violate the confidentiality of a client, but tonight I have no choice. What you saw—Steve clamping that bomb to Sam's forehead—what you saw tonight was an act of a moral man ridding the world of a sick and perverted man. Steve is not a mean or violent man. But he was so sickened by the thought of Sam violating his two daughters—well, tonight he just couldn't help himself. He acted on a very unkind impulse—and took care of Sam."

(Network prez, backseat of limo, later that night, speaking to his mistress/vice president: "So what we do is spin this whole Steve the Gardener into happy-ending-land with the marriage and all . . . but then down the line, Karin finds out that Steve the Gardener is porking both the girls . . . and she shoots him for violating her trust. Then we put her on *You Be the Jury* and the whole freaking world'll go crazy. Now how about them apples? Whose gonna convict her? Nobody!"

"Yeah," says mistress/vice president, "and how about the girls turn lesbo because all of the humpin' they got from dirty old men?"

"My god, you're brilliant," says network prez, "my god, you are. Lesbo. Absolutely freaking brilliant."

HERE TO THERE

by Jane Lindskold

Jane Lindskold is better known for her works of fantasy, but as the repeated appearances of Captain "Allie" Ah Lee demonstrate,* science fiction is near to her heart as well. Lindskold is the author of fifty or so short stories and over a dozen novels. The most recent of these are the Firekeeper novels—*Through Wolf's Eyes; Wolf's Head, Wolf's Heart; Dragon of Despair;* and *Wolf Captured*—and the archaeological adventure fantasy *The Buried Pyramid.* She is always writing something, and enjoys doing this very much. You can learn more about her work at janelindskold.com.

"WHY NOT JUST CALL it off?" I asked. "That's the part I don't understand. It's just a game."

"It isn't a just a game," said Karlsen Knappert. He sat in a chair across the table from me, to all appear-

* Captain Ah Lee appears in "Winner Takes Trouble" in *Alien Pets* and "Endpoint Insurance" in *Guardsmen of Tomorrow.*

ances a somewhat severe-looking dark-haired man. I happened to know he actually was an alien who resembled an overgrown, elongated rabbit as much as anything terrestrial.

"Or rather," Karlsen went on, "it is both a game and an attempt to educate my people about the human race. The competition has been being promoted within the Tesseract sphere for a quarter of a standard year. There is a great deal of anticipation regarding it. If the contest were canceled, the Isolationist Party would turn the cancellation to their political advantage. If it is corrupted—as the message we intercepted gives us reason to believe someone will be attempting to do—the reaction could be far worse."

I nodded, at least partially understanding what he was hinting. Karlsen's race, which humans call the Tesseract, are so technologically sophisticated that they make most human tech seem pretty pathetic. The FTL drive we use in our ships is adapted from a Tesseract model.

However, for all their sophistication, the Tesseract are pretty paranoid about close contact. The trade that had given humanity the FTL drive had been made by a minority government that favored greater contact. The subsequent social upheaval when the general population had learned about the trade had put the most conservative isolationist faction back into power for a long time. Now the tide of public opinion was gradually swaying in favor of more open contact with alien races, and this game was meant to increase that interest.

The other man seated at the table leaned forward. Allen "Spike" West was dark-haired, blue-eyed, lanky, and attractive enough, except for an excess of enthusiasm that reshaped his otherwise completely acceptable features. Looking at Spike, I never failed to feel that I was seeing a twelve-year-old boy—a slightly geeky boy at that—costumed as an adult.

Spike and I had worked together before. He's also my insurance agent, and knows far too much about the details of my life and business for my comfort.

"Captain Ah Lee," Spike said earnestly, "when this came up, I knew you were just the person we needed. You're clever, adaptable, and one of the best poker players I know."

"And this applies just how?"

"You know how to weigh the odds, when to raise, and when to fold. You're also very good at reading human character. We're going to need that skill if we're to find the agent dedicated to turning this good-will mission into an interspecies debacle, one that might even end in interplanetary war."

I looked over at Karlsen. He gave a small, self-deprecatory smile.

"Spike's manner of speech is rather florid," he said, "but he does not exaggerate the seriousness of the matter. Even among humans there is a saying that frightened people do foolish things."

I nodded. The colony where I'd grown up had suffered severe food shortages when I was a child. My petite size was a continual reminder of the foolish—

and cruel—things frightened people do. Despite my desire to remain detached, I felt a chill.

Karlsen went on, "What frightened humans do is nothing to what frightened Tesseract can do. Your people are hardwired with what is usually called a 'fight or flight' reflex. My people are wired with what might be called 'freeze or flight.' However, in cases where they cannot hide or flee, then the panic reaction becomes terrible indeed."

Spike grunted agreement, and there was nothing at all boyish about him now.

"Terrestrial animals have been known to gnaw off a limb to escape confinement," Spike said. "Tesseract historians have documented cases where their race in similar situations committed genocide—both of dangerous creatures and of subgroups of their own kind."

Karlsen picked up the thread. "Humanity has spread more rapidly than even the nonisolationists ever dreamed. Thus far, our inhabited systems have been left alone, but the majority of Tesseract are apprehensive regarding the proximity of alien colonies. If we do not learn to interact with aliens, there may be no aliens left with whom to interact."

I knew Karlsen wasn't kidding. It had long been rumored that while the Tesseract had sold us the secret of FTL drives, they had kept the knowledge of FTL communication to themselves. When Spike isn't recruiting me for some weird job, I'm a communications courier. I know how lopsided a war would be if one group had instant communication while the other suffered under the disadvantage of an extensive lag.

And that communications lag would certainly be only one of the Tesseract's advantages. Humans are pretty good at inventing weapons, but we think in a linear fashion. The Tesseract are born with the power of illusion. They think differently. Humanity might never see the fist until it opened, stretched out long fingers, and crushed us. Nor would our allies among other alien races be much help. They might side with the Tesseract. Humans, aggressive by nature, have a way of making even their friends nervous.

"And you really think this game could make a difference?" I asked.

"Let me state the matter this way," Karlsen said. "If the contest goes according to plan, it will make at least a slight difference in the way in which many Tesseract view humanity—and that difference will probably be positive. If the competition is sabotaged, it will make a large difference, and that most certainly will be negative."

"And my part?" I asked.

"The competition features six players," Spike said. "We want you to be the final competitor. We're in luck in that one remains to be introduced."

"Introduced?"

"The procedure so far has been to introduce each contestant in detail," Spike explained, "using recorded material about their private lives and professions taken from extended interviews."

"In this way," Karlsen added, "my people are given

information about the many and varied human cultures. These profiles have been a great success. Tesseract viewers are already choosing favorites."

"The final contestant," Spike said, "has agreed to resign and give you her place. AASU is paying her an enormous termination fee."

AASU is Spike's employer. Needless to say, the competition was being insured. The losses AASU would take if the entire thing went nova would be staggering—maybe enough to ruin the company. As AASU was a financial force in numerous solar systems, the wide-reaching economic repercussions would be severe, even if the Tesseract didn't decide to attack. And I'd need to find a new insurance company—a prospect I didn't like at all.

"You'll take the sixth contestant's place," Spike said, "and in addition to playing your part in the competition, you'll try to identify the saboteur and, if possible, foil his—or her—plans . . . as subtly as possible, of course."

"Anything else?" I asked dryly. "Would you like me to learn to breathe water or eat fire?"

"That will not be necessary," Karlsen said, missing my sarcasm entirely. "In any case, by agreeing to participate, you will be doing me, personally, a great favor."

"Favor?"

"I will be able to include your relationship with Gittchy in your profile."

"Gittchy?"

At the sound of her name, my pet woke from where

she had been sleeping in my lap. She was a little thing, with lavender fur and five amethyst eyes—three of which are on stalks.

Now Gittchy slid her three eyestalks to their full length and turned one on each of us. I knew her brain could process the complex image, but it still gave me a vaguely unsettled feeling.

"Why," I said, straightening the bow tied in Gittchy's silken topknot, "do you mention Gittchy?"

"Have you forgotten that she is a Tesseract creature? Fluffheads are to us as cats and dogs are to humans—our favorite and beloved companions. If the audience watching the game sees a fluffhead bonded with a human it will create a very favorable impression."

I scratched Gittchy along her spine, considering.

"That's right," I said. "You smuggled out Gittchy and her littermates precisely with something like this in mind. You're just continuing your goodwill campaign."

"This is so," Karlsen admitted.

"As long as I still can keep Gittchy," I said, "you can do as many heartwarming videos as you like."

"Thank you. And you understand what is wanted of you?"

"I'll be trying to figure out which of the other five contestants is greedy or corrupt or just plain crazy enough to want to risk an interstellar war."

Karlsen nodded, but Spike grinned.

"Four," he said.

"Four?"

"Four other contestants. You see, we've saved the best news for until after you agreed." Spike beamed. "I'm going to be the fifth participant. My profile just started running."

"What!"

I nearly jumped from my chair and Gittchy retracted all her eyes, then transformed turned into a fuzzy lace-trimmed pillow. I guess she figured that was about as innocuous as she could get.

Don't get me wrong. I like Spike. He's honest and genuinely brave. He's loyal and true. He also has all the common sense of a rock—or an adolescent male, which to my way of thinking is just about the same thing.

Karlsen spoke soothingly. "Spike had been chosen as a contestant even before we intercepted the message that let us know someone was going to attempt to sabotage the game. My people are fascinated by insurance agents."

"What? I don't get it."

I spoke more quietly this time, and Gittchy risked sliding out a couple of eyes. She stayed a pillow, though. The combination looked very weird. She doesn't normally mix illusion and reality. I must have completely rattled her.

Karlsen continued his explanation.

"Risk management fascinates us. We accept risk. What intelligent creature does not? We do not like risk, however, and it never would have occurred to us to attempt to make a profit from weighing the odds and then estimating a price based upon them. Your entire underwriting process seems rather like magic to us. The complexity of it boggles the mind."

I looked at Karlsen, wishing I could do like Gittchy and extend an eye. "So you're saying that Tesseract find insurance agents fascinating, and Spike is going to be one of the big heroes of the show?"

"Exactly. That's why his profile is only beginning now. We have shown the video star, the soldier, the professional athlete, and the scientist. Next would have been the woman you are replacing. However, we have put Spike in that place so now it's the insurance agent and the . . . interstellar adventurer?"

"There's one thing I don't understand," I said, shrugging off this description of me. "The idea is to have this competition watched, right?"

"That is so," Karlsen said.

"That means you're going to be recording it somehow."

"Yes. We are using several satellite cameras. There will be at least one for each competitor, others to capture area shots."

"Then why not use these to catch the saboteur?"

" 'Shoe,' " Spike interrupted happily. "I call the saboteur 'Shoe.' "

I stared at him.

"Why do you do that?"

"Well, we're going to need a code name, right? We can't exactly talk about it openly. Well, the word 'sabotage' comes from the practice of people sticking shoes into machinery to keep it from working."

"I think I could have lived all my life without knowing that," I said.

"And so," Spike concluded, unruffled, "I call our saboteur 'Shoe.' "

"Fine," I said. I looked at Karlsen. "You haven't answered my question."

"We would prefer not to intervene directly. It would ruin the entire purpose of the game. Also, whatever Shoe is going to do must have been planned with the awareness that it must be done under our camera's extended eyes. Ergo, when it happens, we will not see it."

I nodded unhappy understanding.

"I can think of a couple of dozen ways to foil the cameras," I said, "and that's without trying very hard. You're right. You do need agents there on the spot."

Spike beamed. "So we're the daring duo, Allie. You and me—all for one in a quest for universal peace."

I blinked, but Gittchy stopped being a pillow and announced, "Vrook!"

The time until the start of the game raced by. Most of mine was taken up getting my profile done. Then there were tons of tests, all required by AASU. Most important were the briefings regarding the contest and the potential sabotage. Karlsen handled these.

"We really know very little," he said. "Several standards before Spike initially contacted you, a message was misdelivered. Instead of going to its intended recipient, it came to me. The hotel had been having electronics problems. The message had no return address, and the routing code was garbled—I will return to that in a moment. The message said, 'Deposits made. You may confirm at any time. Instigate interpersonal violence. Death not necessary, but useful.' "

I frowned. "That's it?"

"It is quite enough." Karlsen looked very severe and I realized I was letting my nerves make me rude.

"Go on," I said. "What about the routing code?"

"It contained the prefix for the section of rooms reserved for myself and the five contestants who were then undergoing the more advanced medical tests. Spike was back on Earth being recorded for a portion of his profile. As AASU already insured him, they had the necessary test results on file and we wanted some recent images from Earth."

"So that's why you figure the message wasn't meant for Spike."

"Correct. I made inquiries and learned that the subcodes that routed the messages to individuals had been erased. Since I had made the reservations for our group and there was no return address, the message was automatically routed to me."

"Interesting. You'd think something like that wouldn't have been trusted to public communications."

"It is not as incredible as you might think. As you know from your own experience, our contestants spent much time during the tests without clothing or equipment."

I certainly did remember. It had been humiliating,

like returning to the days before electronic diagnosis. AASU was taking no chances on anyone misleading a scanner.

"Moreover, although cybernetic enhancements are moderately common among humans, they are not among the Tesseract. Therefore, all the contestants have been chosen from among the unaugmented—or at least from those who were willing to have their augmentations removed."

I grinned. I'd heard about how one very popular actor had been eliminated from consideration. It turned out he relied on both a subsonic voice enhancer and a mild pheromone emitter, and he refused to give them up. Until then, no one had realized he used such gimmicks.

"So, this saboteur couldn't be contacted via implant," I said. "But how about a wireless unit? They're easy enough to hide."

"And their signals are easy to interrupt. Because the nature of our project was being kept secret—even now it is primarily known of only on worlds inhabited by Tesseract—a military grade jamming field was in place."

"Wonder if it was good enough to have messed up internal hotel systems as well?" I mused. "You may owe this discovery to your own security precautions."

"I would like to think so." Karlsen twitched in a very nonhuman fashion and I remembered again that appearances are deceiving. "Your people speak of 'luck' with fondness, even court it. Among our mythologies 'luck' is simply another face of unpredictability and so is among the worst of our demons."

I restrained an impulse to pat Karlsen on the hand. It wouldn't go with his image. Or worse he might break down. Too much rested on him keeping things running until Spike and I found Shoe.

"Do you know for certain that the contestant whose place I am taking is not the person we're looking for?"

"We do not," Karlsen said. "If she is, then she is out of the game, and you can simply relax and do your best to win."

There was an informal briefing right before we were dropped onto what was mysteriously—and frustratingly to my way of thinking—referred to as "the game board." I'd protested that Spike and I should be told in advance what to expect. Karlsen had refused.

"You might let something slip. Even the most casual indication that you know more than you should could warn Shoe. Better you play the game as the others will."

Neither Spike nor I could budge him on this. I comforted myself that Karlsen probably wasn't worried I'd make a mistake. Spike, though . . . He'd probably say something like, "Let's turn left. I'm sure the control room is that way."

Or whatever. I had no idea what game we were playing. Neither did any of the others, so the six of us were quiet and alert as Karlsen reminded us what we had agreed to.

"The terms of the game are very simple. A challenge will be set for you. In addition to basic clothing, food, and essential equipment, each of you have been permitted to bring any small items you think will assist you."

I already knew that high-tech items like personal computers or jet-packs had been ruled out. Weapons were also forbidden, though we had each been provided with a multipurpose tool that included a small, sharp knife.

I'd selected a few things, but since we didn't know where we were going, I couldn't anticipate what to bring. I had no idea what Spike was bringing, but based on past experience I had some ideas—none of which filled me with confidence.

"All of you," Karlsen continued, "have received a large payment for your participation to this point. An even more substantial payment will be given to those who conclude the course. Finally, a special payment will be given to whoever is declared the 'winner' by the Tesseract viewing audience. This payment may be taken in the form of currency or in trade."

I had to admire the gimmick involved in offering this "grand prize." We'd all been extensively briefed on Tesseract cultural preferences. Since the Tesseract do not admire violence or brute force, any inclination to use such tactics should be kept to a minimum, because to use them would be to put one out of the running for the grand prize. Basically, the contest had been designed to encourage humans to employ behaviors Tesseract would admire. I only hoped the plan would work.

Anticipating human psychology is not easily done. Indeed, we already knew that in one case the bribe hadn't been big enough.

"But what," asked Carmen Lapageria, the scientist, "is the contest going to be? You have been persistently mysterious about this."

Karlsen smiled. "The mystery is part of the contest. However, you do not have long to wait. From the moment you board the shuttle, the game begins. Every move you make will be recorded and transmitted nearly live to the audience."

They do have FTL communications, I thought.

"One last thing," Karlsen said. "From the time you board the shuttle, you are not to mention this is a contest. You know it is and so does the audience, but for purposes of more enjoyable programming, you must keep references to the contest to a minimum. There are to be no discussions of what you will do with your money or about any of the preparation. The focus must be your goal."

Then, without much ceremony, we boarded the shuttle.

I felt very strange when I realized I was now under continuous surveillance. I'm sure all of us felt odd, but I think it was worst for me. All the rest of them lived within some population group. Most of my time was spent aboard the *Mercury*, alone except for Gittchy. I realized I was getting claustrophobic and struggled to calm myself.

Up to this point, I'd been so busy that I'd both obsessed about my fellow contestants and not thought about them at all. I'd labeled them by profession much as Karlsen had done, spent interminable hours reviewing their official profiles, and done what I could to check their unofficial profiles—in the little time I had.

However, I hadn't really thought about them as living, breathing people. They'd been data packets I had to memorize, with one of them a problem I had to solve. Now as we sat in the shuttle, not talking much, adjusting to the game having begun, I looked them over.

There were six of us: three male, three female. I'd taken a seat toward the rear. Now I started reviewing them, front to back, left to right—just like I was reading a book.

In the front, left-hand seat was Mahliner Zren, the soldier. He was more fair-skinned than usual, his light hair cut short. Armies from Alexander the Great on have favored short hair—it gives the enemy nothing to hold onto in a fight. In modern armies it also means hair isn't being shed into electronics or complicating the fit of vac suits.

Zren (he alone preferred to be addressed by his surname) was very well-muscled, but not at all hulking. In fact, he was distinctly graceful in a sinuous way, like a tiger. My brother had been a Marine, and I'd bet anything that Zren was also a ground-pounder, but he was no Marine, no infantry thug.

Zren wanted to be the leader of our little band, and

I didn't have any problem with that. Carmen Lapageria, the scientist, who was sitting across the aisle from Zren on the right-hand side, clearly did.

When I compared Doctor Carmen Lapageria to Zren it became obvious that Karlsen Knappert and his associates had deliberately recruited to show the variations available within humanity. She was of middle height with very, very dark brown skin. Her eyes were the shade of melted bittersweet chocolate, and her brown hair was a woolly halo cut close to her head.

Carmen's specialization was biology and she also held a medical degree. Like me, she had grown up in a space colony, but she had been educated on Earth. She had never married, but had several daughters. Rumor said they were clones of their mother. Looking at the arrogant tilt of Carmen Lapageria's head, I thought this likely.

Phelps Iorrobino, the actor who sat on the right behind Zren, superficially represented modern humanity at its best. His coloring mingled all of Earth's races, mellowing into warm brown skin, brown hair, and hazel eyes with just the slightest hint of the epicanthic fold that is so distinctive in my own. His features were neither aquiline nor broad but muddled in between. He was slightly taller than average height, healthy-looking, but not unduly muscular.

Phelps had made his career playing a wide variety of roles—anything from soldiers like Zren to freelance adventuring types like me. However, as I saw it, without a script he was certain to be pretty useless. I'd asked Karlsen why an actor had been among the types they'd recruited.

"Much of our population's exposure to human culture," he replied, "has been through dramatic presentations. My fellow organizers and I felt that the inclusion of an actor provided an ideal opportunity to remind that everything we have seen recorded about humans is not based on fact."

"Then Tesseract don't have theater or drama?"

Karlsen smiled indulgently.

"Of course we do. Our ability to project illusions makes such natural to us. That is why it is so easy for many of the less sophisticated elements in our population to dismiss your own abilities. That a people without projection ability can nonetheless create illusions is hard for some to grasp."

"If you say so," I shrugged.

I figured that the last member of our group was likely to prove as useful as Phelps Iorrobino would prove useless. Joellen Wehrung was a specialist in the decathlon, a traditional athletic competition that emphasized personal training rather than technological assistance. She had competed throughout civilized space, and put most of her winnings into creating programs for training new athletes. Not only would her skills be useful, but her familiarity with competitions would also serve us well.

The shuttle was touching down now with a smoothness that spoke well both for the pilot's skill and the quality of Tesseract engineering. An automatic door slid open, and before we had time to register our surroundings, a projection of Karlsen Knappert, minus his human illusion, appeared:

"The sun is just lighting the sky to the east," he said, his voice hissing a little, which it didn't when he pretended to be human. "Your quest has begun. Your goal is simple. Get from here to there before the third sunrise—this is the first."

"Wait!" snapped Zren. "Where is there?"

"That," Karlsen said, "is for you to discover."

The projection vanished. The shuttle, which had risen on its air cushion while we were occupied, now sped off. A moment later, we saw it blast skyward, leaving us perfectly alone.

"Here to there," said Carmen Lapageria. "That's crazy."

"It's what we have," Phelps Iorrobino replied. "I've had crazier scripts. Been in a few projects where they were still writing the end while we filmed the beginning. I've found the thing to do in such cases is not to worry about the end, but to focus on where you are and deal with that."

He made sense, and I found myself respecting him more than I had thought I would. We all started inspecting our surroundings.

We stood on the fringes of a tangled rain forest that stretched pretty much without a break to the west. To the east, just a few meters from where we were, began a broad stretch of beach, pebbly in land, but becoming fine golden sand closer to the water.

The air smelled of salt, rotting vegetation, and

something musky I couldn't identify. Both Spike and Zren removed compact binoculars from the pockets of the lightweight coveralls that, in addition to matching boots and gloves, made up our attire.

Spike looked delighted that his preparations had so closely matched those of the professional soldier, but I had the feeling Zren didn't like having his efficiency upstaged.

While they inspected our surroundings, I inspected the rest of the group. We all had small backpacks, but where mine held little more than the basic gear we'd been supplied, those carried by Zren, Carmen, and Phelps bulged. Spike's pack also was fairly full, and I noticed his coverall was tailored with pockets all over the front, sleeves, and legs. Joellen's pack was nearly as lightly loaded as my own, but she balanced a metal staff between thumb and forefinger.

"Nothing much to the south," Zren reported crisply. "Two kilometers to the north, however, there appears to be an opening in the jungle, perhaps the beginning of a road."

"Did you notice," Spike asked, "that there appears to be a village about a kilometer past the road? Mostly thatched huts, from what I can see."

"What kind of people live there?" Phelps asked. "Humans or Tesseract?"

"Neither," Zren said, and again I had the impression he was unhappy about Spike's anticipating his orderly presentation. "They appear to be bipedal lizards, over two meters in height."

Carmen wiped her forehead on the back of her hand.

"I thought we were going somewhere hot when I got my coveralls," she said, "but I hadn't counted on the humidity. While you folks have been looking in the distance, I've been checking out our immediate surroundings. Have you noticed anything interesting?"

Joellen frowned. "Dr. Lapageria, we have two days—and we don't know how long the days are here. I think we'd better stop the cute guessing games."

Carmen looked momentarily angry, then nodded.

"I stand corrected, Joellen. You are absolutely right. As far as I can tell, there are no birds, no furred creatures. Once the disturbance from the shuttle faded, I noticed numerous insects and several small reptiles returning to their usual routines. I mention this because, at least on Earth, insects and reptiles are more likely to be poisonous than birds or mammals. Evolution may not have been parallel here, but it is something we should take into account."

I noticed that I wasn't the only one who quickly scouted the ground near my feet when she said this. Phelps, who had been standing in the shade offered by the tree line, stepped out into the sun.

"Interesting," Zren said, "and perhaps pertinent. Our next decision is obvious. We need to find what this 'there' is. We have been offered two clues: the road and the village. Time is important. Do we use some to take a look at the village, or do we simply get on the road and see where it takes us?"

"Follow the Yellow Brick Road," Phelps sang.

Zren glowered at him.

"Is that a suggestion?"

"Lighten up, Zren," Phelps suggested. "You know perfectly well they're the words to a song. I think we should talk to the villagers. I bet the road does start us in the right direction, but it's sure to branch at some point. We need something to tell us what direction to follow then."

No one disagreed. As we trudged down the beach toward the village, I cleared my throat.

"Has no one thought about the implications of this? We're about to make first contact with an alien civilization."

Phelps and Spike looked duly impressed, but Zren and Carmen exchanged tired glances, and Joellen actually sniggered.

"What," I demanded, "is the joke?"

Carmen graced me with a forgiving smile.

"I forgot you weren't with us earlier and haven't had a part in our bull sessions. The Tesseract are masters of illusion. It's quite likely this entire setup is virtual."

I snorted. "This is too perfect for a virtual setup."

"Real or illusion," Zren interjected confidently, "doesn't affect our plans. If real, the lizard people— or saurians, as we should more accurately designate them—must have been briefed about our arrival. If illusion, they'll be programmed to respond to our queries."

I thought this overconfident, and was about to say so when Spike reminded us all in a stage whisper,

"Remember. We're to play the game, not wonder about how it was set up."

"Wondering how it was set up," Joellen countered, "may be part of playing the game—like considering the judges' past preferences when going into a competition where style points are part of the final tally."

That reminder of our unseen audience, judging us on how we solved the puzzle shut us all up. I, for one, didn't think this was a virtual setup and resolved to take extra care knowing that several of my fellow players were designing their responses based on the assumption it was.

As we drew closer to the village, Spike and Zren reported more details. There were three structures that stood out from the mass of huts. One was a small stockade built from logs with sharpened tops. As best we could tell, it had one gate. Periodically, different saurians were led in or taken out—always under supervision.

"Slaves," Spike guessed, "or prisoners used for slave labor. We'd better be careful we don't end up in there with them."

The second interesting structure was a thatched longhouse with a fenced area surrounding it. The fence wasn't so high we couldn't see over it, so we were able to glimpse groups of small saurians darting around outside, tended by adults. Sometimes a group rushed inside and another came out.

"A school," Carmen decided, "or a nursery of some sort."

The third structure was the only one that wasn't a variation on a thatched hut. It was built from carved and polished logs—"teak" Phelps said, and no one bothered to argue. The roof was shingled with over-lapping layers of flat shells similar to ones we saw scattered on the beach, but obviously chosen for size and uniformity. Alone of all the buildings, it was built not only well above the waterline, but upon a solid rock foundation. Clearly, every effort had been taken to make certain this building would be preserved in case of hurricane.

"It's too elaborate merely to be a storm shelter," Zren said, "although I'm certain it serves that purpose as well. Nor is it built like a fortress."

"It's a temple," Phelps interrupted. "Obviously. It might be a government center or hurricane shelter or any number of other practical things, but when that much trouble is taken to make something beautiful when all the surroundings are practical, then you have an effort to honor the divine."

We stared at him, but he didn't alter his conviction.

"It just makes sense," he insisted.

"I agree," Joellen said. "It's a good thing we have someone with an artistic perspective to balance us practical types."

Phelps beamed, but neither Zren nor Carmen looked particularly pleased.

While we'd been observing the village, the villagers had been taking note of us. First to notice us were a group of fishers messing with boats down along the shore. The one who first noticed had punched its buddy; then they had called to a third. Finally, all three of these had gone to get a fourth.

This fourth, a sleek figure, naked except for a tool belt, had studied our trudging progress for a moment, then had given orders. Two fishers detached themselves from the main group and headed to inform the village. The fourth fisher—obviously a leader of some sort—had taken the two who had first seen us and headed toward us. The remainder got busy with the boats, though whether they were going back to work or doing something defensive, I couldn't tell.

"The messengers," Zren reported, "are heading toward the 'temple.' Other locals have noticed us, but are staying close to the village."

"Yeah," Spike said, "and the slaves or prisoners are being put back in the stockade. They're taking at least some precautions in case we're not friendly."

"They don't seem too worried, though," Zren sounded slightly affronted.

Phelps laughed nervously, and gestured with a toss of his head toward the jungle.

"Maybe they're used to bigger worries."

Joellen paused and leaned on her staff. "The chief fisher is coming to meet us. Maybe we should wait here? Not seem threatening?"

"Maybe waiting would be interpreted as defensive," Carmen said, "or indicative of fear. I think we should move to meet them, but slowly."

No one disagreed, but I noticed that Joellen hung to the rear as we moved up.

As we closed, those of us without binoculars got our first good look at the saurians. They were thicker through the body than any of us, except possibly for Zren, but gave the impression of slenderness. Part of this was due to how their elongated necks merged into their heads. The other contributing factor were the long tails that counterbalanced from behind.

None of the saurians wore clothing other than tool belts. Their scales were small, close-fitting, and seemed silky smooth. Looking at them, I had an insight into the design of the temple roof. Their coloration was a mixture of iridescent blues and greens, like the shimmer of water.

We had closed to within about ten meters now. Zren cleared his throat, clearly preparatory to giving orders for how we should handle this contact. Spike, however, stepped forward.

He poked at his chest and said, "Spike."

Then he pointed toward the chief fisher. "Who are you?"

I stifled a groan. Apparently, Spike subscribed to the idea that anyone would understand you if you spoke slowly enough and made broad enough hand gestures.

The chief fisher halted. I noticed it had several eyelids and that a translucent one slid over the eye. I wondered what this indicated. Fear, maybe? Or maybe it was a defensive posture, in case your opponent spit poison. Maybe it indicated confusion. I knew I'd be confused.

Spike repeated the pointing to his chest and again said, "Spike." Then he pointed to the chief fisher and spread his hands wide, shrugging.

The chief fisher pointed at Spike and hissed, "Sss-aye-k."

Apparently, its mouth wasn't able to handle plosives, but it was clearly saying "Spike." Then it pointed to itself, "V'reesh."

"Vuh-reesh," Spike repeated obediently, pointing back at the saurian. Then he beamed at us. "Its name is V'reesh."

"Or maybe," Carmen said dryly, "that's the name of the entire village, or the word for 'chest,' or the name of the species. By the way, I think 'it' is female—though with egg layers it's hard to be certain."

However, it seemed that Spike had guessed correctly. V'reesh was introducing her companions with names in which the "eesh" sound was prominent—kinfolk, maybe?

We were about to exchange names from our side when Zren said softly, "Might as well do it all at once. Here come some more."

I'd been concentrating so closely on V'reesh and her companions that I hadn't noticed the approach of the others. Now I saw the messengers had brought a small crowd with them. Of that crowd, two were clearly of paramount importance.

In the front was a tall, heavily-built saurian, wearing armor made from strung bones and leather. A helmet in the shape of a large, crested lizard rested on top of his—I just felt this was a male—head, but could be pulled down to provide pretty decent protection for the top and sides. He carried a heavy club studded with sharp shells and pieces of rock.

Coming up alongside this warrior, its body language somehow reminding me of the precedence games being played within our own group, was what at first glance I thought was a saurian with wings. Then I noticed that the wings were artificial, attached to a heavy vest toggled shut across the saurian's chest. This one also wore a crested lizard helmet, but this model was lighter, more elegantly made—ornamental rather than armor.

These two went into conference with V'reesh, and from the gestures it was clear that V'reesh was telling them what had happened so far. The other saurians, probably a dozen or so, listened eagerly, hissing comments.

"I watched," Phelps said quietly. "The big guy in armor came from somewhere near the temple. The one with the wings came from inside the temple."

"War chief and priest?" Spike suggested. "I wonder why the priest has wings? They're more like bird wings than insect wings, too, but we haven't seen any birds."

"He has something strapped to the tip of his tail," Carmen added. "It looks like a thorn or hook."

We had time to soak in this sartorial oddity before V'reesh turned and made introductions. The big warrior was called Shaash, and the priest (if it was a priest) was called Tra'mash.

We offered first names only, and they handled these pretty well, though Phelps became "Fells" and the *m* in Carmen was so softened it was more like a pause, "Ka'en." They seemed to like "Ah Lee" quite a bit, and "Zren," on which they rolled the *r*.

We were ushered into the village and offered seats in a public square near the temple. I noticed we were kept a good distance from the school. That seemed to speak well for their protecting their young and weak.

Over a meal of grilled fish and a soft, spongy tuber—we ate without hesitation, having been assured by Karlsen Knappert that the environment in which the game was set would not be poisonous in itself— we tried to communicate with our hosts. It wasn't easy. Not only was there a language barrier, but Shaash didn't like us one bit. V'reesh was clearly interested, and Tra'mash neutral.

"We don't have forever," Joellen reminded us when it seemed that Phelps, Spike, and Carmen might get too interested in talking with the saurians. "I want to look around and see if there are any clues."

Without waiting for our approval or disapproval, she rose. The saurians stopped their hissing comments, and Shaash leaped to his feet, his club in his hand.

Joellen stood, indecisive, then she plopped back down.

"I guess I have to wait until the meeting is adjourned," she said with a weak smile.

The others were trying to get the idea of our quest across to the saurians. Added to the language barrier was the fact that we didn't have the faintest idea where we were supposed to go—except that it was within the distance we could reasonably be expected to travel in two days—two days whose length we still didn't know.

"Here to there," Spike said, waving his hand in a loose arc. "Here to there . . ."

"Make the direction clearly east to west," Carmen suggested. "Unless this village is our destination, that's the only road we've seen."

"We could be expected to trudge up and down the beach," Zren objected.

"But in what direction?" Carmen said. "No. I think the road's a clue."

"I agree with Dr. Lapageria," Joellen said, and something in her tone also said, "And I disagree with you."

Spike hadn't waited for the conclusion of this debate to take Carmen's suggestion, and as soon as he started pointing to the road, then making his arc to the west, Tra'mash, the priest, began hissing excitedly to the other saurians.

Shaash was against whatever Tra'mash was suggesting, but V'reesh backed up the priest. Apparently the three made up a local ruling triumvirate, because Shaash reluctantly backed down.

Tra'mash rose from where he'd been squatting comfortably against his tail, adjusted his wings, and motioned for us to accompany him into the temple. We did so, all too aware of the crowd of saurians now following us, and the fact that the hissing chatter had taken on what sounded like a nervous pitch. I thought about the slave stockade, and hoped we wouldn't get stuck inside it.

Once we had passed through the door and through the foyer immediately behind it, none of us had any doubts that Phelps' guess had been right. This was a temple. In the center of what must be the main worship area was a raised dais. On this was a beautifully cast bronze statue of a winged lizard, rearing back and roaring over a cringing throng of saurians. Like its worshipers—or victims—the winged lizard was sinuous rather than heavy. The wings hung in folds, suggesting a vast wingspan.

"A glider," Carmen said, her voice awed.

"Nonsense," Zren returned. "It's clearly a mythological beast. Nothing that huge could fly."

"He's probably right," Joellen said. "I've done some gliding, and even with the best synthetic materials, it's hard to stay aloft for long."

She sounded quite ready for a debate, but Zren interrupted.

"Look more closely. That's not just a tableau. It's a relief map. See, here's the ocean and the beach, then the jungle, and to the west . . ."

"Volcanoes," Spike said, sounding thrilled. "The winged lizard lives in the volcanoes. The saurians go there to visit it, from . . ."

"Here to there!" Phelps said. "That's our destination. We need to get to the western volcanoes."

"And find a dragon?" Joellen asked. "I don't like that."

"It's mythological, I tell you," Zren said. "We'll probably find another temple at the other end."

I noticed he no longer protested the idea this was a temple.

"I don't much like staying here," I put in. "Shaash isn't happy with us, and in my experience people who keep their own kind slaves have even less trouble enslaving other types of people. I vote we get out of here."

No one argued, and the saurians themselves seemed happy to let us go. V'reesh and a couple of the fishers were the only ones who escorted us to where the road began. She talked volubly, but whatever advice she offered couldn't get through the language barrier. Spike invited her to join us, but she pointed back to the boats on the beach.

"That way duty lies, right?" Spike said. "Well, thanks."

"Sss-aye-k," she said before turning away.

"I think you have an admirer," I said, motioning for him to drop back so we could talk privately.

Spike actually blushed.

"So, who does the shoe fit . . ." he said, quickly changing the subject.

"I have some ideas. You?"

"Zren. He's arrogant and keeps trying to direct things."

"I don't know," I replied. "I think that's his nature. I'm wondering . . ."

But what I wanted to tell Spike had to wait. With a tremendous crashing of tree limbs and tearing of vines, an armored, four-legged monstrosity lurched out onto the trail, cutting off our retreat. It was reptilian, and had more than any creature's fair allotment of sharp teeth at one end and a heavy tail that terminated in a spiked ball at the other.

"Run!" yelled Carmen. "It doesn't know what to make of us."

Zren had snatched up a heavy branch and seemed prepared to take on the creature. Now he swung into the intervening space. The big reptile snapped at the branch, leaving splinters.

"It seems to know perfectly well what to do," Zren protested, but he backed away a few steps nonetheless.

"Drop the stick and run," Carmen said, tugging on his arm. "See how widely its nostrils are flared? It can't figure out our scents. We're alien. We're possibly the only mammals it's ever scented. Take advantage of that and run!"

She nearly shouted the last word and, I think as much to his own surprise as to the reptile's, Zren turned and ran.

That wasn't our only encounter with various carnivores along our route west. Apparently, the local predators thought this was a superior game trail and regularly checked it out. However, Carmen's advice held good. I found myself regretting my deodorant. I wanted to reek of human scent.

Our stinking of mammal didn't stop all the predators, but, among them, Spike, Joellen, and Zren had the means to make the more stubborn take time to think about the wisdom of sampling us.

As I had expected, Spike's numerous pockets were loaded with a variety of gadgets. He had smoke bombs and stink bombs, firecrackers and oil pellets. Not all of these proved ideal. One of the stink bombs made us retch, and attracted hordes of ruby-colored, beetlelike insects with long, clacking mandibles. An oil pellet broke before he could throw it, and dribbled slime all over his hands.

Joellen and Zren were more conventional in their approaches. Joellen's staff not only expanded to serve her as a quarterstaff, but was hinged so she could rig a sling to the top. Zren might be short on prudence, but no one could fault him for either courage or honor. Phelps wouldn't have gotten away from the ruby beetles if Zren hadn't carried him after he fell.

But the carnivores weren't the only obstruction the road had to offer. The saurians had towns along the way, and after one nasty encounter with a pit trap, we learned to look out for their workings as well. As we drew away from the coast, the saurians grew more civilized—if installing tollbooths could be considered civilized. At the first one, Spike did his "me Spike, you who" routine, but it didn't get us anywhere. Then Phelps made a suggestion.

"Maybe they know the saurians from the coastal village." He stepped to the front of our little group, pointed back down the road, then said, "Tra'mash. V'reesh. Shaash."

The growing crowd around the toll area where we were being held grew excited and interested. How-

ever, those that were pointing weren't pointing down
the road. They were pointing into their own village.
We were herded toward their own temple, and a saurian garbed much as Tra'mash had been emerged. A
big warrior type showed up almost before we had a
chance to inspect this priest's dragon regalia.

After a lot of mistakes and quite a bit of frustration
on all sides, we figured out that, after all, Spike hadn't
quite broken the language barrier. Tra'mash, V'reesh,
and Shaash turned out to be titles, not proper names.
Head priest, head fisher (or maybe food gatherer), and
military leader.

"The coastal saurians must have thought us the
most overspecialized creatures in the universe," Phelps
said with a laugh. "And given what we've seen along
the road, it makes sense that they differentiate between their hunters and their fighters—keeping back
the predators must be a full-time job."

But I remembered the slave stockades we'd seen at
both villages and thought Phelps was being unrealistic.
Slaves had to come from somewhere.

Where at least some of them came from we learned
at the next village. Darkness was beginning to fall.
One of Spike's pockets held a multizone timekeeper
and he'd confirmed that the local hours of daylight
were quite long.

"We won't know whether that indicates a long rota-
tion period for the planet," he said, "or whether this
planet has irregular day/night cycles depending on the
season."

"We will by dawn," Zren said.

"I'm beat," Joellen said, "and if I'm tired, the rest of you have to be exhausted. I mean, Allie spends most of her time in spaceships, Carmen in labs and stuff. I don't know about Spike and Phelps . . ."

"I'm a city boy," Spike admitted.

"As am I," Phelps said. "Despite these excellent boots, my feet ache."

"We're coming up on another town," Joellen said. Her excellent physical conditioning had made her the natural choice for scout. "Why don't we rest there and continue as soon as there's light?"

"I agree," Spike said. "I brought a variety of artificial lights, but they won't be much help if we're fighting dinosaurs in the dark. Additionally, they'll probably attract insects."

"The pseudo-dinosaurs may become torpid after dark," Carmen said, "if it gets much cooler, and I'm not sure it will. You're probably right about the insects."

Zren tried to push for continuing, but the rest balked. Stim tabs may supercharge your system, but they do nothing for sore feet. All of us wanted to rest. When we approached them, the saurians in the town gave us a place to stay—chained by the ankles in a hut in the slave stockade.

There were other slaves in the stockade, but either they'd been warned away from us or they were simply too apathetic to care about the monsters among them. We were locked into our hut, and heard a bar dropped over the door. Our captors did give us water, food, and a small lantern burning fishy-smelling oil so we could hope they weren't going to kill us right away.

Zren jerked his length of chain between two big fists.

"Cold-forged iron," he said. "I didn't think the saurians were this technologically advanced."

"You forget," Joellen said a bit too sweetly. "The dragon statue looked like bronze."

Phelps hastened to be the peacemaker.

"Likely the coastal saurians aren't as technologically able. However, the inland dwellers may have all sorts of interesting advantages. Geothermal power, probably. Maybe petroleum."

I shook myself from intoxicating drowsiness.

"Phelps, how do you know so much?"

He grinned. "Method acting. I try to submerge myself into the characters I play, and by now I've played almost everything. I can't say I'll equal an expert, but I'm a good generalist."

Zren growled. "That doesn't matter. As Joellen keeps reminding us, we're running out of time."

I leaned over and patted his hand.

"Relax, Zren. We agreed we needed to get some rest. If our hosts leave us be until morning, all the better."

"We have to get out of here," he exclaimed.

I realized that I was comforted by the presence of walls, but Zren was feeling trapped. I glanced around, made sure as best I could that none of the saurians was watching.

"Look," I said. I pointed my foot and slid it, shoe

and all, right out of the cuff. "I don't think the saurians are as flexible as we are. The rest of you can probably manage if you take off your boots. If not, I'm sure Spike would love to have a chance to pick the locks."

I noticed that the saurians had taken his pack, but had missed his pockets. Anyhow, Spike wouldn't be Spike if he hadn't hidden away a set of lockpicks—they're just too romantic for him to have forgotten.

Spike grinned. "I have a set twisted in my hair, just in case we were stripped."

Zren was looking more cheerful as he unlaced his boot. "Any other suggestions, Ah Lee?"

"I'm serious about us all getting some rest. Then, I'll check around outside."

By now, everyone was so wrung out either emotionally or physically, that there was no argument with my suggestion.

To our great good fortune, the hours of darkness seemed to stretch for quite a while. I'm used to sleeping in small installments, and a few hours' shut-eye set me right. Zren, the good soldier, was sleeping sitting up, and his eyes snapped open as I rose.

I held a finger to my lips, and said softly in his ear, "Going to look around."

He didn't move, but I could feel his gaze tracking me in the lantern-lit dimness. I'd brought a few pieces of Spike's equipment with me, and now I removed a collapsible grapnel and a length of line from a coverall pocket. I hooked it to a support beam of the hut and swarmed to the roof. Parting the thatch took a moment, but soon I was outside.

Once my eyes adjusted to the light of the pictur-
esque twin moons, my inspection confirmed what I'd
seen when we were herded in. Our hut was pretty
central and the stockade wall high. The stakes along
the top were sharpened, too. Both within and without
the stockade, however, the saurians were asleep. There
were probably guards along the perimeter, but they'd
be looking outward, worrying about the big predators,
not about us.

Up and over that wall was what we were going to
have to do. I went back inside and poked Spike awake.

"How much line do you have in your pockets?"
I asked.

"In all, about a hundred meters. Not all of it can
bear our weight. Heavy enough to bear weight, about
forty meters."

By the time we woke the others, Zren, Spike, and
I had completed our preparations. I sketched my plan.

"I'm going to anchor a line to the roof of the hut.
We leave that way. Joellen and I are going up first. While
the rest of you get out, we'll anchor a line between the
posts of the stockade. I'll climb and cover the points.
The rest of you follow. Remember. We have to stay
quiet."

There was miraculously little discussion. Maybe
everyone was making an effort to seem at their best
for the Tesseract viewers. Personally, I thought they
were all scared about what morning would bring, and
my plan gave us the best chance of getting out.

"Zren nodded. "I'll go last. I can boost anyone who
needs help."

Neither Joellen nor I needed help. Once outside, I handed Joellen a weighted ball attached to some of Spike's rope.

"We tried to make it about the size of a shot," I said. "Can you put it between two of the posts?"

She hefted the ball, tossed it experimentally to see how the drag from the rope changed things, then got it into place on the first try. I went up the rope, padded the pointy parts as best I could with some smelly bedding that had been in the hut, then lowered the rope ladder we'd cobbled.

Then I dropped back down. I'd seen our gear carried to the temple, and at the very least I wanted Carmen's medical kit. We'd already had to resort to it for various bites and scrapes and we had a long way yet to go.

My ship is named *Mercury* and the god of thieves must have been with me that night, because I got the right pack and out of the temple without being seen. I was sorry to leave our other supplies, but we knew we could eat local food and drink the water. This would have to do.

By the time the night insects were stopping their chirping and the day insects were starting their thrumming, we were well on our way. The air now held the distinct odor of sulfur, and about a third of the water sources were hot. When the canopy of foliage parted, we glimpsed the smoking peaks of the volcanoes.

Early on, when other roads crossed our own, there had been times we were glad for compasses packed by both Spike and Zren. Now there was no doubt about which was the western route. It was far better kept, and the tollbooths more frequent. After our last trouble, we took to the jungle to avoid both these and any other traffic on the road. Zren's sharp eye kept us from being caught by traps meant for toll jumpers, but there weren't many of these, and most could double as impediments for the carnivorous dinos.

"The saurians must be very law-abiding," Carmen said.

"They're religious pilgrims," Phelps replied, "journeying to the home of the gods. They wouldn't want to be anything other than honest."

"Or maybe," Joellen said, "they're just aware that the penalty for being caught is slavery. I'm going to scout ahead."

I thought Joellen was more likely right than Phelps, but I didn't bother to comment. Something else was bothering me more. So far, if Shoe had acted, it had been subtle. Now time was running out. Even with our frequent detours into the jungle, we hoped to reach the volcanic lands that evening—well before our deadline. If Shoe was going to fulfill the contract, action needed to be taken quickly.

Maybe the one I replaced was Shoe, I thought, trying to reassure myself, but I didn't believe it.

Joellen came jogging back.

"Bad news," she said, wiping sweat from her forehead. "There's a huge ravine ahead, running roughly north/south. It splits the ground as far as I could see in either direction. Wide, too. I'd guess twenty to fifty meters depending on where. There's a bridge, but . . .

"It starts in the middle of a village," Carmen guessed.

"Right. And it's no village," Joellen went on. "It's a city, or at least a big town."

"Probably a pilgrim center," Phelps said.

"Probably," Zren agreed. "It seems to me that the farther inland we've gotten, the less open-minded the saurians have become. Even if we had whatever toll they're charging, I wouldn't want to go marching in there. Joellen, is there any way we can get close enough to the ravine so we can cross it?"

"We can, but it'll take time," Joellen replied. "The city spreads to either side of the road, maybe a bit more populous to the north. We can go through the jungle, then close on the ravine."

Spike was fishing through his much depleted pockets.

"Maybe we have something we can trade for passage," he said. "Or maybe we can bluff our way through. I still have lots of smoke bombs."

Zren and Carmen agreed in disagreeing, and even Phelps seemed reluctant. Joellen was already scouting the southern edge of the road for our best route.

"I'm sorry, Spike," Phelps said. "It's not that I don't think you're ingenious, but one night in a prison is enough."

Joellen reemerged from the jungle. "And if we're caught, we're really risking not making it to 'there' by the third sunrise. Come on. I've found a trail."

The trail led us to a comparatively narrow segment of the ravine. The rock was honeycombed with tiny holes, worn smooth in some places, edged like a grater in others. At the bottom of the ravine ran a river of water so hot that the wreathing steam partly obstructed our vision—and happily obstructed anyone upstream from seeing what we were doing.

"If we sling ropes," Zren said, "from Spike's invaluable supply, we might be able to get across. The hardest part is going to be anchoring the rope solidly."

Joellen pointed. "I noticed that projection over there, the cone-shaped one. I might be able to throw something that far."

Carmen interrupted, shaking her head. "I'm sure you could, but what would anchor it? We need a closer point, or maybe to climb down and ford the river."

"It looks pretty deep," I said. "No rocks breaking the surface like they would if it were shallow."

"A bridge!" Spike said, rummaging through his pockets.

"Don't tell me you have a bridge in there," Joellen said.

"I don't," Spike said, "but I do have a better saw than the little cutting blade on our multipurpose tool. We can fell a tree and lower it down . . ."

"Wedge it into place," Zren agreed.

"There's a type I've noted," Carmen said, "that will be perfect. It doesn't have any of the thorns or caustic saps so many of the others cultivate to protect them from the dinos."

The westering sun reminded us we didn't have much time. We cut and hauled the log, and lowered it into place. However, someone would need to go down and make certain it was snug.

"I'll go," Joellen said. "Just be careful how you secure me. I don't want to go over."

I thought about offering to go myself, but Joellen was the acknowledged athlete, and my real purpose here wasn't to gain points with the viewing audience. It was to stop Shoe. I kept quiet, and let Zren splice together a harness for Joellen. Spike stood by, providing a small box of clips and fasteners which he insisted would be far better than the knots Zren intended.

"You've got everything there, don't you?" Joellen said, eyeing him as she tested the harness.

"The insurance creed," Spike agreed. "Anticipate problems before you have to pay for them."

The end of the line was fastened to a tree trunk, but Zren insisted on playing the line over his gloved hands so he could moderate the speed of the drop. Joellen thanked him for his care, but she looked fairly white as she went over the edge.

I wasn't big enough to be any help lowering her, so I knelt on the edge, watching her go down. She went easily enough, then, just as her feet touched the log and she was steadying herself, something snapped. She grabbed onto the log, catching herself before she fell.

Phelps spun on Spike. "Look what you've done! One of those fasteners must have given way."

Spike didn't bother to defend himself.

"I'll go down after her," he said, laying hands on the rope. "It's only right."

"Nonsense," I interrupted, shoving him back. "You didn't do anything."

I whispered very softly, "Shoe . . ."

Spike stopped, glanced back at the others, his eyes narrowing. I didn't give him a chance to say anything.

"I'm smallest and lightest," I said. "As we proved back at the stockade, I'm also probably one of the best climbers. I'll go down, stabilize her, keep her from panicking. Then we'll figure out what to do."

Carmen hurried forward as I was pulling on my gloves.

"Allie, clip this med-kit to your belt. It has pretty much everything you should need in case she's injured—including a sedative patch. Frightened people can be dangerous."

I thought about the last time I'd heard those words. Karlsen had spoken them. Shoe had acted, and I was going to find out just how dangerous a frightened person could be.

"Thanks, Carmen." I glanced at Zren. "Ready to anchor?"

"Ready."

We didn't bother with any fancy harness. There wasn't time, and I was confident of my ability to rappel down—we'd done lots of rope work in my home colony. Besides, two lines could tangle with nasty consequences for both me and Joellen.

I was down almost before I could think about it, the smell of sulfur in my nostrils making me a bit queasy. The log bridge was steady under my feet, and the rough bark gave plenty of traction. That was all I needed for confirmation.

I'd identified Shoe.

Joellen grabbed at me as soon as I came down, but I was quick. I scuttled back a few steps, palming the sedative patch.

"Don't," I warned her. "I'll knock you into the river if you try it—that's the first rule of rescue work. Don't get yourself killed saving the victim."

Joellen stopped. Observers might think she was just reacting to the threat, but I suspected she heard the tightness in my voice. It wasn't fear. It was anger. I was thinking of those words, "Instigate interpersonal violence. Death not necessary, but useful."

Joellen had been trying to set us at each other's throats all along, but maybe the temptation of the grand prize, maybe a real sense of camaraderie had prevented this. Now she'd faked her accident, and once I was parboiled in the river, she'd be blaming everyone else for letting it happen.

Phelps was already on edge. Spike would be mortified. Carmen and Zren would blame each other. It wouldn't take much to show the Tesseract the ugly side of humans under pressure.

"Now we're going to get you up on hands and knees," I said, demonstrating. "That's it. Then we'll try standing."

Joellen levered herself up, then froze, all but her hand which was sliding forward, readjusting her weight.

She's going to make it look like panic, I thought. *A*

drowning person grabbing a line. Got to let her get closer . . .

Joellen lunged, and I almost underestimated what her superbly trained body could do—almost. I narrowly missed the force of her lunge, slapping the sedative patch onto the exposed skin of her face. It clung, and Joellen swayed.

"Grab her line!" I yelled.

My teammates were ready, bigger members on the line, Carmen directing via a set of binoculars. Joellen hung against the rope, struggling limply. Then she was unconscious, and all I had to do was keep her from slipping into the river.

We made it across and up the other side, Zren carrying Joellen across his shoulders until we could rig a stretcher. Darkness was falling when we gained the top, but the volcanoes added their own weird light to that of the twin moons.

Phelps identified our destination, noticing that the smoke from one of the volcanoes was whiter than its fellows and puffed forward at regular intervals. For that, and for his calm rationality under pressure, the Tesseract viewers voted him the grand prize winner. Spike came in second, for creativity. Then Carmen, then me, then Zren. The viewers weren't permitted to vote for Joellen, officially because she didn't finish the course—but actually because Karlsen wasn't about to risk her winning on a pity vote.

We were feted, paid, interviewed, and sent our separate ways. Spike was gone first. AASU need him for some other odd mission. The others went soon after.

I stayed only because Karlsen offered to give the *Mercury* a Tesseract tune-up as a thank you for my services.

"So why did Joellen do it?" I asked Karlsen. He, Gittchy, and I were sharing a final meal before going our separate ways. "She could well have won."

"I doubt it," Karlsen said. "Her approach to problems was too much like Zren's—physical and aggressive. However, winning or not had nothing to do with Joellen's choice to turn saboteur. We have her confession in return for amnesty."

"And since you didn't want this public," I said. "You agreed to deal."

"That's right." Karlsen sipped from a glass of fermented carrot juice. "Joellen Wehrung disliked how dominant technology has become in human society. She thought that if the Tesseract withdrew, if there was a war, that the slate might be wiped clean—a new start acquired."

"Impossible," I snorted.

"Nothing seems impossible to a dreamer who has goals firmly in mind and will sacrifice anything to attain them," Karlsen said. "I believe humans call such dreamers 'fanatics.'"

Karlsen's words haunted me even after Gittchy and I had returned to the *Mercury*. Karlsen had spoken not only with conviction, but with sorrow. I realized that he, too, was a fanatic, and that I owed the profession I loved, my beloved pet, and my new fortune to a creature who empathized with the impulse to throw an innocent person into a boiling river if that's what it took to win the goal.

It wasn't a comforting thought, but I couldn't leave it behind me as I steered again for the stars.

NAME THAT PLANET!

by Elizabeth Ann Scarborough

Elizabeth Ann Scarborough lives in an antique cabin on the Olympic Peninsula with four-going-on-five cats and a lot of paints, paperwork, and beads. She is currently coauthoring the Acorna series with Anne McCaffrey.

"WELCOME TO *NAAAAME THAT PLANET!* The game that tests your powers of observation and knowledge as you try to guess wherein the cosmos you are!

"The game is simple. A three-member panel of intergalactic citizens chosen randomly from our studio audience provides sensory clues they feel are typical or symbolic of each of their home worlds. Each panel member must provide up to five clues to our intrepid space explorer contestant, sealed into a sensory input globe. Though we can see them, the contestants won't be able to see us. Successful contestants win fabulous prizes donated by our sponsors, naturally. But, additionally, panel members who successfully stump the contestants also win great prizes. So let's begin this week's round.

"Our first contestant is the communications officer of a class A starship. Her duties include deciphering alien hieroglyphics and petroglyphs, as well as establishing and maintaining contact between her ship and other cosmic entities. Her hobbies include playing 3-D chess, reading old Terran classics in their original languages, belly dancing, and cake decorating. Let's have a round of applause for Lieutenant Shalula Makira!"

Shalula understood the game show conventions as easily as she understood classical Venusian. She jogged out onto the platform situated high above the heads of the audience members in the stadium below. She bounced. Her white-gold hair and breasts augmented for the occasion lifted up and down—but not too far down since the *Name That Planet!* studio was on the low gravity moon of a wholly owned planetary subsidiary of the FLOG Corporation. The moon was also wholly owned by the FLOG Corporation, of course. FLOG stood or Furthering Logistical Organization Galaxy-wide, one of those meaningless acronyms that took in hundreds of thousands of otherwise unrelated enterprises.

Shalula wore a perky red dress uniform with the gold piping that matched her Galaxy Corps rank insignia. A minuscule skirt showed off a slice of her thighs between the hem and the tops of the scarlet form-fitting, over-the-knee boots. It was actually not a current issue uniform, being from earlier days when the grizzled male upper echelon of the Corps considered that part of the duty of younger female personnel included raising the morale of male personnel. The outfit wasn't hers and she felt a little uncomfortable in it. The coverall uniform she and all other crew members wore on shipboard was far more comfortable. Actually, her idea had been to wear civvies, something floaty and ethnic, possibly one of her colorful gilt-edged thwabs from the flower ships of Griba-Prime, but the producers of the show said seeing a woman in Galaxy Corps uniform made viewers feel safe and gave them a sense of pangalactic pride. So they provided this one. It definitely made her feel feminine and sexy. From communications nerd to communications bimbo with a simple change of clothing. That was show business.

The producers also insisted that contestants enthuse and bubble and preferably jump up and down with excitement when they won something, though they were not allowed to curse if they lost. Shalula agreed to respond appropriately. Accomplishing her mission required that she be on the show so she could hardly disagree, even if she were inclined to do so. Besides, it was interesting to study the intergalactic messaging modes in the theatrical subculture represented by the show's cast, crew, other contestants, panelists, and the studio audience.

When she bounced toward the host and the array of cameras, whether because of the bounce, the uniform, or the vid prompts, the crowd cheered and applauded wildly. She laughed in a manner that did not show her teeth to those present whose people viewed revealing one's dentition as an act of hostility. She waved both hands in the flop-wristed universal gesture of greeting. Among beings possessing wrists to flop, that was.

"Welcome, Lieutenant!" the host cried out to her a full three meters before she reached him. He had no compunctions about displaying his dentition to her or the crowd and let interpretations of his expression fall where they may. Large even teeth on full parade were an age-old badge of the game show host, even on Nilurian Amphibats such as *Name That Planet!*'s own Jiminy Jimson (a stage name, Shalula felt certain). "It's an honor to have you on our show. Are you ready to *Naaame That Planet!?*"

It didn't matter that Jiminy's species spoke by sequencing air bubbles emitted from their nostrils, game show protocol and host behavior was well established in the annals of popular history and custom. A multifaceted universal communication device translated Jiminy's remarks and witticisms into every conceivable method of transmission and disseminated it by appropriate means to the wide and varied audience. Shalula heard the host's words in a smooth, sexy computer-simulated masculine voice as well-oiled as Jiminy's leathery wings. "Indubitably, Jiminy! I mean, I certainly *am*. I've been looking forward to this and studying assiduously to be equal to whatever challenges the panel may present."

"Well, Shalu—I hope I may call you Shalula?"

She remembered to giggle enthusiastically, "Of course."

"Shalula, as you know, it will not be possible for you to meet your fellow contestants or our panel beforehand, so you will have no prior clues to their identities, species, race, and most important of all, planetary affiliation. You must determine that by correctly identifying their clues and answering their questions. You will be allowed to ask one question per panelist in return. With each planet that you name correctly, you will win a fabulous prize and the opportunity to try for another. If you choose to go on after your first success, the game you just won is forfeit and you lose your previous prizes. The clues will be given to our audience as well so they can guess right along with you. Now then, let me just ask, why did you wish to appear on our show?"

She had her answer all prepared. She and the captain and the Galaxy Corps agents had gone over it several times, and crew members of the more exotic species from her starship, the *Havago,* were in the audience to provide verisimilitude to her story. "Well, Jiminy, as I'm sure you've heard, when Sol 169582 went supernova, the inhabitants of that solar system became refugees, homeless. The GCS *Havago* aboard which I serve helped evacuate many of these fine folks. I plan to use any prizes I win to help find them a swell new solar system with life-compatible gaseous exchanges, temperatures, humidities, and other life-supporting factors where they can live in peace and harmony."

"Well, say, Lieutenant Shalula, that's a tall order

even for a plucky little starship officer such as yourself. I'm sure everyone in our audience wishes you luck.'' It was perfectly acceptable for Jiminy to patronize her since presumably he knew all the answers to the questions and she did not.

"Thanks, Jiminy. Actually, some of the refugees are in the studio audience today. May I wave at them?"

"Certainly!' Jiminy said, waggling his forelegs as well. "Helllooo there, all you displaced entities! I know you're all keeping your appendages crossed that your friend wins big for you. See there, you folks at home, our cameras are picking up the encouraging waves, wiggles, color changes, and odor emissions of Shalula's refugees. Everyone give them a big round of applause!"

Shalula blushed. The color change peculiar to her species was by now understood throughout the galaxy as signifying either humility or embarrassment, possibly of a sexual nature. The translator interpreted it as "maidenly modesty" for the benefit of those in doubt of its precise significance. Actually, she was embarrassed at having to lie, even though the lies were crucial to her mission.

"And now, Shalula, it's time for you to step into our sphere and receive the first clue to your first planet! We wish you all the luck in the worlds!"

Shalula laughed, feigning appreciation, though she wasn't sure that the pun translated universally even with the best efforts of the studio's equipment. Humor as humans understood it was totally unknown in some alien societies. Come to think of it, humor was not understood in all human societies either. Or, for that matter, by all humans in any particular society.

She stepped into the transparent globe, which was transparent only from the outside. Once inside, Shalula could see nothing except the matte silver lining of the sphere and the clear plascine chair with the pulldown goggles and keypads at her fingertips. Nasal tubes projected from the bottom of the goggles for olfactory clues.

Shalula settled herself in, aware that although she could not see another living being, the multiverse was watching her every move and listening to her every utterance.

There was a long silence in her earphones as she had been warned there would be while Jiminy introduced the first panelist to the audience.

She sat breathlessly silent and alert, waiting. Suddenly the light inside the sphere dimmed and turned an odd shade of pale periwinkle, while the temperature plummeted. She shivered. The chair extruded a fleece wrap that wound around her like the tendrils of a plant climbing a trellis. Ice began to frost the inner skin of the globe.

"Have you figured it out yet, Shalula?" Jiminy's computer-generated voice asked.

"It's a g–good clue, J–Jiminy," she said earnestly. "I c–can tell that this world is not close to its sun. But I need to know a t–teensy bit more."

"Okay, Shalula, here it comes. This beautiful item is found on the mystery planet."

She started to tell him to wait, that her goggles were

frosting over, and then the frost inside them began thickening in some places, spreading in others, until it formed a perfect three-dimensional blossom shape. Her nose tingled sharply, as if little icicles were forming on the hairs of her nostrils. Could it really be this easy? "That is one of the floral frost folk of Feldstar, Jiminy. So the planet must be Feldstar."

"Must it?" Jiminy asked. "Is that your answer or do you need another clue?"

"That's my answer," Shalula said. "Ah, can the audience see how the frost tendrils are lengthening and shortening at the points of the leaves? This frost fella is congratulating me on my perspicacity." She lifted her hand and, tucking the top knuckles of her middle fingers in, then straightening them, politely thanked the frost person for his felicitations.

The tendrils lengthened and shortened once more, but this time the sequence surprised Shalula. The frost being was telling her to "beware."

She mimicked the sequence and added the knuckle-tip flip signaling interrogatory request for information, but the floral frost fellow's image faded from her screen.

Jiminy's laughter, or the facsimile thereof, burbled out of her headphones. "Looks as though you have had frequent associations with the floral portion of the Feldstar population, Shalula. It seemed quite chatty just now. Don't tell me they are on your ship's regular route? We try to make our little game challenging for everyone."

"Oh, it is, Jiminy. The floral frost folk have interested me in particular since I first learned of them. They remind me of a children's book my paternal aunt used to play for me."

"And a lucky thing that was for you, too. Because— well, come on out here and just look at what your correct answer won for you."

The sphere floated down to the stage and she alighted from it. Jiminy appeared in front of her and waved at a revolving platform containing what looked like some sort of movable furniture. "This *lovely* Etin Island Dinette Set with two pullout sections and seating for sixteen. And that's not all! You will be able to serve your guests from the finest porceplast dinnerware in the classic Rings of Saturn pattern. And in case you don't want to serve them finger food, you will also receive this stunning set of titanium alloy flatware complete with attachments to accommodate the appendages of three different alien species and all serving pieces! In addition, you'll receive this elegant synlin lace tablecloth and serviette set aaaand . . ." The revolving stand revolved to reveal another piece of furniture. "Your dinette set includes this finely crafted buffet and hutch!" His voice dropped to a totally serious tone as he said, "Now, I know it's a hard decision to make, whether to take all of these wonderful prizes or risk it all to continue the game, but our clock is ticking and we will give you five seconds to decide."

She didn't need five seconds, or any seconds at all. What in the world would she do with all that stuff on shipboard? Her quarters were barely big enough for her bed, lamp, desk, and chair. Nevertheless, the producers wanted her to appear to be very tempted. She chewed her lip and twirled her hair around her index finger and just as the buzzer sounded, sighed and said, "Gee, it's really tempting to take that marvelous prize and run. I know it would come in handy for the refugees once they get settled, Jiminy, but I guess I'd better keep playing and hope I can win them a home to keep it in!"

"Spoken like the intrepid officer and explorer you are, my dear! Very well, back into the sphere with you to identify your second planet."

While she awaited the first clue, Shalula pondered how the floral frost fella had been able to communicate with her. Surely it wasn't an actual entity present in the studio? It was far more likely to be a holo chip. So why had it signaled her to beware? Had it been in danger at the time it was recorded? Was it therefore sending an all-purpose message? Common sense said it could know nothing about her, much less her mission or any danger she might be courting. Before she came to a conclusion, music filled the sphere.

Music was, of course, a valid form of communication based on mathematics and therefore far more universal than language per se, but like many alien art forms, it could seem incredibly unattractive to a human. However, Shalula was highly trained and had taken courses 1 through 6 in Galactic Musical Appreciation at the academy. Although the piece was played on instruments with which she was so unfamiliar that she could not rightly say if they were string, wind, or percussion, its melodic structure was not unappealing.

Judging from its time signature, it would be from one of the peripheral moons of the fourth planet in the Scathach Galaxy.

But which one?

She shook her head.

"Stumped you, did we?" Jiminy crowed. "Well, never mind, little lady, here comes clue number two."

Another holo appeared, this one of some sort of rectangular mauve-colored fruit. The goggles extruded a flat wafer, which pushed at her lips.

"Have a taste of this, Shalula! It is considered quite a delicacy by the people of the mystery world."

She bit down. It was slimy and bitter but with a surprisingly pleasant aftertaste. She had never tasted anything like it, which was saying something. The *Havago* had an extremely adventurous chef. "I'd like to ask my first question if I may, Jiminy," she said.

"Certainly! But remember, only one per panelist."

"If I were actually biting into the foodstuff depicted in the holo, would it be toxic to my species?"

There was a long pause for consultation. During this time Shalula felt her tongue growing numb and her throat beginning to close. Finally Jiminy said, laughing heartily, "Oh, dear, our panelist says that is entirely possible. Bite down on the antidote now, won't you, before the next clue?" Another flat object extruded itself from her goggles and she bit, then, when she was able, drew a long breath. Jiminy's levity was highly inappropriate.

When her tongue moved freely again, she said, "I'm ready for the next clue, Jiminy. I hope it won't be as hard to take as that last one."

Was the clue a simple mistake or an attempt to murder her? Had the producers somehow learned about her mission? Was this one of the ways in which the previous six Galaxy Corps personnel who had appeared on this show had disappeared from their lives after it?

"Well, as we on the program say, considering the many and varied species with which we deal, one contestant's meat is another one's poison."

How did an ancient Terran aphorism find its way to this alien moon? Shalula wondered. She had been briefed on FLOG's ownership and supposed corporate structure, but it was as vague and difficult to pinpoint exactly what the corporation did or who was in charge of which section as any other intergalactic enterprise. *Name That Planet!* was a fairly new show. It had been airing for only part of a single season, but it was already tremendously popular. Dinette sets were definitely at the low end of the prize spectrum. The top prize, for contestants who met the ultimate challenge, was an enormous amount of credits. So far, only two contestants had come close to winning that prize, but both had given an incorrect answer just one step away from their goal. Both were also starship personnel. Four other Galaxy Corpsmen, from lesser ships, made it through several rungs of the game before failing. All were given very nice consolation prizes, which were duly delivered to their units. The crewmen never returned to their units to claim the prizes, however. All were now considered AWOL. The common theory was that the contestants were too humiliated by their public failures to show their faces among their fellows again. Shalula didn't believe it, and neither did Corps headquarters.

As one of the brightest officers with the most versatile knowledge of alien peoples and places in the Corps, Shalula was recruited to investigate, posing as a contestant. She had never done undercover work before. So far she found it stimulating, though a bit confusing since her usual goal was to clearly communicate a message rather than to dissimulate. Perhaps this would be useful training for a diplomatic post later in her career?

"Ready for your next clue, Shalula?" Jiminy asked in a challenging tone—or rather, his translation device made it sound challenging. Perhaps it was programmed that way.

"You bet, Jiminy! Bring it on!"

And with a quick shift of color and space she found herself inside a cascade of swirling turquoise-and-blue rock. Light shot through translucent sections turning them to orchid glass. Mint-green lichenlike growths clung to some of the surfaces.

"Where are you now, Shalula?"

"Lost in wonder, Jiminy! My stars, but this is beautiful! Who would think that the dung heaps of the ancient Zanticoran Pzitsaaurus would be so lovely that their interior, once dried to a hollow shell, would make ideal housing for vacationing monarchs from surrounding star systems? I am on Zanticora, Jiminy. Therefore, that toxic fruit you offered me before must be no fruit at all but the solidified resin from the sap of the Tatatata tree. It's now widely believed that once great groves of the Tatatatas covered Zanticora and their bark and sap provided food as the trees themselves provided habitat for the Pzitsaaurus. The Pzitsaaurus is thought to have consumed sixteen acres of trees every lunar cycle. It then shat so copiously that . . ."

"Yes, yes, right you are, Shalula! Come on out now and see what you've won."

She stepped down, but the surroundings of her last clue didn't change, except to become larger and more spacious. She gasped appreciatively as a group of muscular blue-tinged avian Zanticoran males danced onto the platform, their antics engineered to showcase the pieces of sleek and serviceable luggage each carried. "Yes, Shalula, it's a good thing you are so intrigued by Zanticora's colorful history and culture. In place of your lovely dinette set, you have won a lunar cycle leave from your duty station aboard the *Havago* to vacation on Zanticora. You will bask in the blue light of Zanticora's sun! At night you will dine, dance, and rest in a luxury suite within one of the deluxe structures you so aptly described. To properly equip you for the journey, you will have this full set of fabulous Saturite Luggage—it dehydrates with the push of a button so that the entire set will fit into this convenient, pocket-sized packet. To fill the luggage, we are also equipping you with a fashionable wardrobe of

Zanticoran resort wear courtesy of Tzany Design Studio, Designers for the Stars. You will attend shows, gamble at the casinos, and may either take a companion of your choice or choose from among a bevy of Zanticoran escorts such as these here with us today. So what do you say, will you claim this prize or go for the big jackpot?"

Shalula had carefully punctuated each of Jiminy's revelations with a little hop, a squeal, and a clapping of her hands. Sometimes a gasp was in order. But now she took her clasped hands away from her mouth and said seriously, "I think we should let your audience know, Jiminy, that as swell as all these prizes are, none of them are actually what I will win."

"That's right, Shalula. Ladies and gentlemen and beings of all species, this generous little lady will not actually receive any of these things, though she could have them if she wished. Instead, by special arrangement with our sponsors, Shalula has asked that credit prizes of equal value be substituted for the prizes you see here, to go toward the resettlement of her refugee friends. Isn't that special? Isn't she an exceptional contestant and an exceptionally fine example of her species? Let's have a round of applause for this little lady!"

The crowd went wild, in a controlled way that ended the applause and cheering when the prompter went blank.

"What we haven't told her is that our sponsor values altruism such as hers and wishes to reward her unselfishness. If she chooses to take these prizes now, the money will go to her friends as agreed. However, if she wins our jackpot, she will receive not only the cash value of all the prizes but the prizes themselves for herself!"

Shalula gasped, squealed, and jumped up and down. The down part was difficult, given the light gravity. "Oh, Jiminy, that is so wonderful! And I know just who I'll bring with me if I win this prize. There is a little orphaned Beltarian boy who could really use cheering up. I think Zanticoran beaches are just the ticket!"

"I am filled with admiration," Jiminy said, fluttering his wings and baring his large teeth again. "Always thinking of others. So I gather you're going for the jackpot, then?"

"You betcha!"

"You do realize that so far on our show, no one has managed to go aaaalllll the way and score the grand prize!"

"There's always a first time, Jiminy, and I am, after all, a professional pioneer of previously unexplored places and experiences! Not to mention my own personal potential."

"Well spoken! Okay, then, Shalula, pop back up inside the sphere and prepare yourself for a ree-aaaallly tough round."

"Ready and willing, Jiminy!" she said, regaining her seat. Even though she knew the game was rigged against her, she couldn't help feeling a sense of elation. She had watched vids of all of the previous show episodes prior to embarking on the assignment. She was by far better prepared than previous contestants, she felt sure. Her hunger for and grasp of esoteric knowledge of the people, places, and languages of the multiverse was vast and comprehensive. She also had a photographic memory courtesy of the implant her parents had given her for her third birthday.

"For your first clue to this world, the panelist will ask you to answer a question, Shalula. Are you ready?"

She nodded enthusiastically.

A voice did not so much speak as rearrange its secretions. Its supposed language sounded like phlegm being hacked up, rearranged, swallowed, and hacked up again. The very sound of it gave Shalula goose bumps she thought the studio audience probably could see clear to the back row. She was at a loss as to what tongue contained such fearsome noises. It had none of the common features that distinguished a tongue from a mere set of subvocalizations.

Watching the vids of the shows on which her fellow Corps members were contestants, Shalula had noticed that among the last set of questions, the clues were usually a bit indistinct in sound or image. Audience members were meant to think that the puzzle was simply extremely difficult but now Shalula wondered. Perhaps the clues were hard because they were not actually legitimate clues at all?

To test her theory, she scoured her throat to make similar sounds, as if she were about to vomit. It took several moments, probably while Jiminy decided how to respond. She waited for him to say, "What was that you said?" or something of the sort, but instead he said, "Our panelist says that was the correct answer. For the benefit of our audience, the panelist asked Shalula if she spoke the native language of Emeticus Trine and she replied that she did, a little. However, Shalula, that was a trick question as the planet in question here is *not* Emeticus Trine, though the panelist speaks the language. You must tell us which planet is the panelist's home world. Do you need another clue?"

"Yes," she said, and then added, or should I say, "Hrrracchacch."

"Heh heh. Very good. Here it is, then, for the grand jackpot, tell us where you will find our next clue."

A lacy tracery of interlocking outwardly expanding ripples of multicolored lights filled the interior of the sphere. At the center of each set of ripples a strong clear light pulsed. There was something familiar about the sequencing of the pulses—three short ones bursts, three long, then three short. Versed in ancient messaging modes as she was, Shalula, to her amazement, recognized that the light beams were signaling SOS, the once well-known distress signal in a system of dots and dashes used by obsolete antique communications equipment. Who could be sending such a message except another communications expert? Like, for instance, the one who had preceded her on this show, and who was presently listed as AWOL from the GCS *William Gates*.

"Well, Shalula, do we have your answer?"

"Help," she murmured, still considering the message.

"Does that mean you wish to ask the panelist a question?"

"Er—yes. Yes, it does Jiminy. Except my Emeticus Trine isn't quite up to it, so I'd like to ask my question in Standard."

"And your question is . . . ?"

"It is . . . it is . . . what does the dominant species on your planet look like?"

"I'm not sure that is the sort of question that is authorized, Shalula," Jiminy told her cautiously.

"Oh, gee, Jiminy, nobody told me there were restrictions on what I could ask."

Jiminy's teeth looked bigger than ever as he smiled. "Gee, I'm sorry, too, Shalula, but that question is just too broad. We might as well let you ask 'what planet are you from?'"

"Yes, well then, let me rephrase my question. We know your language is from Emeticus Trine, but the planet we are speaking of is not Emeticus Trine. Are you yourself or your species dominating *another* planet?"

There were more gurgling, hawking, choking sounds. Shalula had identified them now that she read the feeling behind the noises rather than trying to make words of them. For the sounds represented to her as language were merely the predigestive utterances of a hungry slavering bestial being in search of a meal.

Jiminy looked extremely skittish. "I don't think that question is quite authorized either."

"Oh, but it should be, Jiminy. Because the answer to it holds the key to many of the riddles posed on and by this very show! I *did* recognize the light show from the last clue. It's the transmission waves from this station bouncing off FLOG's world below us and back out into space. And the rulers of this planet, FLOG's board of directors, are dominated by the beings who make those horrible noises. I wonder if the audience can see the Emeticus Trinian as it really is. Because it is my contention that if they saw the true nature of this being, they would see it as one of the data-devouring demons of the Damaclesian Delta. No wonder no one guessed before. The demons are shapeshifters and can assume any form. In fact, Jiminy, I wonder if you yourself are what you seem to be?"

"Ladies and gentlemen of all species, we are going to cut to our commercial now. It seems our contestant is suffering from space sickness that is making her delusional."

Shalula, still suspended inside the sphere, could see nothing outside except what Jiminy projected into her sphere. She could only hope her fellow crewmembers were advancing on the stage.

"What better cover than a game show for a race that devours the data transmission and reception waves of living beings?" she continued. "Your so-called sponsors are these beings and *you,* Jiminy, are their leader! Not being content to manipulate from behind the scenes, you assumed the guise of a Nilurian amphibat and sought center stage yourself!"

Jiminy said nothing, but through her earphones Shalula heard the scuffle of feet, the futile flap of wings, and the voices of her comrades barking orders.

A moment later her captain's voice reached her. "We're bringing you down now, Shalula."

Her sphere was lowered to the stage and she stepped out. Jiminy was blurring around the edges.

"Aha!" she said. "I was right. For a data-devouring demon, being the host of a show such as this would allow you to satisfy your appetite before any of your fellows. If you had left it at that, Jiminy, or whatever your real name is, you would not have sparked a Galaxy Corps investigation. But six Galaxy Corps troops disappeared after playing your game. We want to know their fate and we want them or their remains returned at once."

Havago's special task force waved weapons at the blurry but still grinning host.

"Calm yourselves," Jiminy said with a flutter of rapidly fading wings. They were morphing into a huge warty hump behind his head, which was also changing shape. The teeth now looked vaguely green and instead of being broad and square, were pointed. "We eat intellectual energy, not the beings that possess it. Your colleagues are all unharmed. We have simply given them the vacation we promised them, though we extended it somewhat. They are safe on one of our farms, hooked up to computers feeding them data indigestible to us in electronic form. They are more like cooks than meals to us. It takes very high-level intellects to absorb some of this material and, even so, some of what we are given is indigestible. This we recycle as questions for contestants."

"Aha!" Shalula said. "That is how two of our peo-

ple were able to get their mayday messages to me—
one implanted a message within a frost flower holo
and one in the pulsing of those lights."

"But that's cheating!" Jiminy said indignantly. "I'm
afraid we can't award you any prizes after all, Shalula."

"No need," she said grimly. "Breaking up your operation will be prize enough."

Later, when the contestants, civilian and Galaxy
Corpsmen alike, had been rescued, the off duty members of the *Havago*'s crew sat around the recreation
lounge feeling at loose ends. Usually, this was the time
when they could tune in for another game of *Name
That Planet!* But now, of course, that was no longer
possible. To her dismay, Shalula, who had been hailed
as a heroine, now found herself the target of resentful
glances. But as a second-voyage replicator technician
was flipping frequencies, the ship's intercom crackled
to life.

"Lieutenant Makira, please report to the bridge. We
have an incoming communication for you from Corps
headquarters."

Shalula arrived on the bridge to see the captain and
other personnel standing at attention before the com
screen. General Azimblii herself stood beside an amphibat much like the one Jiminy Jimson appeared to
be. The amphibat also had large teeth and carried
a briefcase. Shalula snapped to attention in front of
the general.

"At ease, Lieutenant Makira. This is Consul Flaabaat of Flaabaat, Flaabaat, and Smith, Attorneys of
Intergalactic Law, Incorporated. He is representing

the being known to most of us as Jiminy Jimson and the FLOG corporation, who have brought a lawsuit against the Corps.''

"I thought they would be incarcerated by now, General!" Shalula said indignantly. "Why are they suing us?"

"It's complicated," the general said, "But they have a great deal of power and money and the Galactic Congress has recently cut our own legal budget. Therefore, I hope you will consider FLOG's proposition, which they wished Consul Flaabaat to present to you personally."

"With respect, ma'am, I will not, even for the Corps, become one of FLOG's data feeding drones."

Consul Flaabaat fluttered his wings in a soothing sort of way that indicated her assumption of his purpose was unwarranted. "Once your dramatic rescue of your colleagues (which by the way caused extreme public humiliation, harm, mental suffering, and constituted an invasion of privacy) was broadcast, beings throughout the cosmos realized what our sponsors required. All positions for data processors vacated by former contestants have been filled. We have quite a waiting list of applications, in fact."

"Then, what?" Shalula asked.

"Well, our clients wish to invite you to appear as a hostess on another show they have in production. You see, the show on which you appeared garnered the highest ratings *Name That Planet!* ever enjoyed in its brief history. Viewers simply ate up—if you'll pardon the expression—the drama of a game involving a live rescue. Our clients quickly realized that reality game shows are the wave of the future and you, you intrepid pioneer you, showed them the way. Therefore, they have agreed to drop their suit against Galaxy Corps if you will sign a contract to host the first six episodes of *Save That Alien*. So what will it be, Lieutenant Makira? Will you risk losing your commission in Galaxy Corps or go for the big rewards of hosting another popular FLOG TV production?"

Shalula said, in the appropriate communications mode for the situation, "I choose option number two, Consul Flaatbaat."

SCENES FROM THE CONTEST

by Robert Sheckley

Robert Sheckley was born in Brooklyn, New York, and raised in New Jersey. He went into the U.S. Army after high school and served in Korea. After discharge he attended NYU, graduating with a degree in English. He began to sell stories to all the science fiction magazines soon after his graduation, producing several hundred stories over the next few years. His best known books in the science fiction field are *Immortality, INC.; Mindswap;* and *Dimension Of.* He has produced about sixty-five books to date, including twenty novels and nine collections of his short stories, as well as his five-book *Collected Short Stories of Robert Sheckley.* In 1991 he received the Daniel F. Gallun Award for contributions to the genre of science fiction. Recently, he was given an Author Emeritus Award by the Science Fiction Writers of America. He is married to the writer Gail Dana and lives in Portland, Oregon.

IT'S A WIDE, CIRCULAR OLD plaza, made of stone and brick. The stands are full of men and women in their Sunday best. Overhead, a sultry sun comes in and out of clouds. Cameramen in the front rows look to their apertures and filters. It's the bullring in Almeria, Spain, and they're taping an episode of *You Bet Your Planet.*

Beneath the stands there is a changing room with a door sloping upward into the arena. From here, the matadors make their appearance. But we have no matador today, only Ron James, dressed in bullfighter's red, silver, and gold, but carrying no sword or any other weapon. This isn't a regular corrida. Today, the GGS corporation has hired the arena for a special episode of the *You Bet Your Planet* show, and handed out complimentary tickets all over the city.

The stands are packed. Everyone's interested in what the Americans are up to now. The mayor of the city is not in his special booth. He's down in the stands. He has rented out his covered booth to the GGS corporation, who are using it to house their cameramen and commentators. These men will record and tell the huge American television audience what they are watching. American audiences have seen too many special effects, they must be assured that this stunt is dangerous.

In the room beneath the arena, Ron's trainer gives him a final slap on the back. He tells Ron, "Don't forget, this bull hooks left!"

Ron nods. He is numb with excitement and fear. At the touch of the trainer's hand, he grimaces. He doesn't want to do this. But he is ready. He gets up and runs out into the arena. He waves to the crowd. He spots the bull just as the bull spots him.

The clouds disappear. The sun is bright, the shadows black and sharp-edged. The audience leans forward expectantly.

"Here comes our contestant, Ron James."

Today there are two commentators for the vast TV and radio audience. The one who has just spoken is Red Carlisle, a former quarterback with the Forty-niners, a very popular sports announcer, a tall, strongly built man with the look of a star.

"He just has to cross the arena, folks," Carlisle says. "Get across and behind the barricade at the other end. And then he has to come back to where he began. Sounds simple. Ah, but he has to get there despite the best efforts of the bull. This bullring may be old, friends, but the bulls are fully modern. They have been changed a bit in the laboratories of GGC, the Galactic Gaming Commission. 'Enhancement' is what they call the process. These bulls are a lot faster and smarter than anything nature ever produced. They are man-eating. They are skilled hunters. They eat lions for lunch. A unmodified lion has no chance against one of these modified bulls!"

"A man is a lot smarter than even a modified bull!" the other commentator says. She is Marne Ducheny, a popular talk show hostess.

"True," says Red. "But is a man smart enough? Is Ron smart enough and savvy enough to get across the arena and back? Has he had sufficient modifications to permit him to cross the hot sands unscathed?"

Consulting a paper on which Ron's and the bull's modifications are listed, Marne says, "According to the modification specifications, Ron's got the legs of a champion sprinter. But in a timed heat the bull can beat him easily."

Red says, "Our contestant has received no training as a matador. He doesn't even carry a sword. He is an American, he doesn't fool around with swords."

"It's starting!" Marne exclaims. "Look at that bull bearing down on him! A ton of beef on the hoof, coming like an avalanche on wheels. See that sort of low thick fence at the far side of the ring? That's the barrier. If he can duck behind that, he's safe. But I don't think he's going to make—"

"There, see what he did?" Red says. "Just as the bull overtook him Ron curled up into a ball and dropped to the sand. Got away with it, too. The bull overran him."

"The bull did score a wound in Ron's back," Marne says.

"That's one for the bull," Red says.

"Right," says Marne. "But now Ron's up again. He's feinting, the bull is confused. And now Ron is running for the far side barrier, and the bull is after him. Another slash of those big horns—a miss—and now Ron has ducked in behind the barrier."

"The bull is slamming into it, but they build these barriers pretty good."

"Ron gets a ten-second rest. Any longer will be charged against him . . ."

"He's stepping away from his protection slowly, moving with small steps, trying not to provoke the bull."

Marne says, "The bull looks him over for a moment or two, paws the ground, and charges."

"He's coming hard and fast, too fast for Ron James to do much about it."

"Yes," says Marne, "but due to the alchemy of fear, Ron James probably feels that time is slowed down. But so are his responses. His legs must feel filled with glue, his feet are paralyzed, his whole body is laggard and not responsive to his command to 'Move!' "

Red Carlisle took it up: "But there is something in him that overcomes this fatal sluggishness."

"That's right, Red. Something not his own, something engineered into him, as his limbs were rebuilt and engineered to his trunk through the wonders of science, as his hearing and eyesight were both enhanced to provide him with better defenses. Some manufactured willpower existing within his natural willpower enables him to act."

"Ron James has reached the barrier. The bull shakes his head, looking around for someone to charge. If it were capable of wonder, it might ask, how could my rush, my charge, so unerringly performed, have missed its purpose? He snorts, he stamps his hoof, he looks around for someone to kill. But Ron is safe behind the barrier, and it's time for us to leave sunny Spain and proceed to the next event."

"He got away with it," Red said.

"That's good for him. And vitally important for his brother, Timmy."

Red said, "I heard he's doing all this to pay for Timmy's hospital costs."

Marne nodded, "It's a very moving story."

*   *   *

The moving story began when Ron was ordered to pay a visit to Doctors Burnham and Rees in New York, the physicians appointed by the corporation to look after the contestant's health.

The doctor's office to which he was told to come was very fancy, slick. A piece of articulated action sculpture in the waiting room. Polished wood floors, a receptionist.

The doctors—Charles Burnham and Joshua Rees— were both tall young men in their mid-thirties. Rees was a little overweight. Both were good-looking men. Keen. Attentive to their duty.

Rees said, "Mr. James? We need to give you some memory transplants."

"There's noting wrong with my memory."

"Never said there was. But we need to give you some new ones."

"Hey, I'm okay with the ones I have."

Burnham shakes his head. "The corporation doesn't think so, Mr. James. They're afraid audiences won't find you sympathetic enough."

"So what will a memory do for me?"

"It'll give you someone else to think about other than yourself."

"I'm not sure I want to do this."

"Please don't argue with us about it, Mr. James. The memory implant is company policy. Either get it now, or take a hike."

"A hike? Where to?"

"Horseturd, Oklahoma, or wherever you came from."

The doctors stand up. The interview is over.

In James' mind, leaving the contest was not an option. He was prepared to do whatever he had to do to stay away from where he had come from.

"Can you tell me what kind of memory you're going to implant?"

"As soon as the operation's over, you'll be the first to know."

They had a nice operating room, right there on the premises. There was a lot of equipment, flashing lights and wires and stainless steel probes. They had an anesthetic that put Ron into a deep sleep state.

When Ron woke up after the operation, his first thought was of Timmy. Where was the kid? Was he all right? What was his condition now?

Timmy. His kid brother. The sickly younger brother he had promised Ma and Pa to take care of, look out for. The one who was so ill in the New York hospital.

He never quite got it straight that the memory was implanted, was not real. You could tell him over and over that he had no kid brother. He might even agree with you—but he remembered him, remembered growing up with him. What was he supposed to believe?

He caught a taxi over to the hospital where he had put Timmy. He wanted to see the kid badly. He had told Ma, many years ago, that he would look out for Timmy, take care of him, make sure he was all right.

Beth Zion was a big private hospital on New York's

Upper East Side. Nothing but the best for Timmy. They had put the kid in a private room on an upper floor. The views of Manhattan, out the big windows, were breathtaking. The cost was breathtaking, too, but only the best was good enough for Timmy. He had promised Ma.

When he walked into the room, there was Timmy, propped up in bed, head bandaged, eyes closed, evidently dozing. Sandy, the private nurse Ron had hired, was seated in a chair in the corner, writing some notes.

"Hi," James said. "How's the kid?"

"He had a pretty good morning. It's quite remarkable, after the surgery earlier. He was asking about you."

They kept their voices down, but Timmy opened his eyes and said, "Hey there, bro."

"Hey yourself," James said, coming over to the bed. He took Timmy's slender hands in his own. "How they treating you?"

"Very well. It's just that I'm so weak."

"Well, that's to be expected. Sandy here says you're improving."

"I'm glad to hear it. Look, Ron, this must be costing you a fortune."

"That's what money's for."

Sandy came over. "Mustn't talk too much, Timmy. You have to rest, get back some strength."

"I won't tire him out," James said. "I have to get back to the studio. Hang in there, kid."

Sandy walked him to the door. She was very pretty, Sandy was, with pale hair and a heart shaped face. A good figure, too. James knew she worshiped him, and he was starting to think, maybe with a little practice he could feel that way about her, too. Maybe they could get married and move to some place quiet, like Ireland. It would take Ron out of the action, but what the hell, it was worth it if it helped Timmy. Pubs, cows, leprechauns . . .

"I'll come back as soon as I can," he told Sandy.

"That's good, Mr. James. He so adores your visiting."

And you do, too, James thought. *I can see it in your eyes, you've got a thing for me, haven't you kid?* He didn't say any of this aloud, just squeezed Sandy's hand and left the room.

James had his own dressing room at the studio. Mr. DeMario the Boss had arranged it for him. Mr. DeMario had a lot of pull. He had gotten James into this contest in the first place, a gift in repayment for something James' father had done for Mr. DeMario a long time ago.

His dressing room was a whole small suite of rooms. There was even a bedroom. It was a good place for entertaining. And Mr. DeMario had also loaned him Pat and Giuseppe to act as waiters and gofers, and to make sure everything stayed cool. Well, he hadn't exactly loaned them. He had posted them. "Just to be safe," he had said. Sometimes people got crazy ideas about stars. And James was definitely a star. The boss wanted to make sure nothing bad happened.

Pat and Giuseppe were seated on folding chairs with a little folding table between them, playing pinochle.

James said hello and went into his room. He went into the bedroom to change. He opened his closet door and someone said, "Surprise!" and there was a naked woman in his arms.

"Claudia! What are you doing here?"

"I couldn't stay away from you, Ron. You didn't come into the bar last night. I waited for you until closing."

"Get dressed," James ordered. "Did anyone see you come in?"

"I don't think so. I came by the service door."

"Come on, get your clothes on."

"The coat's all I wore. Ron, we have a little time—"

"Christ, Claudia, get your coat on, you know you shouldn't be doing this. If Mr. M ever found out—"

"I don't care about Mr. M," Claudia said. "I've got a life, too, I've got needs, too. You're what I need. Give me a kiss, Ron."

"You have to get out of here! How do you button this coat?"

"It doesn't button. Take it easy, don't push! When will I see you?"

"Tonight, at the bar." He got her out the service entry and closed the door.

He sat down and thought about it. Mrs. M was good-looking and built, but he should never have begun with her. What had he been thinking? And anyhow, now there was Sandy, or could be once he decided he loved her.

A moment later, by some unfathomed chain of asso-

ciation, he decided he was hungry. He went to the
front door, opened it. "Pat? I need a club sandwich
and a Coke. Could you have somebody get that for
me?"

"No trouble at all." Pat took the cell phone out of
his pocket. Before he could dial, James asked,
"Where's Giuseppe?"

"Had to take a leak. Hello? Shimmer's Restaurant?"

James went back inside and closed the door. He
wished he'd remembered to tell Pat to order hot sauce
with it. He wished Giuseppe had been there, too. It
was probably okay, sometimes guys had to take a leak.
James liked to keep an eye on the guys keeping an
eye on him.

"Good morning, Marne."

"Good morning, Red."

"I believe you've been in Guatemala before."

"I have. It's a splendid country, Red. I've got a little
house outside of Guatemala City. The fruit trees are
just coming into bloom . . ."

"No fruit trees around here, are there?"

"I should say not. Folks, we're in Chichén Itzá, in
a camera booth near the edge of one of the sacred
wells of this country. The approach is all flag-
stone . . ."

"That must be why there are no fruit trees."

"I'm sure you got that right, Red. Anyhow! MMT
has arranged to install special machinery in this well.
It is where our contestant, Ron James, will undergo
his next and perhaps most significant ordeal."

"What we have here, Marne, is a big limestone well, maybe thirty yards in diameter. The well has been flooded to a depth of ten feet. Ron will enter the well, and more water will be introduced, raising the water level. There's another twenty feet to go before the water reaches the top. But that's not where Ron's going."

"You did your homework very well, Red!"

"Well, it's a little like one of those dazzle plays we used to use with the Forty-niners."

"Sure it is. Only Ron will not be carrying a football. He has to float in the water until he can get into that drain hole in the side of the well. See it? It's got about a four-foot diameter. He has to scramble into it and crawl or swim through it to the far end."

"Sounds straightforward enough."

"But the game designers have introduced a couple of wrinkles. For one thing, there are piranha in the well. Those are those horrible little man-eating fish. And once he gets into the tunnel, there are the insects."

"Insects!"

"Oh, yes, insects. Our cameras have cut to them now. No, friends, those aren't spots in front of your eyes. Those are bugs. You can see they're sort of brown-colored with little red spots on them. They have all the normal complement of legs, antennae, stingers. I've been told they even have wing covers. You won't find these guys in your garden, folks. The guys at the company's labs brewed these up. They're artificial, they live only one generation. Can't reproduce. The science people made them extra special nasty. They've got no sexual drive, no reproductive urge, only hunger. They bite, they claw, they'll do anything to satisfy themselves, and they're always hungry, never satisfied."

"If you know all that, maybe you can tell me why all those bugs are in the pipe?"

"To make it difficult for Ron, of course. I understand they unloaded a bag of ten thousand or so of these guys into the tunnel. With government permission, of course. Those bugs are trying to get out the far end, which is where Ron has to go. There's nothing to eat in the tunnel. Except each other. And Ron."

"So the question is, can Ron get through while there's still something left of him to get through with?"

"I guess that's a fair enough assessment . . . Look! There's Ron. He dives into the water!"

"He's coming up. On the surface now, he spots a roiling in the waters."

" 'Roiling.' That's very poetic, Red."

"Not much poetry in those piranha fellows. What's Ron doing?"

"He seems to be spanking the water. What an odd sound it makes."

"And look, the fish are backing off. Is he doing that with his hands?"

"I think he modified his hand especially for this contest. But how did he know . . . Never mind, he's making some sort of noise in the water, and most of the piranha are backing off."

"Look! One of them got in behind him. Tore a chunk out of his thigh."

"Ron caught him and squeezed him to death. What a set of reflexes he bought."

"Ron is turning in circles, he has to stay there until the water level has risen high enough—"

"Wow, did you see that? He came up out of the water like a seal and he got into the hole!"

"Impressive. I don't suppose you can train for that."

"Not unless you're a seal. He's in the tunnel now. We're switching to a minicam."

Red: "This is a big one, folks. The only way out of here, out of this pit in which the water is constantly rising, is through the large drain hole in the side of the pit, clearly visible to our cameras, and circled in yellow so there'll be no misunderstanding. The contestant has to tread water until he can get himself into the drain hole. Then he has to crawl through to safety on the other side."

Marne: "Nothing too difficult about that, is there? You could do it yourselves. So we thought we'd make it a little less savory, a little less heroic. We're bringing one of our remote cameras into the hole. The view you see now is from another camera filming the progress of the first one. You see, the camera slips into the hole, and you can see what's in there."

Red: "Ron is moving through the tunnel now, with stylish flips of his swim fins. Way to go, Ron! You went in there with a flourish. Now all you have to do is crawl through to the far end, and try to do it before

these little critters take all the skin off your hide. Before they strip you and feed on your bones, your
nerves, your sinews. It's a race, Ron. In the short run,
what you can win is most of your hide. If you slow
down, get confused, you can get killed. Don't know if
we can help you if that happens, Ron. We don't have
any skin to spare. Don't bother clapping your hands.
These bugs can't hear . . ."

Marne: "It's lucky for the company that it is to be
held blameless if death happens to Ron or any other
contestant. Death is just another way of losing. You
did it yourself, pal."

Red: "And, audience, how do you like these shots
we're bringing you? You can really see those bugs
work. The bottom of the tunnel is alive with them,
I don't see any way Ron can get through all this.
Our planners might have gotten carried away this
time . . ."

Marne: "Did you see that, folks? Ron rolled around
and attached himself to the ceiling of the tunnel! How
did he do that? I'm looking over Ron's statistics
now . . . Here it is, one of the modifications he had
performed was the attachment of suckers to his wrists
and ankles. So he can go upside down on the tunnel
like a goddamned gecko reptile! The bugs come after
him, but Ron is scampering like a goddamned gecko
and he's at the end—and he's out of there! Congratulations, Ron!"

When I came in, Timmy was asleep. He woke up
in a moment, however, and sat up in bed. His head

was just starting to grow out hair from the last radiation treatment. It looked like fuzz on his head.

"Hey, bro," he said.

"Hey, Timmy," I said.

"I watched almost an hour of you today." He nodded at the TV. "You looked great! But then I couldn't stay awake anymore. Those pills they give me are just too much."

"It's okay," I said. "That stuff is all helping you."

I'm not really sure what Timmy had. I think it was a version of Lou Gherig's disease, but with complications you wouldn't want to hear about. It wasted him and crazed him and should have killed him six months ago and would have if I hadn't gotten a spot on the *You Bet Your Planet* show. It's money from that that pays for all his attention. I've got Sandy and two nurses working in shifts. I've got specialist doctors coming out of the gi-gi. I don't mind. Timmy's my only kin, and now that Ma and Pa are gone, it gets lonely. If I win this contest, I'm going to buy a place for Timmy and me. House, garden. And maybe I'll marry, maybe it'll be Sandy, she gets along with Timmy.

Man, I did it! I won! And then I was in my own spacecraft, which I had learned how to pilot. I was on my way to my asteroid. The ship was all automatic control, anyhow, nothing I had to do. The excitement was something, I can tell you. I was going to my own world, and already I had plans to bring Timmy and Sandy there, to lay on a medical system for Timmy, import some friends for Sandy, and maybe a couple of poker buddies for me. I could make my world as large as I wanted, and bring in as many people as I wanted. And I'd be in charge.

I was right in the middle of these thoughts when my telephone light flashed.

That was funny, because I had understood that all my calls were being blocked, since half the world wanted to call up and congratulate me. I hadn't had time to hire a secretary yet. I had asked that my calls be blocked until I got this new situation figured out. But the light was flashing, so I picked it up.

"Ron? This is Pat."

My bodyguard! What could he want?

"Ron, I gotta talk fast and you gotta pick up fast. You need to bail out of that spaceship. You've got an airtight spacesuit, right? So bail out of there. With a little luck, someone from NASA will pick you up."

"What are you, crazy?" I asked.

"Here's the straight dope. I think Giuseppe saw you and Mrs. M. Mr. M is going to blow up that ship before you reach the asteroid. He's going to blow you and the ship sky high. Mr. M is not pleased about you and Claudia. I gotta get off now."

"Pat, wait!" I cried. But the phone had gone dead.

Bail out? How was I supposed to do that? And anyhow, Pat must be crazy, Mr. M's arm couldn't reach that far, could it? I had to get this asteroid for Timmy, and for Sandy, too . . .

The explosion came while I was having that thought. Luckily, my brain wave recorder is still on. So I have a chance for some last minute thoughts before I am evaporated into the nothingness. I just want to say, I did it all for you, Timmy. I know now that you were just a figment of my imagination. But you were still the best part of me.

THE HOLLYWOOD DILEMMA

by Russell Davis

Russell Davis currently lives in Arizona with his wife, Monica, and their three children. His short fiction has appeared in numerous anthologies including *Sol's Children, Single White Vampire Seeks Same, Space Stations, Villains Victorious,* and *Little Red Riding Hood in the Big Bad City.* His most recent collection is *Waltzing with the Dead.* He's currently hard at work on several novel projects.

THERE ARE TWO THINGS you need to know right up front. Chuck Woolery is Satan and all game show hosts go to hell. I wish it were otherwise—at least the part about where game show hosts end up—but it's as true as what women say about men hogging the remote and channel surfing.

My name is Milt Seevers. You've probably heard of me, maybe even watched me. I was the host of *The Hollywood Dilemma,* the longest running reality television game show spin-off, for three years, two months, and one week. My last appearance is still among the highest rated shows in history. Then I disappeared.

All because I met Chuck. And made the deal.

Energetic music with vague, but ominous undertones blared from the speakers. Audience applause, generated by a digital sound system rather than live human beings, joined the decibels in a growing swell, while the electronic voice-over, a gender neutral, but still decidedly male voice said, "It's the show that all of America's talking about . . . classic challenges with a twist . . . welcome to another edition of *The Hollywood Dilemma!*" The music and the audience volume increased then faded, as the voice added, "And now, here's your host . . . Milt Seevers!"

Oh, for god's sake, I thought, watching myself step into the spotlight from stage left, grinning like a fool. *I hate my job.* I grabbed the remote and shut off the television, then stood and walked with the careful stagger of the almost drunk to the minibar. "Hello, Mr. Walker," I said, "guess it's just you and me tonight." I added two ice cubes to the glass and filled it with the scotch.

Drunk people talk to themselves, and I was no exception. "The problem," I told my glass of scotch, "is that it's all stupid. It's a stupid game, with stupid contestants and a stupid host. The only ones who aren't stupid are the people at home." I took two long swallows of the scotch, about half the glass, and said, "Hell, I'm stupid for staying."

The Hollywood Dilemma had been good to me. I knew it, admitted it in the occasional interview, but that didn't mean I had learned to like it, let alone love it. I was plain sick of it. Five nights a week, I had to become someone else—Alex Trebeck, Pat Sajak, even Bob Barker, for chrissakes. You can't imagine how hard it is to do Bob Barker. The man had a leer that wouldn't quit.

I had to know the rules of every damn game show from the 1950s to the early 2000s—and while the contestants played for money and prizes, *I* was judged by the television audience, voted on, and if my performance wasn't up to their standard, whatever it happened to be on that night . . . they would penalize me. Sometimes, they'd vote to dock my pay, which wasn't so bad. It was when they voted for things like "The Host Challenge" or an electric shock. My hair had gone completely white six months into the gig, and now I had to wear a wig every damn time I went out in public.

I drank off the rest of the scotch and added ice and booze again. "I just can't stand it anymore," I said to the bottle of Johnny Walker Red. "It's been three years." My contract, I knew, ran for five and there wasn't an out clause for "sick of being tortured."

Sometimes, a whole week or two would go by, my performances dead on, the games going well, and the pay and perks would skyrocket—also voted on by the audience—but other times . . . like last spring during sweeps, when they'd pulled out all these old shows I hadn't even hard of . . . goddamn, that had been horrible. Four straight weeks of hell. At one point, the audience had voted for me to be cut on the hands and feet then dunked in a piranha tank. I still have the scars.

"It doesn't have to be that way, you know," a smooth voice said from behind me.

Startled, I dropped my glass and did my best to spin around, though the booze made it more clumsy than graceful.

"Chuck Woolery?" I said, surprise taking the slur from my words. "Aren't you dead? Why are you in my house?"

Chuck moved smoothly to the bar. "Walker Red? Milt, you've disappointed me already. Surely on what you make you could afford a *decent* scotch." With a sigh, he poured a shot into a rocks glass.

I shook my head. Was I dreaming? "I grew to like it when I was a lot less wealthy. Never bothered to acquire a taste for anything else."

"That's one of your problems, Milt," Chuck said. "You've always chosen to settle."

If it was a dream, it had all the texture of reality—or at least as much as a game show, which in my case amounted to the same thing. I decided to play along. "Okay, fine," I said. "I'm a settler. Why are you in my house?"

Chuck drank the scotch and put the glass back on the bar. "If I were, in fact, Chuck Woolery, that would be a good question, Milt, a damn good question. But I'm not Chuck Woolery—I just look like him for right now."

"So you're not Chuck Woolery," I said. "Fine." *I am hallucinating*. "Then who are you?"

"I'm Chuck's boss—his ultimate boss."

"A producer?"

"No," he said, laughing, "though I *am* a producer of sorts." He shook his head. "Why don't you sit down, Milt? I'll explain the whole thing."

There was a strange . . . *force* behind the words, almost a compulsion, and I felt myself walking to the couch and sitting down before I'd even consciously chosen to do so. "Okay, I'm sitting," I said. "I'm not sure why."

"Because I suggested it," he said. "So, where to begin . . ."

"The beginning," I said, "like why you look like Chuck Woolery but aren't—you're his boss who's like a producer, but isn't."

"Ahh, but the real beginning goes back so much farther—it always does in these things, you know."

"No, I don't."

Chuck sighed and sat down. "You probably don't at that." Reaching out with a finger, Chuck touched me lightly on the cheek. I felt a small surge of electricity, almost like the kind of shock you'd get from walking on wool carpet, and I was suddenly—painfully—sober.

Which, to tell the truth, was a rare condition for me in those days.

"How . . . how'd you do that?" I asked.

"Just one of my talents," Chuck said. "I prefer my interviewees to be sober. It tends to make things easier in the long run. Fewer complaints."

"Interview?" I asked. "I don't remember applying for anything."

"A figure of speech, Milt. Now listen close, because I'm on a schedule and I don't have a lot of time."

Compelled once more, I nodded. I could do little else.

"For our purposes, you can call me Chuck—it's stuck in your mind already and will make things easier. But the real Chuck Woolery, as you know, died some years ago."

"Yes—right after they tried to revive *The Love Connection*."

"*He* tried, Milt, *he* tried. But he'd never hosted the first one, let alone anything else. That was me."

"So you are him?"

"No, we made a deal."

"A deal?"

"Yes, a deal. I—or is it better to say one of me?—became him for a time while he lounged about on a private island I own. I made him famous. *The Love Connection* was the perfect show, the perfect irony. Once he was safely established, I went on my way and he took over. Of course, he screwed it up, but he still got to enjoy the fame and the fortune for quite some time."

"But I—"

"Shhh, Milt. I'll make it clear for you in a moment.

Now, when Chuck died, he had to complete his part of the deal."

"His part?"

"Yes, he now works for me."

"But he's dead."

"All right," Chuck said, "his *soul* works for me."

"Then you're . . ." my words trailed off as the proverbial lightbulb came on. "You're Satan?"

"Call me Chuck."

"Chuck Woolery was *Satan?*" Milt asked. "Are you serious?"

"It *is* a perfect fit, don't you think?"

I thought about it for a long minute, remembering the laugh (*hee-hee-hee*), the smooth grin (*a well-fed shark*) when Billy somebody or another *didn't* make a love connection. "I suppose it does at that."

"I knew you'd agree, Milt."

I stood and headed for the bar. "I think I could use a drink," I said. "Do you mind?"

Chuck smiled again. "Not at all—you won't be able to get drunk now anyway. Mind if I join you?"

I poured for us both and we drank together. In the silence, I realized that if I was dreaming, it couldn't hurt to play along and if I wasn't, it could hurt in ways I'd never imagined if I didn't play along.

"So what's Chuck doing these days? In hell, I mean," I asked. It's like any other game show, I told myself, just make him comfortable.

"Oh, he hosts a little show for me down on level nine," Chuck said. "A somewhat hotter version of *The Love Connection*." He chuckled softly. "I call it *The*

Shove Connection. There's a burning pit and everything."

"Must be something," I said, imagining the losing—or perhaps the winning—or perhaps all the contestants—being pushed into a pit of burning fire.

"Number two in its slot," Chuck said.

"You've got ratings in hell?" I asked.

"Sure," Chuck said. "We've got to compete with the heaven networks, don't we?"

"I . . . guess I hadn't thought about it," I said.

"Look, Milt, this is a new age in the afterworld. It's all about the ratings. My opposite number, he went with the dramas, the epic movies, that sort of thing. I could name ten or fifteen actresses that he's got up there right now working their buns off. Me? I went with game shows. I've got *all* the hosts—or I will when they die. People like games."

I nodded in agreement. "They sure do. Even one as annoying as mine."

"And that's where you're wrong, Milt. You're too burned out to see it, but your show is great."

"Really?" I asked. "I'm sick to death of it."

"Really," Chuck said. "But I know how you feel. That's why I'm here."

"I'm not following you," I admitted.

"I know you're sick of the show, Milt, and I've come to offer you a deal."

"A deal?" I said. "But then I'd go to hell when I died, right?"

Chuck nodded. "All game show hosts go to hell anyway, Milt. God hates 'em. Says they offer false hope to an already dark world. He likes that uplifting bullshit they show on Lifetime and Pax."

"Sometimes people win," I said, a bit defensively. "Besides, why should I go to hell for my job?"

"I don't make the rules, Milt," Chuck said, "I just play the game."

I refilled our glasses and thought about what he'd said. "So, what do you want from me?"

"Your soul, Milt," he said, holding up a well-manicured hand to stall my protest. "But not just yet. Eventually. When it's time to launch the best game show the afterworld has ever seen. I'm thinking of calling it *Hell's Dilemma,* but that's not quite right."

"You want me to host this show . . . when I'm dead?"

"Exactly," Chuck said, grinning with pleasure. "You're very good, you know."

"Uh-huh," I said. "Thanks. And what do I get out of the deal?"

"Out," Chuck said.

"Out?"

"Of your current contract and into something better. What kind of show would you like to be doing?"

"One where I don't get tortured," I said. "Something a little *less* real."

Chuck snapped his fingers. "How about *The All New Family Feud?*"

"The one where the families beat the hell out of each other for cash and prizes?"

"That's the one. The host never gets hurt—he stays in that glass booth the whole time."

I thought about it. Chet Marker had been hosting that show for quite a while—and he made loads of cash. "That wouldn't be too bad," I said. "What will happen to Chet?"

"Oh, I'm sure I'll figure out something for him to do," Chuck said. "So, do we have a deal?"

My sudden sobriety had apparently woken me up enough to ask for more. "I also want something else," I said.

"Name it," Chuck said. "I want you in the next world. You're too good to go to the other side."

"I want an autobiography deal—a big one. The world needs to know what being the host of *The Hollywood Dilemma* is really like. Maybe they'll pull the plug on the damn thing." I thought a moment more, then added, "I also want to pick the next host."

"You really hate it, don't you?" Chuck said.

"Like you hate Lifetime movies," I said.

Chuck smiled. "Where I'm from, we call it the Victim Network. Who do you want to replace you?"

"Stuart Steadman," I said.

Chuck went silent for a long time. "Can't say as I know him," he finally admitted. "Who is he?"

I smiled. "The show's creator."

Chuck laughed, long and low. "That's perfect, Milt," he said. "I think we've got a deal, yes?"

"Where do I sign?" I asked, anticipating long hours of watching Stu try to live up to his own brainchild.

Snapping his fingers, a scroll appeared in his hand. Chuck unrolled it carefully and removed an ink pen from his suit coat. "Right here," he said, pointing to a line at the bottom. "It's all there—the new job, the book deal, and Stuart Steadman as your replacement on *The Hollywood Dilemma*—for as long as it lasts, that it."

I took the pen. It was a Mont Blanc. "No signing in blood with a quill?" I asked.

"You've got a sense of humor, Milt," Chuck said. "I like that about you. But to answer your question, no, we haven't done the signing in blood thing for quite a while. There's no need. It's the *intent* that counts."

"I suppose so," I said, then placed the pen on the line and signed.

When I handed it back to him, he quickly scrawled his signature on the line next to mine. The writing wasn't in English, but I'd be hard-pressed to tell you what language it was for certain.

Chuck rolled the scroll tightly, and placed an end in each hand, then clapped them together. The scroll disappeared with a vague flash of light and a sound that made my ears pop. "Well, Milt, that should do it. As I said earlier, I'm on a schedule, so I'd best be going."

"That's it?" I asked. "Nothing's changed!"

"Even for the Prince of Darkness, making changes to *The Hollywood Dilemma* takes a bit of time." He clapped me on the shoulder. "Don't worry, Milt. The changes will happen—you'll see."

Reminding myself that this was a dream, I said, "Okay, Chuck. Thanks for coming by."

Chuck smiled and for a moment—maybe a second,

and certainly no more, mind you—I saw something in that smile that made me think that Chuck *wasn't* a dream. "I know you don't believe me, Milt. But you will," he said, laughing. "In time you will."

And with that, he stepped out the door and into the Beverly Hills night beyond it.

And I went back to the bar to resume my communion with Johnny Walker Red.

But no matter how much I drank that night, I couldn't feel a thing.

I told you at the beginning that Chuck Woolery was Satan and that all game show hosts go to hell. Of course, you had no reason to believe me then—why would you now? All because of a story?

Would it help if I told you it all happened? All of it? *The Hollywood Dilemma* let me go three days after Chuck's nighttime visit, and poor Stuart—he only lasted one week before one of the Host Challenges killed him. I watched the episode—he had to climb a wall of razors and glass shards naked. After that, they canceled the show. Couldn't find a new host, I guess.

I wrote an autobiography in less than three months—it spent almost six on the best-seller lists.

And I hosted *The All New Family Feud*. I quit after a month—this time, my contract had more out clauses than channels on television. But my heart just wasn't in being a host anymore.

When it was all said and done, and I decided to retire to a life of playing pool and drinking scotch (the good stuff, for what it's worth), I got an e-mail from

Chuck, reminding me of the terms of our agreement and that he'd lived up to his end of the bargain.

And he did, I tell myself late at night when I'm lying here in the darkness. Everything happened just as he promised. Just as I'd wanted.

But I've read that e-mail time and time again because it only occurred to me *after*. Chuck never said how long I'd have to host *Hell's Dilemma,* and he never said when the job starts.

I'm guessing it will be soon now. And I'm sure the job will last a very, very long time.

YOU'D BETTER WIN!

by Josepha Sherman

Josepha Sherman is a fantasy novelist, freelance editor, and folklorist. In addition, she has written for the educational market on everything from Bill Gates to the workings of the human ear. Forthcoming titles include *Mythology for Storytellers* and the *Star Trek: Vulcan's Soul* trilogy. Visit her at www.sff.net/people/Josepha.Sherman.

" . . . aND NOW IT'S TIME to play— *You'd Better Win!*"

The audience, both those crowding into the stands surrounding the flat yellow surface of the gaming field and those watching from the viewscreens all over it, cheered, yodeled, screeched, and made whatever other noises from whatever orifices their particular species used. *Yeah,* I thought, *laugh it up. Enjoy the show.*

The announcer was a male Traie in full plumage.

Picture a skinny cross between a man and a wingless bird covered in a jarring mix of neon-orange-and-green feathers, with a great orange-and-green crest trailing down his back. He preened at the crowd's adoration, crest rising and falling, and turned, waving to everyone.

And I— well, I stood in the wings, or rather in the shadow of an archway leading out onto the field, trying not to feel nervous. Like a gladiator, I thought, from those old Roman times. Or maybe a clown. Yeah, that was more like it. A clown in snug, slightly worn blue tunic and trousers, spacer's wear and the only gear I had, with more Traie crowding behind him to make sure he made his entrance and didn't try to turn and run. Why in hell I'd ever thought to enter the damned game . . .

Erase that. I knew why. I needed the money that winning would get me. A quick flash of memory showed me standing, dumbfounded, on the docking bay, watching that contrail fading away against that too-blue Traiea sky. Things happen—bar fights not avoided, travel connections not made—and sometimes a guy can get left behind on some foreign world, with nothing left to him but to watch his ship soar away. Never thought that sort of thing would happen to me— but then, who does? If that left-behind guy doesn't have the money to get himself back to one of the human-held worlds, things can get grim pretty quickly.

The problem gets doubly serious when the guy in question happens to be stuck on Traiea. They don't actually do anything as crass as attack humans on this birdie world. No, they simply won't hire humans for anything, and I do mean anything.

Bigots, after all, come in all sizes and species, and humans haven't cornered the market on prejudice. So there I was, down to my last few credits, doing the cliché bit of sitting in a bar—a spaceport one that tolerated all kinds, even mine—and nursing my drink. Yeah, and by that point, I was beginning to wonder if I had the guts or skill to rob a Traie-type bank or hijack a ship off world.

The bar's viewscreen was on, of course, since speaking of clichés, that seems to be one in every bar in all the unknown worlds. Lost in my dour thoughts, I hadn't really been paying attention to it. But suddenly the shouted words, "You'd Better Win!" cut into my musings. They'd been in Standard as well as Traie'e. Some sort of quiz program, I guessed—a popular one, judging from the way everyone was suddenly staring at the viewscreen.

No, wait a minute. I looked up again when I realized that this wasn't the show itself, it was an ad for the show, and yes, it really was in both Traie'e *and* Standard, which was interesting. Turned out that they were looking for new contestants for a game starting up right here in this city, and species wasn't an issue.

I sat bolt upright when I heard the amount of prize money they were offering. Hell, that was a lot better than starving or getting shot for bank robbery! Knowing the general layout of the city by now, I headed off at just under a run to the show's headquarters.

The crowds parted as I went, Traie fastidiously getting out of the way of the hurrying human.

The address turned out to be as flashy as anything else Traie, the whole building blazing with colors that never should have been put together, pinks and oranges and yellows, with the words YOU'D BETTER WIN! flashing on and off in gold-and-crimson lettering over the doorway, in both Traie'e and Standard. I've seen landing beacons that were less dazzling.

I was the first would-be contestant to answer the ad, but the Traie who perched at the registration booth didn't seem at all surprised. She showed no more expression than any other Traie. Nothing personal: Those beaked faces don't allow for much expression even when they're outrageously happy. She didn't draw back *too* blatantly from a human either.

Unfortunately, she also couldn't give me too much information about the show, other than that yes, it was real-time, fake reality, test your real-life skills. Again, nothing personal in the lack of data: Very few people on the planet spoke Standard. Which was how I'd gotten into difficulties to begin with.

But from what I could make out from her broken Standard and my few words of Traie'e, the theme of this session of *You'd Better Win!* did seem to be "work in space," a game that tested space skills. Hell, I had those. I could, no false modesty, out-space any Traie ever hatched. There was, this Traie managed to assure me, no prejudice against humans in the game either: Any and all contestants were welcome. She also assured me that the show's staff could provide a space suit for my species and size. So, I told myself, this was definitely worth the shot: get the money, get out, get home.

It was only after I'd finished signing the forms and was fully entered that I was told one little extra complication. With the language difficulties, I couldn't be sure if it was accurate or just another mistranslation. But if what she was telling me was right, during the game, "worth a shot" could be quite literal, and trying to back out could be fatal.

Clearly, they took their game playing seriously on Traiea.

What the hell, it was this or nothing. I assured her that I had no intention of backing out.

So there I was, standing in the gateway to the game, and watching the flamboyant announcer wave to the audience.

"Today," he chirped in Traie'e and Standard, "today, we have a matchup of three of the most exciting players yet! First, from world known as Ututchai, comes one who claims the name Trath-I-Gorick."

Oh, hell. I hadn't thought about the other contestants. I'd been sure it would be an easy win over those less space-savvy Traie. But of course, if a human could enter, so could other aliens.

So much for that easy win.

Roars of approval from the crowd. None of whom, I'd wager, had a clue as to what the announcer had just rattled out meant.

Neither did I. A . . . thing that I assumed was Trath-I-Gorick lumbered out from one of the other archways,

and the audience's roar grew louder. Not surprising: This
was definitely an alien Mr. Muscle. At least, I assumed
it was a "he." For all I knew, this could be Ms. Muscle. Picture a dull yellow scaly biped brick on short,
sturdy legs, with a hairless dome on top, as no-neck
as some old Earth footballer. Yellow eyes, nose slit,
mouth slit. All muscle, yeah, taller than me, and if
there was any justice, dumb as a brick as well. Though
you didn't judge a, uh, brick by its cover.

"Next," the announcer chirped, "from world known
as Ithacala, comes one who claims the name of Prrulit
ca Elel."

Another roar from the crowd, a little less enthusiastic
this time.

Okay, not a clue for me. What was it? Bird? Reptile?
Feline? Slim, sleek, and lithe, with pale blue skin, a
narrow, pointed face and big, slit-pupil eyes blinking
in the bright light. No hint as to gender here either.
Wiry strength, I'd guess, and no telling what intelligence hid behind those eyes. Those light-sensitive
eyes, I added to myself, and stored that bit of data
away.

"And last," the announcer chirped, "from world
known as Urth," nice try, I thought, "comes one who
claims the name of Sam'l Stefens."

Just a slight mangling of "Samuel Stevens." I'd
been hearing worse mutilations of my name ever
since I'd first had the bad luck to land on this world.
I strode out onto the yellow field with as much bravado as I could field, trying to pretend I was some
sort of hero, not just some out-of-luck spacer. Yeah,

I got sort of a roar from the audience, too. It didn't reassure me at all: They would have cheered a rock by that point.

I glanced at the other two contestants, guessing that they had to be left-behinds on this foreign world like me. A shame to have to defeat two stuck in the same boat as myself, so to speak, but hey, there's a limit to charity.

They stared back at me, presumably thinking the same thing. "You guys speak Standard?" I began.

"No, no!" the announcer cut in, crest rising. "Contestants do not speak to each other!"

But I guessed from the flicker I'd seen in the other two contestants' eyes that the answer to my question was yes. For what that was worth, it meant we would understand each other.

A sudden blaring of, well, call the cacophony music, made me nearly jump out of my skin. Out of the corner of my eye I saw Muscle and Bird-Cat start, too. The announcer cheerfully chirped, "And now, and now *it is time!*" Crest fluttering he screeched, *"Let the game begin!"*

The roars of the crowd were drowned out by the shrill whine of a shuttle craft descending—here, now! The three of us contestants raced for cover, swearing in our native tongues. Damned idiot Traie, sending a shuttle down almost on top of us. Hell of a short game that would have been, three squashed lumps of charcoal!

One last thrust of superheated air sent me tumbling helplessly into Bird-Cat. "Get off!" it hissed, and shoved. Those thin blue arms were strong as wire. I scrambled to my feet, spitting out sand.

During all this, the brick, of course, hadn't even been swayed.

"Come, come, aboard!" our host chirped, apparently unperturbed by it all.

It was the most ridiculously over-ornate shuttle possible, clearly meant to give the viewers a thrill—particularly viewers with the gaudy natural coloring of the Traie. Feathers, cushions, glittery fabrics—you name it, it was there, again in every pink, orange, and green possible, plus enough cameras to catch every sneeze or scratch.

We three contestants didn't get much of a chance to do more than glance at each other before we were up and away. Three ships sitting out there, and as the announcer was happily chirping, they were in a triangle, equidistant from each other. And sure enough, it was a case of one contestant per ship. The shuttle dropped us off, one by one.

As soon as the three of us were onboard, the three ships started unfurling between them a . . . net? Yeah, a really big one made up of some type of wire mesh, with rigid ribs snapping out to hold its shape in space. A three-dimensional game field?

Before I could ask—assuming that anyone would answer—I was being all but shoveled into a space suit. The computer scanning they'd done of me back on Traiea had been a good one. The suit fit pretty well, and to my relief seemed to be spaceworthy, with breathable air. I knew those facts pretty quickly, because before I could run any tests, almost before all the suit's seals were sealed, I was shoved out the air lock into the area defined by the net. So, I saw, were the other two contestants. Easy enough to see them, since all three ships had their exterior lights blazing. And yes, Traie ships have far more lights than are really needed in space. Particularly these, which were now studded with cameras.

Okay, basic tests made, maneuvering jets working, oxygen working, good flexibility to the suit. Could have been worse. Now what was the contest going to—

Whoa, what? What looked like swarms of bright red, green, and yellow . . . beach balls were being hurled out of the ships. Couldn't be real beach balls, of course, not in the vacuum of space. Something colorful and round—hell, it didn't matter what they were, because the announcer was chirping directions:

"You, you are red," to Mr. Muscle, "you, green," to Bird-Cat, "and you," to me, "yellow."

The point of this game, it seemed, was for each of us to get as many of "our" beach balls out of the big net and into smaller wire cages, one for each color. There didn't seem to be any other rules.

This is it? I mean, this is the whole "real test of space skills" contest? Some dumb sport?

Hey, don't argue, I told myself. Maybe the whole point to the game was for the Traie to just watch three aliens making fools of themselves. No problem with that. I'd look a lot sillier if it meant getting out of here. And I'd always been good at working in a suit. Firing up one maneuvering jet, I aimed myself at the nearest yellow ball. Yeah, good. I closed my arms around it—

Mr. Muscle crashed into me. Of course, in space that meant we both ricocheted off each other: Every action, equal and opposite reaction and all that. The yellow ball, naturally, went flying in yet another direction.

"No rules." Muscle's voice was thin and rough.

No rules, huh.

I could hear the announcer in my headphones, chirping enthusiastically to the distant audience. Damn. No way to shut him out.

Okay, then here's something to make you really chirp! As I said, I'm really good at working in space. I caught myself against the side of the wire mesh, fired up my maneuvering jets, caught one of the yellow balls, did a neat 180-turn past the floundering brick, and dunked the ball into the right wire cage, which promptly pulled it in and sealed it away. *How about that, you damned bird? Score one for me!*

No time for triumph. That lithe Bird-Cat had just gotten not one but two of the green balls into its cage. I'd better hurry up. Pushing off into space again, I took aim at another yellow ball. Two choices were suddenly in front of me: Hit Muscles and knock him away from a red ball, or stay on target. Which got me more points?

I went for the ball. Muscles went for his. I missed.

He didn't. Cursing under my breath for having been too nice, I went hunting for another yellow ball. Fortunately, a sideways glance told me that Bird-Cat had missed, too.

By pure luck, I caught a yellow ball with the toe of my suited foot as I turned and—whoa, go humans! It shot right into the right cage as neatly as though I really had aimed it. Bird-Cat and I were tied now, and ha, Mr. "No Rules" Muscles had wasted time going after Bird-Cat. While those two were busy bouncing off each other, I started after another ball—

"Round Two!" the announcer shrilled.

What the *hell?* Those pretty beach balls had suddenly come alive, moving under their own power, zipping about wildly. Great. Now we not only had to figure in the speed of the things, we also had to figure in how far off course we'd be thrown when we did catch one and its momentum dragged us with it.

I hung in space for a moment, trying to catch my breath—you run out of breath fast working in space, no matter how experienced you are—and trying to figure out my next move. One ball zigzagged that way . . . another headed to the left . . .

Okay, no one had promised this would be easy. Firing a maneuvering jet, I dodged a red ball that seemed to be trying to take my helmet off, struck a green ball with my hip, sending it ricocheting away, and grabbed at the yellow ball that had been—damn! It shot right out of my grip. I turned—and collided with Bird-Cat. I got one glance of those large eyes, wide with surprise, heard an "Ooof," then we both were hurtling backward. I slammed helplessly into the wire mesh and bounced off it again before I could get my maneuvering jets working and myself under control.

Hey, look at this! I'd trapped one of the yellow balls between me and the mesh, and it had bounced off with me. I caught it in both arms before it could zoom off, and then fought it, trying to damp its speed, both of us spinning dizzily, till I could manhandle it into the cage.

Mr. Muscle had, meanwhile, forced a red ball into his cage. Bird-Cat was doing what looked like a ballet in weightlessness—yeah, if a cat did ballet, because the creature had snared two green balls with predatory ease and pitched them into the right cage.

Lord. I was losing count. Who was ahead? How many balls were left? Hell, how could you tell, when they were darting about and—

"Round Three!" the announcer shrieked.

Now what?

No way! The damned balls were suddenly sprouting spikes—no, blades, glinting in the ship's lights, looking definitely long and sharp enough to cut right through the tough skin of a space suit.

"Oh, that's just not right!" I heard myself say like an idiot.

Bird-Cat protested, too, voice shrill and angry in the headphones of my suit. Mr. Muscle said nothing.

Gee, what a wonderful day this was turning out to be.

Okay. There had to be a way to catch the damned things without getting sliced. I let one go zooming past my helmet—whoa, and here came another, right toward my face. As I ducked, using my jets to get me out of the spin, I caught a close-up look. Where the blade jutted out from the ball was a flat casing, a guard to keep the blade from cutting the ball itself.

I liked this game less and less with every second. Yeah, the Traie didn't like humans or presumably any other foreign species either, but I had never thought that they could be downright sadistic. That guard hadn't looked like more than a few inches long.

Think of Earth, I told myself, and grabbed. Pure luck: I got the hilt, not the blade. Quickly I caught a second hilt, then hung onto the ball with both hands and grim determination, realizing that now I had no way to get to the control of the maneuvering jets.

More than one way to do it. I wriggled and kicked, not as effectively as it would have been if I'd been in water or atmosphere, but enough to steer myself more or less in the right direction. A quick jackknife bend—as much of one a I could manage in a space suit—and a flip—yes, right into the cage! I turned (carefully so I wouldn't spin), counting the remaining balls. Two yellow balls, three green balls, three red balls. Well, what do you know? I was actually ahead in this stupid game. Now if only I could get the remaining two yellow balls without killing myself . . .

Mr. Muscle crashed into me, this time, I think, by

accident: I could hear him panting. A brick isn't the best shape for agility. Just as well we collided, though. Otherwise I would have collided with the knives of a green ball I hadn't seen coming. I recovered from zooming backward with a few careful blasts from the maneuvering jets (I didn't like what the fuel gauges were showing me, not that much fuel left), and shot off in pursuit of a yellow ball—damn! It changed direction, heading right at me. I got out of the way just in time and managed to catch the flat of a blade between both gloved palms. Couldn't hold onto it . . . Glancing over my shoulder in the suit's rearview mirror, I timed this, let go, grabbed the ball again by the guard, and flipped the thing over my head, right into the cage. All right! Maybe I'd get out of this in one piece and even win this damned stupid—

And then I heard it. That unmistakable combination sound of a gasp of horror and a hiss that every spacer learns to dread—yes. Bird-Cat's suit had just been deeply sliced across one arm.

All thoughts of winning left my brain. I did what every decent spacer does in this situation: I dropped everything and rushed to Bird-Cat's side. The being was clutching the slice. Those big eyes stared at me in blank panic.

"It's okay," I said hastily before the alien started to struggle, glad we could both speak Standard. "Don't fight me. Let me see. Come on, relax, don't be afraid."

I winced. Bad news. Really bad slice, through the suit and down into the flesh: Blood was boiling out in neat reddish balls.

"Stop the game!" I shouted to the announcer. "Emergency! Stop the game!"

"Not possible!" the announcer chirped.

"What the hell do you mean, not possible!"

"The orbs cannot be recalled now. The game must be finished!"

What I said back to him was pure old-fashioned Anglo-Saxon. But there wasn't any time to think about anything but Bird-Cat losing air and blood—

Yeah? Yeah! That would do it. "Hold still," I said, and something in the tone must have gotten through to the alien: I know what I'm doing.

God, I hoped I did. Carefully, I held the slit sleeve so that blood would completely fill the opening—

Yes! Expose enough liquid to the infinite cold of space and you had instant quick freeze, instant emergency seal. Bird-Cat would have to hold that arm perfectly still till we got into a ship. But at least that ominous hissing had stopped, and blood wasn't still flowing. Bird-Cat and I exchanged glances, gratitude in those big eyes, relief in mine, and we understood each other perfectly.

Whoa, but where were those damned barbed balls? I looked over my shoulder—well, what do you know? Mr. Muscle was busy swatting them away from us. Not so surprising at that, since spacer law kind of overrules anything as superficial as a game.

Except for that damned announcer, who kept chirping, "The game cannot be stopped!"

No recall? No fail-safe? Gee, wasn't this going to look great on Traie viewscreens?

Hah. It probably would be their top-rated episode.

"Stay put," I said to Bird-Cat. "Stay absolutely still." I didn't like the look in those eyes: Shock was setting in.

Muscle and I worked in unspoken agreement. Ignore the game, ignore which ball belonged to which contestant. We were a team, getting ball after ball into the nearest cages. The announcer must have nearly been having avian apoplexy by now judging from his increasingly frantic shrieking, but Muscle and I kept going, our suits scored a dozen times but mercifully not pierced, keeping Bird-Cat safely between us.

"We got them!" I yelled. "Got them all!"

"Game's over!" Muscle roared. "Let us back in!"

"No winner!" the announcer shrieked in what sounded like utter hysteria. "No winner!"

"Wanna bet?" I yelled back. "We're all still alive and nobody's suing your feathered butt—so let us back in or you're going to have to kill all three of us, here, now, *and on camera!*"

Even Muscle gave me a wild stare at that one. But after a heart stopping few seconds it turned out that I'd guessed right. Sure, killing off contestants live and in real time would be dramatic enough to garner high ratings and publicity—but it would also mean the end of *You'd Better Win!* Who'd compete on a show that was so realistic it guaranteed death?

You probably have figured out what happened next. No prize money, of course, since we didn't actually win that last round. But the three of us ex-contestants didn't really care about that. We got something better: ship passage that rushed my fellow contestants and me off Traiea, and some good old-fashioned hush money.

During the flight from Traiea, we three had time to talk together and get to know each other. Misfits, the three of us, but when we analyzed our skills, we realized that hey, the three of us misfits made a pretty good crew. We're going to use that hush money to buy us a nice little freighter, work up a small business.

You'd Better Win!? Yeah, we did.

DISH OF THE DAY

by Susan Sizemore

Susan Sizemore lives in the Midwest and spends most of her time writing. Some of her other favorite things are coffee, dogs, travel, movies, hiking, history, farmers' markets, art glass, and basketball—you'll find mention of quite a few of these things inside the pages of her stories. She works in many genres, from contemporary romance to epic fantasy and horror. She's the winner of the Romance Writers of America's Golden Heart Award, and a nominee for the 2000 Rita Award in historical romance. Her available books include historical romance novels; a dark fantasy series, *The Laws of the Blood;* science fiction; and several electronically published books and short stories. Recent books include the hardcover publication of *The Children of the Rock* duology, *Moons' Dancing* and *Moons' Dreaming* with Marguerite Krause.

"WHAT THE HELL are we doing here?"

"I, for one, Marc, am here to win,"

Venus Baxter answered her sous chef. *Don't be afraid,* she thought. *Some of them can probably smell fear.* Some of them were probably telepaths, too. She spoke loudly, for everyone to hear. "Team Terra can outwit, outplay, and out sauté anybody in the galaxy."

Her words were pure bravado, of course. She was as daunted by the alien sights and sounds around her as anyone on her seven-person team. But she was the leader; at only thirty-three she was acknowledged as the premier chef of her species. She had to appear confident and focused and ready to take on all comers in the *Grande Galactic Challenge* as they stood at the top of the entry staircase awaiting their introduction and the long march down to the competition area. God help them.

Terra had only been part of the Bipedal/O_2 Bloc of the Galactic League for a couple of decades. This made her species very much the new kids on the block, and none of the neighbors were particularly friendly. Venus was no history buff, but the Terran Department of State had insisted on briefing the whole team on the reasons why being invited to participate in the GGC was not just an honor, but a patriotic duty.

"This isn't your average chili cook-off," they'd been informed by an annoyingly folksy official. *"We can't play nice-nice and feel like it's an honor just to be chosen to compete."*

This comment caused a near riot among the team. For, after all, in any competition reputations and careers were made and broken. It was obvious this man had no idea he was talking to a group of dangerous people. The practitioners of any profession where the most important tools of the trade were knives and fire were not sissies.

Of course, the news the official gave them after they calmed down was enough to quell any remaining sense of outrage.

"The Galactic League doesn't allow outright bloodshed among its members. War, as such, was outlawed a long time ago," he told them. *"You grew up being told that the League is all about peaceful coexistence. Which is, of course, bullshit. The League is all about competition. Competition for trading rights, competition for resources, competition for technological edge. We Terrans need to compete. We need territory and trading agreements. Up until now we've had very few chances to get ahead. This is our chance. You are our chance."*

Venus and her team had looked at each other in confusion, and then they had begun to babble questions. Once the official had them all worked up, he explained, *"Terra has its first chance to be allowed to colonize a star system with a Class 3 rating. We need to move population outside our own system. We need this new resource. We need to win it. That's where you come in.*

"The League sponsors every sort of competition between member species, from spelling bees to fight-to-the-death gladiatorial games. Every League media outlet covers these events—you can't turn on a vid or holo station

broadcasting from outsystem without seeing some contest or sports show. The games have been popular for thousands of years in the League, and we Terrans now feed on the same excitement. We want to take part. More importantly, we need *to.*

"What's not known outside the Terran Government is that the games are how the League regulates tension among worlds. Winners of the contests are rewarded with power, privilege, and prestige. Terra has not had many opportunities to participate in these competitions. And when we have . . ." He'd shaken his head. *"Remember our athletes' terrible showing in the last Invitational Games?"*

They'd all nodded dismally. The games had gone on for a year, and excitement ran rampant all over the Terran System at the thrill of finally facing off against all the aliens in the sports from other worlds that Terrans had so enthusiastically adopted. It had been a year of humiliation and heartache for humans back on Terra watching on the giant screens set up to catch the action in every city and town of the home world.

"Our finest Olympic and professional athletes went up against the finest athletes of the rest of the League." The official shuddered, and shook his head. *"Damn, that was ugly."* Then he looked them over. *"Now, you—cooks—are our people's hope for a better life and brighter future for our species."*

"I wish he hadn't said that," Venus muttered now.

"What?" Alice Damiano the baker asked.

"Just remembering our briefing."

"Oh, god!" The words came from Connor the pastry chef as a fervent prayer.

"The Gourmet Society of the Bipedal/O$_2$ has invited Terra to participate in the Grande Galactic Challenge." The official's words echoed in Venus' mind. And the memory of his hopeless sigh. That made her grit her teeth. *"The prize in the Challenge is the right for the winning species to colonize and exploit that star system. Your species is counting on you. You* have *to win."*

With those words ringing in her ears, Venus took a deep breath and finally made herself take a good look around the huge arena. Even the very word "arena" brought images of bloody combat that made Venus' knees go weak. The scope of the place, the sight of thousands of spectators, the noise, was staggering. The colors and shapes and sounds were, well, completely alien. All the other teams had been introduced and she could see them milling purposefully in their kitchen areas below.

All the beings the Terran team was up against were *technically* humanoid in shape—at least everyone had two legs and two eyes, breathed oxygen, and could digest the same minerals and nutrients. The contestants were all similar—in the loosest possible translation of the word.

Now Venus understood why Terrans were known as Soft Skins. Scales seemed to be a popular evolutionary outer covering for many of her fellow oxygen breathers. Some of the beings were covered in scales as slinky as snakeskin, some skins were rough and bumpy, or sharp-edged like obsidian blades. There was one group that resembled green-and-pink two-legged triceratops. The scaled beings came in colors ranging from palest orchid to one armored species whose bodies flashed iridescent black, red, and green.

After scales, the next most popular body covering seemed to be fur. A lot of the furry species sported tails, huge claws, and fangs. She was willing to bet there weren't any vegetarians among that lot. There was one alien team that looked like animated tree bark with eyestalks. Venus couldn't help but wonder if the catlike creatures used the bark creatures as scratching posts.

The only thing that didn't disturb her was the heat.

"If you can't stand the heat . . ." she murmured, and took another hard look, this time at the layout of the vast cooking arena. Even though she'd had a week of training in a simulated combat kitchen, the complexity of the cooking equipment they were required to use was still daunting.

And the rules of the competition . . . Good God, the rules . . .

Calm down, girl.

She took a deep breath, and let it out in a rush just as Connor said, "Look at the scrolling reader board where the rules are posted. Does that really say that points will be deducted for poisoning judges?"

Venus looked up, and up, above the spectator stands to where holo projectors spun information around the arena in dozens of languages. "Yep," she answered. She wondered if she was the only member of the team that had followed procedure and memorized the rules.

The voice of the announcer filled the air, somehow drowning out the cacophony of the crowd. "Finally, in red, welcome first-time participants, representing the Sol System—Team Terra!"

"Touch that and I'll bite your paw off," Connor Marsh warned the Kaparian team leader as the big black cat moved too close to the judging table.

Connor was a genius with sugar. Venus was had come to admire him not only for his gift for creating dessert fantasies, but for his pugnacious defense of Terran territory as the competition grew more intense over the last two days. Mind games were an important part of any good player's stock-in-trade, and Connor was the best of them at adapting well to the unwritten rules of this contest. He put on a game face and talked trash.

"I don't think you should threaten it," Marc cautioned Connor. "The rules state—"

"Shut up, you weasel," Connor answered Marc. He continued to glare threateningly at the cat. "Move along, furball."

"Ethnic slurs are—"

"Being tossed all over the place," Venus cut Marc off. "Or haven't you noticed?"

The cat pumped a furred fist in the air, said, "We conquer all!" and marched off, lashing tail barely missing the delicate spun sugar tower Connor was guarding so fiercely.

Marc gave an offended sniff. "I've been concentrating on cooking."

Marc, her second-in-command, was proving to be something of a liability. Marc was brilliant at following a recipe, but creativity and improvisation were not his strengths. He whined and complained at every little infraction of the official rules, which he had bothered to memorize. He took credit for every point they won, blamed Venus and her bad management style for every deduction. He was riding the team like he was already planning on opening a seaside restaurant on the planet the Terrans hadn't won yet.

"Calm down, everyone," he cautioned as the team was lined up behind the display table awaiting their turn to be judged in the day's second round. "We have to stay calm, professional. Our planet's counting on us."

Marc had been saying that a lot. Venus sighed. She gestured toward the alien teams, some waiting like the Terrans were, some in their kitchen areas, some milling around, checking out the competition like the big black cat. "Their planets are counting on them, too," she told Marc.

"Don't you want to win?" Marc demanded. "Don't you think we can win?"

Venus took note of how the undertone of hysteria in his voice increased the tension among the Terrans. She really wished the whole team wasn't stuck standing in a double row behind the table, waiting while each portion of the contest was judged. It would be a lot more fun and far less stressful if the ones not involved with each specific project were allowed freedom of movement during the judging. At the moment she yearned to follow the cat chef's example and roam the arena floor. She was as glad as she was nervous that the judges would reach the Terrans' display area next. She wanted to get this over with, and get away for a while.

"Look at the scoreboard," Marc said.

She didn't want to, but her gaze was drawn up to the holographic screen above the spectator stands. There was so much information displayed that each team was assigned an interpreter to aid them with understanding all the symbols, signs, and commentary. The one thing that was easy to read was the scores.

"We're still two points behind the Arrhaians," she said.

"Second place," Marc said. He shook his head, and tugged on the hem of his red team jacket. "We can't stay in second place. We wouldn't even be in second place if it wasn't for the dim sum." Somehow he made it sound like this victory earlier in the day had been some sort of mistake.

Venus glanced proudly at the Li twins. "Terrans invented dim sum. It'd be pitiful if we hadn't taken that one, even if Asian cuisines are trendy in the space lanes."

"I'm sure the judges gave us extra points because it's Terran cuisine."

Venus noticed Zhin Li casually draw a cleaver out of his utility belt. "We won because our team's the best," she spoke up.

The last couple of days had been even rougher than Venus had expected. The vegetable sessions had been the worst for her. Team Terra was abysmal at preparing dishes from the alien plants they were given to make into salads, terrines, and side dishes.

Venus blamed herself for most of the mistakes, but at least she hadn't thrown up until after she got out of the kitchen area. They'd done much better with breads. Yeast and flour, even if they came in strange colors and textures, were pretty easy to work with. Venus found working with Alice Damiano a joy, and everyone on the team was a good baker. Their bread presentation did a lot to make up for the vegetable fiasco. At least for the dessert portion, every species was allowed to use native ingredients.

"We're doing fine," she assured her team.

"No we're not," Marc insisted. "This *thing* Connor's made is going to lose us points."

She patted Marc on the arm, not gently. "Calm down."

"And shut up," Connor added. "The judges are heading toward us."

Venus watched as five judges dressed in elaborate robes and headdresses moved with stately grace up to the Terrans' table. None of these alien persons were members of species participating in the event. All five judges were members of senior League species from the Bipedal Bloc, all from the founder worlds that controlled the League High Chamber. There were two tall avian Kalans, one with blue feathers and a purple beak and eyes, the other gold all over. They were rather like parakeets with opposable thumbs. The third judge was a black-and-green-striped cat being, taller and broader than any of the competing felinoids. He had a thick dark-green mane, and sported many gold rings in his tall, tufted ears. The fourth judge was a squat, red-scaled Millopid, with four cyes, three nostrils, and two large mouths. The Millopids were the most sophisticated gourmands in the League. The fifth judge was a stick skinny Kelbi. The Kelbi were elfin creatures who lived on fermented nectars and delicate sprays of sweet dews.

Or, as Connor put it, they were drunks who liked sugar any way they could get it. He'd taken that into account when putting together the creation for the Ornamental Dessert portion of the contest that was now being judged.

What he'd designed and they'd carefully constructed was a water garden of fountains and pools and streams flowing through flowering meadows of multicolored spun sugars, meringues, marzipan, and frosting. The tiny pools, streams, and fountains were created with the finest, most richly flavored and colored liqueurs Terra had to offer. Pure booze and sugar, as Connor said. And damn pretty to look at.

This was Connor's show. Too nervous to watch and unable to leave, Venus distracted herself by glancing at the dessert presentations on the tables to their left and right. The table on the left held a miniature alien city done all in white. There were even what looked like cotton candy clouds circling the delicate spires of the tallest buildings. Quite pretty, she thought, but not as elaborate as the Terran design.

Having just been judged, the alien team on the left had already moved away from their display table. Since no scores were posted until every entry was judged, standing around and watching the scoreboard was a waste of time. Several were using the time to work at the computer stations in their combat kitchen, preparing for the next challenge. The rest had joined the crowd in the aisles.

The raucous crowd in the stands was not allowed near the arena floor, but there was endless cheering and booing as each entry was displayed on the holo screens. Synth recreations of each dish would be distributed to spectators after the judging.

The red-scaled Arrhaian team on the right stood waiting with the same nervousness as her own crew. She wasn't sure what their creation represented, but it was round, mottled green and brown—and it was smoking. On Terra, this shape for a dessert was called a *bombe*. Whatever the Arrhaians had made, it certainly looked more dangerous than delicious to her Terran eyes.

Though there was noise all around, Venus was aware of the tense silence as the judging seemed to go on for hours.

"They've been bent over Connor's fairy garden for

nearly two minutes," Marc complained behind a fixed smile and gritted teeth. "What's taking them so long? How many faults can they find?"

Venus didn't answer this, or even throw Marc a dirty look. She did sigh in relief when the judges moved on to the next table a few seconds later. It was a whole body sort of sigh, all the tension draining out of her and leaving her limp. Good or bad, at least one more trial was over with.

"I'm going to party now," she said.

"Me, too," Connor said.

"Wait! There's work to be done."

Marc grabbed them both by the sleeves of their jackets as they started around the table. This probably saved their lives, as the Arrhaians' dessert exploded just as he pulled them back.

"The Arrhaians are protesting the point deductions," Marc said.

"I heard that," Venus answered.

While Marc paced, she didn't look up from the recipe computer. They were coming up on the meat course portion of the competition. While she was executive chef in charge of the whole team, this round featured her specialty. Despite their excellent showing in the dessert round, Team Terra was down three points.

Marc circled the workspace, then came back to her. "You're not taking this seriously. If the Arrhaian protest results in voiding the penalty—"

"The explosions killed two judges," Connor spoke

up. He touched his badly bruised face and neck. "It nearly killed us."

"They got the recipe wrong," Alice said. "That's what all the commentators are saying. Never mind the casualties, they screwed up the cooking."

Venus did mind the casualties. She couldn't close her eyes without seeing gold feathers and green fur everywhere. She shuddered. She'd wondered why the whole Grand Galactic Challenge hadn't been called off after the horrible accident—only to find out that fatal accidents were not unusual in any League game. The mess had been cleaned up, alternate judges had taken the late judges' place. The show went on.

"Let's not talk about this," she said.

This didn't stop Marc. "They could be reinstated on a technicality. The rules state that contestants cannot *poison* judges. No one was poisoned."

"That's crazy," Zhin Li said. He shook his head.

"It's the rules," Marc said. "If we want to play on League level, we have to be as ruthless as everyone else."

"We have no control over the judging," Venus said. "We can only control our performance." She turned from the computer to face the team that was gathered around her. "Let's concentrate on what we're good at."

With the expected exception of Marc, she got nods of agreement, and a general feeling of determined pride from her crew.

"Places for the final round," the announcer's voice

cut through the arena noise. "Team leaders to the front."

While her crew scattered to stoves and prep tables, Venus took a deep breath and walked as calmly as possible to the display table to see what ingredients and instructions waited there.

There was a cage set in the center of the table. She stopped and stared in surprise at the sight of the frantic blue creatures bouncing off the glowing bars of the cage. The first thing she realized was that the bars were actually an energy field. The second was that there was only one animal with many legs, and a lot of speed. Moving closer, she made out six legs; a plump, round body; a large head with a wide muzzle full of shark-sharp teeth. All six paws sprouted five long curved claws. She was obviously going to butcher it before she cooked it. She had no problem with that, except that the animal didn't look like it was going to cooperate with its own demise.

"You damn well better be good eatin'," she muttered.

The animal screeched loudly, almost as if in answer to her comment.

Alice came up behind Venus and looked over her shoulder. "Oh, isn't it cute!"

"Please," Venus told her. "Don't personalize something I'm about to turn into hash."

"Hash? The finest cook in the solar system is going to make hash?"

"Of course not— *What is hash?*"

"What?"

Venus shook her head to clear it, but the movement brought on a stab of pain in the center of her forehead. She grew slightly dizzy. This was not a good time for the stress to be getting to her.

It didn't help that the announcer intoned loudly. "The final challenge—Kabaca—the rarest delicacy in all the worlds of the League!"

Huge cheers and gasps went up from the spectators. She could see some of the nearby beings in the audience salivating. The place reverberated with growling stomachs.

Venus peered closer at the blue bundle of fur and fangs in the energy cage. The creature's big blue eyes peered back. "Guess you are good eating," she told it.

Eating is good?

She looked over her shoulder at Alice the baker. "That's the whole point of the contest, isn't it?"

Alice frowned at her. "What?"

Another shot of pain lanced through her.

Venus put her hands over her ears as the announcer went on. "Each team has been provided with one rare Kabaca. The challenge is to serve the Kabaca in the way most appropriate to their own species. The timer is set."

Alice gasped. "We've only got half an hour!"

Venus made herself look at the animal again. The Kabaca was chasing its tail, whirling madly around the cage. *Eating! Eating! Eating!* It stopped and met her gaze. Saliva dripped from its oversized mouth. *Eating.*

"Get ready . . . The challenge starts—now!" With the dramatic end of the announcement, the energy cages disappeared.

All over the arena Kabacas skittered across tables and leaped into the air. Chefs shouted and ran after them. Venus' Kabaca's powerful muscles bunched, and it sprang at her. Alice screamed.

All Venus saw was the fangs and claws flying toward her. Her impulse was to duck, but instead she held her arms out and caught the Kabaca in midair. It squirmed and scratched and bit at her, but she held on tight to the creature's thick blue fur and turned toward the prep area.

Her team gathered around. Li Zhin held up his cleaver.

"We've got twenty-nine minutes," Marc announced. Chaos reigned around them as the alien teams chased the rampaging six-legged blue creatures around their prep kitchens.

"What do we do first?" Connor asked. "Break its neck, then skin and gut it?"

"I looked up Kabaca recipes while the announcer was talking," Lao Zhin said. "Easily adapted for Terran cuisine. Want to try flash-braised in a red wine reduction?"

"That's one mean teddy bear you've got there," Connor said while the Kabaca continued to struggle. "You okay, Venus?"

Her arms and hands were bleeding, but she wasn't about to let go. "Fine."

"What do we do?" Connor asked.

"Hurry," Marc urged.

"Wait." She tilted her head to one side. "I'm listening."

"Listening? For what? We're on the clock, Venus!" Marc was outraged. He stepped forward. "Give me that thing!"

Venus whirled away, and pressed the creature to her chest. It scratched at her chest with its hind feet, ripping her red chef's jacket, and drawing more blood.

"Calm down," Venus told the critter. "Calm down."

"Don't personalize it," Alice parroted Venus' earlier warning. "We have to cook it."

Venus turned back to her crew. "We have to cook," she agreed. She took a deep breath. "I know exactly what we need to do. Li, put down that cleaver and put on a pot of water. I want somebody to chop and sauté potatoes, peppers, onions, and garlic. Marc, a béchamel sauce—right now. Alice, you've got time to make a batch of biscuits."

As she spoke the Kabaca clung to her, growing calmer by the second. This calmed Venus, and helped her to think. She kept the blue beast close to her when she went to the dry goods cupboard and began rummaging for corn. Someone screamed in the distance, but she paid it no mind. What other beings did with Kabacas was none of her concern. She intended to serve hers in the Terran style.

"I do not believe this," Marc complained. "What were you thinking?" He stopped glaring at Venus long enough to turn his annoyance on the rest of the team. "How can you have let her get away with this?"

"She's team leader," Connor answered. "It was her call."

"And her fault. I'm not taking any of the blame when we return to Terra in disgrace."

Alice shrugged. "If we lose—we lose."

"What happened to your competitive spirit? If we lose, we lose a colony world for our species."

The whole team was gathered behind the display table once more, waiting for the judges to make their rounds. On one side of the table sat a chafing dish full of vegetable hash. On the other was a bowl of buttered popcorn. The Kabaca was in the center of the table.

It was eating the popcorn. It had tasted the hash, just to find out what it was, but preferred the corn.

The judges were making their way quickly down the row. They'd be at the Terran table in a minute. Venus glanced at the nearest display tables, taking in all the various dishes prepared by the alien teams. She noted that several of the Kabacas had managed to elude capture, but most of the blue creatures were now the centerpieces on the display tables. They'd mostly been roasted, but there was one bubbling pot of Kabaca stew sending mouthwatering fragrance into the air.

Connor noticed where she was looking, and leaned closer to Venus. "Maybe we made a mistake," he whispered.

"Maybe." She sighed. "But I couldn't cook something that talked to me."

Of course, Marc overheard this. "It's your imagination," he said. "You've snapped under the pressure." He looked at the others again. "You should have let me take over when I tried. You should have followed my lead. You're all going to be in trouble for this. You'll never run a kitchen on Terra again."

He was probably right. They were going to lose. The contest. The colony world for their species. They would go home in disgrace. Their careers were in the toilet. It was all her fault. She realized how badly all the scratches and bites hurt. Then every muscle in her body tensed as the judges stepped up to their table.

Silence reigned, but for the Kabaca noisily stuffing popcorn into its large maw. Five pairs of eyes critically surveyed the Terran display. Three of the judges made notes on their handhelds. They glanced at each other.

Venus held her breath until she was ready to faint, then Connor nudged her, and she let it out in a gusty sigh.

The Millopid moved closer to the table. He turned the gaze of all four eyes on Venus. He spoke with both mouths, the sound oddly echoing. "This is the Terran way of serving Kabaca?"

Venus had to swallow a couple of times before she found the nerve to answer. "This—this is how I serve my guests," she answered. "I serve them the food that interests them." She gestured toward the busily eating blue creature. "He asked for popcorn."

The Millopid peered at her critically. "How did he ask?"

Venus touched her forehead. "In here." This sounded so stupid! "He's sentient," she added defiantly. "I—Terrans—do not cook sentient beings."

The Millopid nodded. "No civilized species does. A pity when it comes to Kabacas, really. They're delicious."

With that, he and the other judges moved to the next table in line.

"You see," Marc spoke up. He tapped Venus on the shoulder. "We should have cooked it."

Venus spun around to confront the other chef. "All right, so we lost! I don't care." She did care. Terribly. "But I couldn't do it."

"Then you should have let me. Now we go home empty-handed."

Losers? The Kabaca thought. Venus could tell that this time everyone could hear him. *Good hash. Eat.*

"All right," Marc conceded. "It can talk. It's mimicking. That doesn't mean it's intelligent. It's edible. All's fair in cuisine warfare."

"It's too late now," Connor said. "We've lost. Just shut up."

"Or Venus won't be the only one bleeding," Li Zhan promised.

Losers look now. Up, and up.

Venus did look up, past the crowd, past the multiple data screens, to the scoreboard high overhead. She didn't want to look. Her heart was pounding, her nerves stretched to the breaking point. She didn't believe what she saw. She wasn't reading it right.

"Oh, my god!" Alice shouted. She clapped her

hands to her cheeks and began to jump up and down. "Oh, my god!"

Connor laughed, and pounded Venus on the back. She stumbled forward, and caught herself on the edge of the display table.

"That's impossible," Marc said.

"We won," the Zhan brothers said.

Venus was blinded by sudden tears. She couldn't talk past the lump in her throat. The scoreboard flashed. Bells and whistles went off. The crowd cheered. Holographic balloons and streamers floated in the air, along with simulated fireworks explosions. The judges were heading their way, a huge gold trophy balanced on a gravity sled floating before them. The other teams were facing toward them, clapping, growling, and yapping congratulations in the spirit of good sportsmanship.

They had won.

The Kabaca threw himself into Venus' arms. *Not losers. Good food. Better people. Win planet. Now more popcorn,* he demanded.

So, Terrans were good people huh? Who'd have thought that being good would win the game? No, they hadn't won a game. They'd passed a test. A test that brought Terra into the wider membership of the League, and that was far more satisfying.

Venus laughed, and squeezed the blue-furred troublemaker tight. "Sure, you mean little teddy bear. Anything you want."

Not bear. Ambassador to Terra now.

"Marc," she said after the Kabaca thought at her

some more. "Will you prepare a batch of pancakes?"
She passed the Kabaca over to the frowning sous chef
as the judges arrived. "I'm going to go collect Terra's
trophy now."

ENTERTAINING FOLLY

by Bruce Holland Rogers

Bruce Holland Rogers is the author of over one hundred short stories. Among the honors that his stories have garnered are two Nebula Awards, the Bram Stoker Award, a Pushcart Prize, and a nomination for the Edgar Allan Poe Award. In addition to writing, Bruce teaches practical creativity to workers and managers in government and business. His nonfiction book *Word Work: Surviving and Thriving as a Writer* helps writers to meet the psychological challenges of a committed writing life. He is a frequent speaker at writer's conferences and has delivered keynote addresses to writers' groups across North America, from British Columbia to Florida. Bruce is a master of the short-short story. Readers in over a dozen countries subscribe to Bruce's stories-by-e-mail at the Web site www.shortshortshort.com. He lives in Eugene, Oregon.

D EREK, VAJRA, SUSAN, AND CLARK were in their usual post-seminar hangout, the darkest corner of The Prince of Wales, at the one table that had no view of the televisions. The place was busy.

Hockey Night in Canada was on every screen, and now and then the bar erupted in a common cheer or groan, depending on what the Maple Leafs did on the ice.

In Derek's pocket was a piece of paper. He wanted to show it to the others, and at the same time, he didn't. He didn't want to look like an idiot.

Clark sipped his beer and said, "My brain hurts."

"Because we stuck to English," Vajra told him. "Do some math before you go to bed tonight, and you'll feel better tomorrow."

Susan laughed. "You guys are such nerds."

Derek said, "And you're not?"

"Of course she isn't," Vajra said. "She's a nerdette."

Susan pretended to pout, but Derek could tell she wasn't offended. "Nerd" was hardly an insult among grad students who ran an interdisciplinary seminar on nonlinear systems on their own time. Today they had discussed Susan's paper, which modeled the spread of democracy using cellular automata. Derek had liked it. It read a bit like theoretical biology.

Clark, a Jamaican, was in particle physics. Vajra studied human learning. Time spent in their seminar wasn't getting any of them closer to finishing their doctorates, but none of them was in a hurry to finish, anyway.

Derek reached into his shirt pocket and took out the scrap of newsprint with the ad. He tried to sound casual as he asked, "Did anybody else happen to see this?"

Susan glanced at the piece of paper. "Oh, yeah. And I thought of you immediately, Derek."

"Because you want to get me off the planet?"

Susan smiled. "Well, you don't always seem to like it here."

"It's not that I dislike Earth," Derek said. "I just wish we had more than one example of it."

"What is this?" Vajra asked. He dragged the slip of paper across the table. Clark read it, too.

"A hoax," Clark said.

"Yeah, probably," Derek admitted.

"Probably?" said Clark. He read aloud. "The aliens have landed! Compete on TV reality show for a chance to meet the aliens and travel to the stars!" He looked at Derek. "And you think it's *probably* a hoax?"

"If it is real," Vajra said, "Derek would kill himself if someone else got to meet the aliens before him."

Derek wasn't sure if Vajra was making a joke. In fact, that *was* Derek's thought. Even if the chances of this being real were vanishingly small, he had to respond to the ad. "Insufficient data to conclude that it's a hoax," Derek said. He retrieved the ad. "I mean, if aliens *had* arrived, wouldn't they want to break the news to us gradually? And if they're looking for someone to meet them, well, I'm the man."

"Amazing," Clark said, looking at Derek.

"What?"

"That someone so smart can be so dumb."

At that moment, a dozen other bar patrons groaned. The Leafs must have blown another opportunity.

*   *   *

The lineup for interviews stretched down Yonge Street to Frichot Avenue and back to McMurrich Street, almost all the way around the block. Derek found himself in line between a grandmother who hoped the aliens would take her to visit heaven and a teenaged girl who hoped that being on a reality show would help her launch her singing career. "Honey," the grandmother said, "the aliens aren't going to ask you to sing on their show."

A chill wind blew off Lake Ontario. The girl's arms and midriff were bare, and she hugged herself. "How do you know what the aliens want?" she said. "Besides, I don't have to sing. I have to be seen. I need exposure."

"Well," said a man with a turban, "you are certainly getting that."

Derek said to her, "Want to borrow my jacket?"

"No, thanks," the girl told him. She jumped up and down in place. As she jumped, Derek thought about other paths by which an animal could become bipedal. What if the forelimbs became the primary way for a quadruped to get around? He imagined the girl with long arms ending in feet and short legs ending in hands. How would she eat?

"Why do you want to go to heaven?" the turbaned man asked the grandmother.

"My husband is there. I want to see if he needs anything."

"Madam," the man said, "in heaven, I am sure your husband is well looked after. But I am not at all sure that aliens could take you there. If there are aliens."

"What do you mean, if?" said the grandmother. "They have to be real." She dug a copy of the ad out of her purse and waved it. "Says so right here. They couldn't print it if it wasn't true."

"My dear lady," said the turbaned man, "I am a writer. I assure you that untrue things are printed all the time."

"Maybe in books," she said. "Not in the *National Post*."

The writer turned to Derek. "What about you? Why are you here?"

"I want to see them," Derek said. "If they're real."

"And if they aren't?"

"Then I've wasted my time."

"For me, there is no wasted time," the writer said. "If it's a hoax, I'll write about the hoax. If it's real, well, that's going to be a best-seller for sure!"

"They probably won't take Canadians," said a man farther back in line.

"What do you mean?" said the girl. "Of course they'll take Canadians. The show is going to be on CTV."

"They're having tryouts like this in the States, too," the man said. "They'll take Americans and *maybe* one Canadian. Who gets voted off right away."

"Not just the States," said the writer. "India, too. Haven't you heard? All over the world, people are in lineups. I think every large television market gets its own version of the show."

That surprised Derek. "All over the world?" What would it take to generate a globally coordinated effort like that? It raised his hopes slightly that the aliens could be for real.

"These shows lie," said the writer. "People watch to see other people get fooled. If the producers want their lie to work in more than one place, they have to tell the lie simultaneously everywhere."

"Well, if they *are* lying," said the grandmother who wanted to go to heaven, "I for one will not be fooled."

At the end of the line, the actual application process disappointed Derek. It was so mundane. He sat with other applicants at a table and filled out a form. The form was printed on both sides with tiny print and cramped space for his responses: name, address, phone number, and years of education. Also on the form were questions about whether he had ever been arrested and how much television he watched in an average week. (Never arrested. One hour or less.) Had he traveled internationally? (To conferences, yes.) Only one question was interesting, and the space allowed for his response was minuscule. What do you think of extraterrestrials?

Derek had written a monograph on the subject even before he was admitted to grad school. Environmental conditions shaped evolution, but the same environment could generate a wide variety of dominant life-forms. The Earth that teemed with Orthoceras was later the Earth ruled by dinosaurs and eventually humans. Life could almost certainly emerge in radically different forms starting with its biochemistry, and every order of complexity up from that offered more chances for divergence. If there were extraterrestrials, they were likely to be a total surprise even to someone who had thought a lot about biological possibilities.

He wrote in tiny letters: "Morphogenesis bound to be surprising. I like surprises."

After Derek handed in his form, he was sent to a room to wait for an interview. While he waited, he thought about chlorine-based metabolisms.

The sound of the door opening startled Derek out of a reverie on electron exchange. The man who came in to talk to him was a mundane oxygen breather. He looked tired. He glanced at the clipboard in his hand. "Derek. You want to go to outer space, eh?" he said.

"I'm more interested in meeting aliens than traveling between the stars."

"But would you mind space travel?" The man looked at his watch.

"It would be interesting to see where other life-forms had evolved."

"What if I could tell you right now that you could meet the aliens and see where they came from, but you couldn't ever come back?" He tapped a pencil against his clipboard.

"What do you mean, couldn't ever come back?"

The man sighed. "Say it has to be a one-way trip."

"Why?"

"I don't know. Budget restrictions."

Derek thought about it.

*   *   *

At The Prince of Wales, Clark raised his beer glass. "Here's to folly," he said.

Susan and Vajra raised their beers.

Derek said, "I didn't think they were going to call me back for another interview, much less to be on the show."

"Come on," Clark said, "join the toast."

Derek lifted his glass. "To folly." He took a sip. "I thought they'd choose only average people or weirdos. I'm not average or weird."

"Think again," said Vajra. "You model imaginary biochemistry for fun. That's weird."

"I didn't go to the interview dressed in aluminum foil," Derek said. "I don't think that I've already met the aliens in a past life."

"Derek does seem like the wrong kind of weird for television," Susan observed. "He's weird, but not television weird. Seems like they'd want wackos."

"Wait until you see who else they chose for the show," Vajra said.

Clark shook his head. "The whole world is going to hell. I can't believe that you're doing this, Derek."

"Taping only lasts a week."

"It's a week of lost work that you'll never get back."

"Clark, I'm always working." Derek tapped his forehead.

Frowning, Clark shook his head. "The whole thing is obscene. Did you read about the two guys who shot each other in the lineup?"

"In New York," Vajra said. "That's New York."

Susan said, "That's America."

"Twisted sick," Clark said. "The whole idea of reality television is a decadent sign."

"Lighten up," Vajra said.

"So, guys . . ." Derek reached under the table for his briefcase.

Clark set his beer glass down heavily. "All I'm saying—"

"Please," Derek said. "I want to ask you guys a favor." He put the briefcase in the center of the table. He put a key on top of the case.

"What's this?" Susan asked.

"Maybe the show is a hoax," Derek said. "Maybe I'm going to end up embarrassing myself."

Clark said, "How can you doubt it?"

"They told me that if I win, I won't come back."

Clark rolled his eyes. "I can't believe—"

"Hear him out," Susan said. She was looking right at Derek. He looked away from her.

"If I never see you again—" Derek said.

"Oh, for Pete's sake—"

Vajra told Clark to shut up.

"I wrote letters. To my mother, to my grandparents. To old friends. I don't want to mail them if it's all a hoax, or if I don't win."

"Sure," said Vajra. He pulled the briefcase toward himself.

"There are letters inside there for the three of you, too. I don't want you to read them. Unless."

"Understood." Susan picked up the key. "Vajra keeps the case. I keep the key."

Clark burst out laughing. "All right, my friend," he

said. He stuck out his hand. "If this is good-bye, I will miss you. Boy, are you going to feel silly in a week."

Derek shook hands with all of them. "One more round on me," he said. "We need to drink another toast to folly."

"At least," said Vajra, "let it be entertaining folly."

After hours of driving past the lakes and pine forests of the Canadian shield, Derek drove through a small town and turned onto a secondary road. There at the end was the motel, surrounded by trees. The motel windows had been painted over with the same greenish-gray paint that covered the whole exterior of the place, right down to the doorknobs. The motel looked as if it were about to be demolished. There were cars in the parking lot, though, with plates from Quebec, BC, and Manitoba. Derek parked next to one of them and checked his letter once again. *Meet in the motel office,* it said.

Derek got out of the car, feeling like an idiot. He was being taken in by a hoax, and a low-budget hoax at that. Extraterrestrials would be able to do better than a decrepit hotel in northern Ontario as the setting for their show. He stood in the sun for a moment, considering whether to proceed to the office and commit his gullibility to video. Up until now, there was no solid evidence of what a fool he'd been.

Well, what a fool he had *probably* been.

With that thought, he realized that he was hooked too badly to shake himself free. Even as everything told him that the supposed aliens were a lie, he was still thinking . . . *but what if they are real?* What if they had their reasons for making contact with humans in such an improbable way? Since their biology would be surprising, wouldn't their psychology also be a surprise?

Inside the office, he found three people sitting in mismatched armchairs. An elderly woman among them was saying, ". . . bound to be an adventure either way. So here I am."

"That is a good atti*tude,*" said a black man, nodding.

"Am I in the right place?" Derek asked.

The black man smiled, wagged his finger, and said, "There are no wrong places, my friend!" Then he laughed, and so did the two women. "I am Chrestien Boisvert."

The younger woman stood. "I'm Nina Leone." With dark eyes and black hair, she looked as if she might be First Nations, or maybe Metis. The older woman's name was Maggie Mackenzie.

"We were just talking about what an elaborate practical joke this all is," said Maggie. "Someone's gone to a lot of trouble to make us look foolish. But the joke's on them because my foolishness was already well established."

Everyone but Derek laughed.

The talk continued with speculation on what an alien might look like. Chrestien, Nina, and Maggie's ideas struck Derek as simplistic, limited to grotesques of terrestrial life-forms. A real alien would be more exotic than any of their ideas. But Derek kept his

mouth shut. There was something comforting about
their conversation. They were ordinary Canadians who
might lack scientific imagination but were eager for
whatever happened next, whether it was the arrival of
a gigantic worm or the revelation that they'd all been
taken for a ride.

The door behind the registration desk opened. An
attractive woman in a pinstriped navy suit came in.
She smiled and said, "Welcome! I see you're all getting to know one another!"

"Indeed," said Chrestien Boisvert. "We feel as if
we are old friends."

Derek didn't feel that way himself. But it did seem
as if the others had already established that they had
something in common. Perhaps he should have come
earlier. If the show involved voting someone off, he'd
be the one who didn't fit in.

"Are you an alien?" asked Maggie Mackenzie.

The woman smiled. "I am."

This time when everyone laughed, Derek laughed,
too. "You look pretty terrestrial," he said.

"I should hope so," the woman said. "I've been
practicing. But what you're looking at isn't the whole
story. You can call me Avi. That's short for Avatar.
You don't have the anatomy for pronouncing my real
name." Suddenly, she grabbed the edge of the
counter. "Crap!" She froze for a moment, unmoving,
unblinking. Then she came back to life. "Sorry
about that."

Derek looked at the others. Chrestien smiled and
shrugged. Nina and Maggie looked bemused.

"Ah," said Avi. "Your sensory apparatus isn't subtle. You didn't feel it. *I* felt like I'd just been kicked in the ass. Anyway, they'll be more careful with deceleration."

"You're telling us that we're moving?" said Derek.

"Near light speed. Yes."

Derek snorted. "I see. You're telling us that we just accelerated to relativistic speeds without feeling any g-force. You want us to believe we're in space."

"We have left your atmosphere, yes."

"Oh, really." Derek stepped to the door. "And I suppose that on the other side of this door, there's hard vacuum?"

"Yes. Now, we'll be docking in a few minutes. Before then, I have a few things to tell—"

Derek twisted the doorknob and opened the door.

Instead of the motel parking lot that he expected to see, Derek found himself face-to-face with a greenish-gray surface that filled the doorway. It was the same color in which the motel was painted. He touched the surface. It was warm and yielded slightly.

"Hm," said Nina, sounding interested and totally uncommitted to any conclusion.

"Please close the door," said Avi, "and pay attention."

"I don't know what this is," Derek said, soundlessly rapping the surface with his knuckles. "But it's not vacuum."

"Oh, the vacuum is out there," said Avi. "'But do you think we'd let you kill yourselves? Now the first thing I want you to know is that you've been deliberately misled into thinking that our reality show would be a contest. It is and it isn't. Or rather, it *was,* and it's over. The four of you have been competing with thousands of candidates since you first expressed an interest in our show."

Derek scanned the bare furnishings of the room. "You're recording this, aren't you? Where are the cameras?"

"We don't have cameras. We use quantum resonance to record events. And that's one of the things you've been allowed to misunderstand. We have recorded your lives since each of you lined up to try out for our show. That's the show we'll give to viewers, the drama of your struggle between skepticism and a willingness to believe. We've recorded your every interaction for weeks. You've already won. You're all going to get to meet aliens."

"My dear girl," said Maggie, "we'll believe that when we see one. A real one."

"That was better," said Avi.

"What?"

"The docking. We're inside the mother ship." And when Avi said that, the walls of the hotel office melted. The ceiling disappeared. The chairs and registration counter sat in a little island of illuminated space in a vast blackness. There was no source of light overhead, though there was somehow still light in the room. The air smelled of acetic acid and something vaguely floral. Out of the darkness shambled a huge assembly of . . . Of what? The thing emerging from the darkness had many legs, with joints bending and bobbing. It had two domes riding on flexible tendrils, domes that might have been heads riding on necks. Or maybe they were sex organs. Perhaps the rising and falling cylinder of flesh in the center was the head, and all those black dots were eyes. It stopped behind Avi, legs quivering.

"This is the rest of me," Avi said. And as Derek peered over the registration counter, he could see that, indeed, a column of wet flesh now connected her calves to the main body mass of the alien.

"My word," said Maggie.

"Incroyable," Chrestien said.

Nina said, "Wow!"

Derek moved past the counter without a word. He stood close to one of the enormous legs. Little spikes of black hair stood out from the vibrating flesh. He reached out, paused. He looked at Avi, at the humanoid part of Avi. "May I touch . . . you?"

Avi nodded.

Derek brushed his fingertips over the black bristles, then pressed his whole hand against the moist skin. It was warm. "You're an endotherm," he said.

"Partly," said Avi. "My metabolism is variable. It depends on . . . energy sources. Type of air."

"You're real." Derek started to laugh. "You're real!" He felt flooded with questions. What was Avi, the Avatar? Had the rest of the organism grown her? How long did it take the creature to make a humanoid, a humanoid . . . puppet? Where had this organism evolved? It breathed different kinds of airs? What kinds? What sort of environment exposed an organism to variable atmospheres? "You're real."

"I am real," said Avi. "And there are others that are not so similar to you as I am. Many others."

Derek looked up at the legs rising above him, at the extensions of pale flesh that curled and uncurled on the creature's underside. Breathing, perhaps. Or circulating blood. "You are similar to us?"

"Relatively. In all, we are more than twelve thousand sentient species, plus some individuals of near sentience, such as yourselves."

"Near sentience?" said Chrestien. "Does that mean how I think it means?" He laughed. "Should we take this personally?"

"Well," said Avi, "that brings us to why you are here."

The room looked like a real restaurant diner, just as their bedrooms looked like the rooms of an ordinary motel. But the aliens could make the rooms and their furnishings come and go as the schedule required. Right now, the schedule called for the Canadians to have dinner together, without Avi. Elsewhere on the ship, other groups from other countries on Earth had their own schedules and were having their own discussions in many different Earthly languages.

"I can't help but feel a wee bit insulted," said Maggie.

"It is an insult that we have earned, I suppose," said Chrestien as he buttered a roll. "One look at human history or at the way things are these days, and you must admit that they could be right."

"They're not insulting us," said Nina. "They're trying to help us."

"Not help us," said Chrestien. "They are giving us a chance to help ourselves. That is very different. That is better."

"Is it?" said Maggie. "I'm all for pulling ourselves up by our bootstraps. I'm an Alberta girl, so of course I believe in self-reliance. But with so much at stake, why couldn't the aliens just give us a hand?" She smiled. "Or a tentacle? Heaven knows, I always try to help people who need it."

Derek kept his peace while the conversation continued. He was still staggered by the thought that among thousands of sentient species, Avi's was the closest analog to Homo sapiens. What else was on this ship? Avi had said that the ship's upper decks had hundreds of times more surface area than the Earth. Different decks maintained different environments, different levels and types of radiation, different liquids and gases. Avi had also revealed that bilateral symmetry was a statistical outlier in the galaxy's life-forms, almost an aberration. That was what made Avi and the humans similar, for all of their other vast differences.

And how Clark's mind would have been blown by what Avi had said about the ship. The alien starship was enormous. Its black exterior circumference, she said, was greater than the Earth's. And it was that big out of necessity. Light speed could be surpassed only with a really massive object. Derek chuckled at the thought.

"Yes, my friend?" said Chrestien.

They were all looking at Derek.

"Something is funny?" If Chrestien was irritated, he didn't show it. He seemed simply to be asking Derek to share.

"Sorry. My mind wandered."

"You know, we have a problem here to discuss," said Chrestien, still without any hint of irritation. "We are only here with the aliens for a short time. They say that the TV show will help us to convince people, but then we have the problem of how do we fix everything? What do you think, Derek?"

"I think the aliens have pretty much helped us as much as they are going to."

"But, Derek, dear," said Maggie, "if they're so sure that we're doomed, why can't they just . . . fix us! Take us in! Make us a Good Samaritan project "

"Because we're dangerous," said Derek.

"To them? When they have technology like this?' Maggie picked up her water goblet. "This feels real. It could have come from my own kitchen at home. I can drink this water. I can eat this food—and we must remember to say that it's delicious."

"And the wine," said Chrestien. "Very good."

Maggie said, "The aliens can make these things come and go like turning lights on and off. They can cross the galaxy faster than light. How can *we* be dangerous to *them?*"

"Like cancer," said Derek. "If we don't have what it takes to survive on our own, then it means that we're . . . wrong. Inviting us to join their galactic civilization would be like accepting a cancer into their body. All the problems that Avi talked about, all of our aggressive and destructive tendencies would make it dangerous to have us around."

"Well, they certainly don't seem to think our chances are very good," said Maggie.

"No," Derek agreed. Out of every ten thousand semisentient species, Avi had said, two survived for a thousand years beyond their discovery of radio. "They don't."

"If the problem is difficult," Chrestien said, raising his glass, "it calls for more discussion. And more wine! Do not worry, Madam Mackenzie. Human beings are resourceful!"

"We have wisdom," said Nina. "We just need to remind ourselves of it."

"To wisdom!" said Chrestien. "And to the *persévérance!*"

"If anyone can teach the world to get along," said Maggie, "Canadians can."

There was no sunrise or sunset inside the ship. The days were defined by when the aliens turned on the lights in their hotel rooms or summoned them to meals. Derek's wristwatch showed that Avi was letting the humans sleep and eat an hour later each day. Somehow the aliens knew that in the absence of sun, humans fell into a twenty-five-hour circadian rhythm. Was there an alien guide to humans, sort of like *Caring for Your Gerbil?*

Days were filled with meeting different species. Communication was often difficult even with Avi's mediation. They met with one alien that looked like there gray toy balloons tied onto the crown of a big jellyfish. The jellyfish part crept along the floor. The balloons rose and fell on the stringlike necks, and the creature vocalized with what would have been a rude sound for humans. Derek never could figure out where that sound originated, from the balloons above or the jelly below. It seemed to shift. Along with the sound, the balloons sometimes flashed colors. When Avi replied, her human-looking skin also turned gray and flashed colors. Her shape also wavered a bit. She sagged, as if at any moment she might lose her human form and turn into something else.

Every utterance of the balloon aliens, the Vkirrik, required that Avi explain the creatures' social structure and folklore so that what it said would make even a trace of sense. A two-hour conversation seemed to sum up as, "Do not kill except to eat, and do not kill to eat either. Except to eat."

"They are difficult," Avi admitted. "Very subtle. But wise."

Each interview seemed to leave the other Canadians a bit bemused, but never discouraged. Nina, Chrestien, and Maggie seemed to be comfortable with their responsibility of trying to save the Earth. "We will do our best," Chrestien said merrily at dinner. "What has changed? We will live and love and die. We will hope. And in the end? *C'est la guerre.*"

Maggie Mackenzie said to him, "No more *guerre,* Chrestien. *C'est la vie.*"

Soon they would be returning to Earth. The TV series would air. In spite of the simultaneous shows all across the globe, many viewers would decide that it was a hoax. Avi said it was best that way, for the human species to begin to believe only gradually. The Earth would start getting used to the idea that there might be truly intelligent life in the galaxy. Humans might take baby steps toward the long view that their long-term survival would require.

One morning, the light came on in Derek's room, waking him. According to his watch, this was two hours ahead of schedule, if they were all still on a twenty-five hour cycle. He washed his face, dressed, and stepped into the corridor. The light was dim. When he closed his door, light from his room glowed in the gap under his door.

No light glowed in the gaps under the other doors. He was the only one who had been wakened.

Derek made his way down the hall to the dining room. Inside, he found Avi, but a changed Avi. The main part of Avi, alone.

From somewhere in the body mass, Avi's usual voice said, "Come in. Let's talk." The voice sounded a bit muffled.

Derek approached.

"Sit," said the alien.

Derek pulled up a chair. "Where's the humanoid avatar?"

"Here." The front of the alien's body opened wetly, and the avatar's head emerged, but hairless and glistening. "I thought you might let me dispense with appearances," the head said. "It is tiresome to keep my tongue sticking out all the time."

"Your tongue?"

"Like a tongue. It is more elaborate than your tongue," said the head. "My ancestors hunted. Our tongues were . . . lures."

"I can do without the avatar," Derek agreed. With hair and dry, the avatar was appealing to look at. But bald, wet, and sticking out of alien lips, she wasn't quite so attractive. He was a bit relieved when the avatar head disappeared again. "What's your name?" he asked. "The one I won't be able to pronounce?"

A series of clicks and trills issued from some other part of the alien.

"I think I'll still call you Avi," Derek said.

Avi laughed. "Derek, you know that you are not like the others."

"I figured that out."

"They would be dismayed if we kept them here, if we denied them a chance to save your species. And you would be sad . . ."

"If I had to go back. Yes."

"But you must know the restrictions, Derek. If you stay, you may fraternize with others of your kind who will also stay. We expect about a hundred will remain with us. You will soon know all of them. But you may not reproduce. You will not have a vote. You will not be a citizen."

"I understand."

"You may visit your home again one day. You will not age or sicken. But what you know of Earth will die. And if your kind survives long, it will be because they have changed. They will no longer be your kind. They will be your inheritors."

"You know what my answer will be, whatever your terms. You selected me because I will stay. You selected the others because they will go back."

"Yes. They will struggle for your kind. We hope against hope."

"I know why I want to stay. Why do you want to keep me?"

"Diverse life. We love it."

"You're like me."

"Yes."

"I'd rather not say good-bye to the others."

"No?"

"I am saying good-bye to a lot. I have already left my planet behind." As he said those words, Derek thought of whales and cicadas and *Plasmodium* and giant redwoods. He thought of gigantic slime molds, tiny shrews, and far tinier *Drosophila*. All of the Earthly organisms that had ever amazed him, he might never see again. There was only one Earth, and it expressed life in a limited number of ways. But even Earth was amazing. And his friends and family . . . "I have already said all the good-byes I want to say."

"You will have," said Avi, "new friends."

And so he did. Many of the humans who stayed on the alien ship spoke English. But he was soon spending much of his time with an Egyptian woman who did not. She was a painter. She reveled in the forms and colors of their hosts, and some aliens seemed fascinated with her representations of them. Arabic wasn't an easy language to learn, but they had time for teaching and learning. And Arabic was a language for which he had the suitable anatomy, even if it didn't always feel that way when Bardriyah laughed at his vowels.

He made other friends as well. A trio of Roon hatchmates liked to visit him. They were trying to learn English, and since they vocalized by vibrating an organ very similar to a stereo speaker, there wasn't a human sound that they couldn't perfectly mimic. They were bilaterally symmetrical, so even though they had ten appendages and spit chemical messages to one another with two of them, they were like kin to him.

Derek and Bardriyah took long sojourns through the oxygen-atmosphere-decks, across different illumination zones, seeing who there was to see. One day they came across four Vkirrik, the jelly-body balloon-heads. Derek had found that Vkirrik were numerous across most of the oxygen zones. He was quite used to seeing them. But their behavior was new. Bardriyah was puzzled, too.

On the floor of the deck, a hundred silver-colored disks had been materialized. Each Vkirrik would stand on one for a while, then slide off onto another to linger a while before moving on.

Bardriyah said something in Arabic, and a chair materialized for her to sit on. She started to sketch the Vkirrik.

"Question, Avi," Derek said into the air.

In the empty space next to him, Derek heard Avi's female human voice. "Yes, Derek?"

"What are they doing?"

There was a pause as Avi somehow imaged what was happening close to Derek. "Ah. I see." Feminine laughter. "How funny that you're happening upon this right now. Try it."

"Try what?"

"Stand on a projector," said Avi's voice. "Stand on this one." One of the nearest disks glowed white.

Derek stepped onto the disk . . .

. . . and he was in standing in a room on Earth. There were people sitting in rows of chairs, all facing toward a stage with a podium. The podium was crowded with microphones. It was a press conference. And at the front of the room, Chrestien Boisvert was taking a question in French from a CBC reporter. Behind him stood Nina Leone and Maggie Mackenzie. Chrestien answered the question, and then repeated his reply in English. "Of course we know that many people think that our experiences with the aliens is nothing more than an elaborate joke, and I say to you this. So what? Let it be the joke that saves us from ourselves. We must learn new ways to be human."

"That sounds impossible," the francophone reporter followed up in English.

"Mais, oui, c'est impossible," said Chrestien with a smile. *"Naturellement!* But that is no excuse not to try!"

Derek stepped back. He was on the ship again.

He tried another disk. This one found him in a room where two men were having an earnest conversation in Spanish across a desk. It was a big desk. The room suggested power. A big yellow, blue, and red flag was draped behind the desk.

Another disk. This one put him in the middle of a village of huts made of sticks. The ground shook with explosions. Derek turned, and the ground before him was blasted into blinding dust. He heard human voices, a man shouting, a child screaming. More explosions. He stepped back.

"Question, Avi," he said.

"Yes?"

"I still don't understand."

"Semisentient species almost always destroy themselves," Avi's human voice said. "Will they change? Will they die? We hope for the best."

"And you watch it happen?" Derek said. "Like . . . a TV show?"

"Yes," Avi told him. "It's terrible. It's sad." She made a sound that might have been a chuckle. "But it's very entertaining."

OTHERLAND

TAD WILLIAMS

*"The Otherland books are a
major accomplishment."*
–Publishers Weekly

"It will captivate you."
–Cinescape

*In many ways it is humankind's most stunning
achievement. This most exclusive of places is also
one of the world's best-kept secrets, but somehow,
bit by bit, it is claiming Earth's most valuable
resource: its children.*

CITY OF GOLDEN SHADOW (Vol. One)
0-88677-763-1

RIVER OF BLUE FIRE (Vol. Two)
0-88677-844-1

MOUNTAIN OF BLACK GLASS (Vol. Three)
0-88677-906-5

SEA OF SILVER LIGHT (Vol. Four)
0-75640-030-9

To Order Call: 1-800-788-6262

C.S. Friedman

The Best in Science Fiction

CJ Cherryh
EXPLORER

"Serious space opera at its very best by one of the leading
SF writers in the field today." —*Publishers Weekly*

The *Foreigner* novels introduced readers to the
epic story of a lost human colony struggling to
survive on the hostile world of the alien atevi. In
this final installment to the second sequence of
the series, diplomat Bren Cameron, trapped in a
distant star system, faces a potentially bellicose
alien ship, and must try to prevent interspecies
war, when the secretive Pilot's Guild won't even
cooperate with their own ship.

*Be sure to read the first five books in this action-
packed series:*

FOREIGNER	*0-88677-637-6*
INVADER	*0-88677-687-2*
INHERITOR	*0-88677-728-3*
PRECURSOR	*0-88677-910-3*
DEFENDER	*0-7564-0020-1*

0-7564-0131-3
To Order Call: 1-800-788-6262

CJ Cherryh
Classic Series in New Omnibus Editions

THE DREAMING TREE
Contains the complete duology *The Dreamstone* and
The Tree of Swords and Jewels.   0-88677-782-8

THE FADED SUN TRILOGY
Contains the complete novels *Kesrith*, *Shon'jir*, and
Kutath.   0-88677-836-0

THE MORGAINE SAGA
Contains the complete novels *Gate of Ivrel*, *Well of
Shiuan*, and *Fires of Azeroth*.   0-88677-877-8

THE CHANUR SAGA
Contains the complete novels *The Pride of Chanur*,
Chanur's Venture and *The Kif Strike Back*.
                                        0-88677-930-8

ALTERNATE REALITIES
Contains the complete novels *Port Eterntiy*, *Voyager in
Night*, and *Wave Without a Shore*   0-88677-946-4

AT THE EDGE OF SPACE
Contains the complete novels *Brothers of Earth* and
Hunter of Worlds.   0-7564-0160-7

To Order Call: 1-800-788-6262

Julie E. Czerneda

Web Shifters

"A great adventure following an engaging character across a divertingly varied series of worlds."—*Locus*

Esen is a shapeshifter, one of the last of an ancient race. Only one Human knows her true nature—but those who suspect are determined to destroy her!

BEHOLDER'S EYE
0-88677-818-2
CHANGING VISION
0-88677-815-8
HIDDEN IN SIGHT
0-7564-0139-9

Also by Julie E. Czerneda:
IN THE COMPANY OF OTHERS
0-88677-999-7
"An exhilarating science fiction thriller"
—*Romantic Times*

To Order Call: 1-800-788-6262

Julie E. Czerneda

THE TRADE PACT UNIVERSE

"Space adventure mixes with romance...a heck of a lot of fun."—*Locus*

Sira holds the answer to the survival of her species, the Clan, within the multi-species Trade Pact. But it will take a Human's courage to show her the way.

A THOUSAND WORDS FOR STRANGER
0- 88677-769-0

TIES OF POWER
0-88677-850-6

TO TRADE THE STARS
0-7564-0075-9

To Order Call: 1-800-788-6262